TREACHEROUS WATERS

First Edition: May 2018
Printed in the United States of America

Printed by Professional Office Services, Inc.,
of Waite Park, Minnesota, 56387

TREACHEROUS WATERS

Book 2
The Chronicles of an
Unlikely Voyageur

Nikki Rajala

CHAPTER 1

André hurried on the slushy narrow path along the French-Canadian waterfront, his feet skidding. October was early for this much snow, but it was not yet cold and it might not last.

He lurched in the slippery mud and lost his balance, toppling into an icy puddle. Splat!

As he pushed himself up, he glanced at the swollen St. Lawrence River cascading nearby. *What if I had fallen in there?* The water swept by, carrying dark dead trees with shocking speed. In the twilight, the upthrust branches looked like arms beseeching the heavens.

Like Basile Roche struggling for his worthless life. He shivered—he'd mostly forgotten about his family's enemy, since Roche had drowned only a half a year earlier on a dark and rushing river in the wilderness west of Lake Superior. *But that's over and done. And it's well past supper—time to get home or Berthe and Joseph will worry.*

He clambered to his feet, looking at his dripping and grimy clothes, and hurried on.

André was returning home from delivering a packet of medicinal herbs, a late-evening errand for Berthe Didier, his foster mother. Their hamlet was too small to attract a doctor—Berthe's knowledge of herbal remedies made her an often-needed substitute.

He was worried, his mind like a caged bird flitting from place to place—proud, sad, happy, lonely, fearful, troubled—but never settling in one place for long.

What if Antoine doesn't choose me to paddle to the rendezvous? Or to clerk at his wintering fur trade post in Ojibwe country beyond the Grand Portage? He should, because I proved myself as a clerk, even if I am only fourteen. But he has many good men to choose from.

A year and a half ago, he had left Lachine in a birch bark canoe with a voyageur brigade led by Antoine Felix, a top canoe brigade guide and leader. André sucked in a cold breath. The word "voyageur" thrilled him! Wearing the *capote*, a blanket coat, was a badge of honor and made him proud. *I was—I am one of them.*

In his village he had no friends, and André felt lonely. No one else his age studied with Father Goiffon. The other boys of his village had become men, and had long since left school to work, helping their families, earning money. They scorned him for wasting his time with lessons in mathematics and geography, English and Latin.

Those studies, however, had made his adventures in the New World possible. And he had gained new friends—his canoe-mates and Ojibwe natives. He glowed with warmth.

Then he frowned. He missed his brother, Denis, who had sailed to France with his new wife, Marie-Thérèse, less than a month earlier. A brother lost, then found, had brought him wholeness and connection—they were family. Then lost again, so far away. *Somehow Denis saw into me, understood me, though we had little time to learn about each other as brothers. Will I ever see him again?*

CRAAACK!

A massive limb overhead snapped and plummeted toward him with astonishing speed. Its load of heavy wet snow smacked him on the chest, hammering him backwards. The branch snagged into his *capote*, hooking its wide sleeves and fringed hood. He lost his balance and his feet slipped once more.

André grabbed at the tree to steady himself. But his fingernails only scraped painfully against the bark. The limb, thick as his body, knocked the air out of him, and propelled him towards the river. Suddenly he was powerless. His arms flailed in the air.

He tumbled down the slick muddy bank. His hands clawed at the mud as he tried to free himself from the heavy branch.

Head first, André toppled into the river. It enveloped him in a full-body icy grip. He choked, nearly inhaling water.

The river, swelled with meltwater, rushed him away from the bank at a furious rate. The current twisted him, rolling him deep underwater.

André thrashed. His head popped above the surface. "*M'aidez!*" he gasped. "Help me!"

There was barely time for a single yelp before the force of current sucked his sodden *capote* and dragged him under.

André couldn't swim. Like most of his French-Canadian neighbors. Panicked, he fought for breath, and tried to control his terror.

The river curves. And slows. Can I get to where the current is slower?

His hands scrabbled for anything to grab onto—but came up empty.

No, this can't be.

The churning water whirled him around—he struggled to stay right-side up. *I can't breathe!*

Terror struck.

His face broke the surface and he coughed, gagging, drawing in the river water. The icy water felt like nails stabbing into his chest.

Like a dark beast grabbing him, his heavy wet clothing drew him deep down, spinning him so he had no sense of up or down.

His mind started going black, dotted with stars.

Ow! His knee banged against a submerged boulder.

Underwater André's eyes flew open—he saw vague blurs of light.

A rock? It could help spring me to the surface.

He reached halfheartedly but could not find another boulder.

His lungs burned.

His brain dimmed.

He could not …

Am I going to die?

Suddenly his body jarred to a crumpled stop.

"Got him."

Crisp beautiful air washed over him. He oozed out bitter-tasting river water. His lungs wheezed—it hurt to breathe. His hands were numb, refusing to cooperate, and his arms went limp as rags. His head ached. André's eyelids drooped shut.

Hands latched onto his leg. He was yanked, hauled over a slippery pile of snow.

"Who is it?"

"Joseph and Berthe's boy."

"The stone cottage people a league inland?"

"*Oui*, 'tis the one."

"But, is he still alive?"

"Perhaps."

"Good eyes, Sam. Now run for the priest."

André couldn't draw in air. He couldn't move, think, speak. Warm fingers on his wrist probed for a pulse.

Without warning, he coughed, then shuddered violently.

"Alive then. A quilt anyone? Let's get him to shelter."

Several men rolled a heavy blanket around him and carried him to a nearby cottage, but André remembered no more.

CHAPTER 2

By the time Joseph Didier, his foster father, arrived with a cart, André had barely regained enough clarity to gaze gratefully at his neighbors. After Joseph's profuse *"Merci, merci beaucoup,"* they left, bouncing along the rutted road.

With André wrapped in furs, nothing was said on the way home. Berthe's warm poultice relaxed his breathing until he slept.

That night, he writhed with restless terrors—of the river sucking his life away, of Basile Roche, the man who'd vowed to end his brother Denis' life. And André's. In the nightmares, Basile was alive—but André was dead, drowned.

He jolted upright and cried out, sweating from his intense fear. He shook his head to clear the memory, panting to catch his breath and slow his racing heartbeat. The river water yet in his lungs rose up and filled his mouth with a dead earthy taste. Then he shivered, confused.

Though Berthe and Joseph came immediately to soothe his fears, an overwhelming dread weighted him down—he could not return to sleep. Nor could he let go of the memory.

Roche, a cruel man, had died after falling into a rushing river, his arms reaching upwards, before disappearing under the roiling water forever. *He deserved death, I didn't—but I almost suffered the same cold watery fate. Was it like this for him? Am I guilty of his death?*

Logic told him that Basile had died. André had watched him attack Denis, had watched Silent Wolf intervene, had watched Basile plunge over a raging rapids. Nobody could survive that. Denis and Ghost Wind and André had witnessed it—no one had rescued Roche.

Basile had pretended to be a *windigo*, an Ojibwe evil spirit. *Could he be a real windigo? Had Roche rescued himself? No, he is dead. I am not. I am not.*

After Berthe and Joseph had returned to their beds, André recited it over and over, to help himself believe it. He did not hear their midnight murmurings in the cottage's kitchen hours later.

He awoke to a sharp rap on the cottage door and the smell of coffee, a rare treat.

With a mischievous grin, Antoine Felix peered around the bed curtain at André. Not a single gray hair showed in his curly black hair and full beard. Long fringes and bone buttons adorned his red and black *capote*.

"André, what are you doing? I hear you are swimming. Why you do that?" Antoine squared his wide shoulders, his eyes twinkling. "*Nous sommes voyageurs.* We are voyageurs—we paddle, not swim!"

At the word "we," André leapt out of bed. He needed to hear more—*Will I be chosen for the next brigade?* He dressed speedily.

Berthe and Joseph exchanged a private smile. She offered Antoine a large slice of fresh bread loaded with butter and jam, and pointed to the empty bench near Joseph. The table was set with delicate china cups, used only on special occasions.

"Ah, Berthe," Antoine said. "It is not so often, no it is not, that I eat such gooseberry jam as yours."

"André, my elbow is weak today," she said when she saw him. "Please carry the coffee for me."

As he placed her china pot, hand-painted with yellow roses, on the table, Antoine's piercing black eyes sized him up.

"You are growing again," Antoine laughed. "This you must stop. A few more inches and we cannot fit you into the canoe. Oho, not many men get bigger than five feet and six inches and work as an *engagé* in the fur trades."

The word "we"—André heard it again. He glanced up hopefully.

Joseph held a china cup to his lips, and breathed in the aroma of coffee. "So when will you begin to make up your brigade?"

"Already they come to me, and say, 'Choose me. I can paddle with your brigade.' But I look and look and look—only for the best. This year it is not so easy. Some of my old friends, they have the sore shoulder or aching knees. They say, 'Me, I want to paddle—but my knees, they do not like me to carry the packs.' And yet they want to go with me. Others, they say they are too old to brave the river rapids or the cold lakes that look like mirrors. Them I pity!"

Antoine sighed and looked longingly at the jam.

"Help yourself to more, Antoine." Berthe sliced the loaf of bread and slid it all closer. "You have no wife to bake for you."

"Me, I fear for Emile. Will he paddle on my brigade?" Antoine's huge hands spooned jam onto a second slice. "Emile, he is moon-eyed over a pert black-haired beauty. He carries her milk buckets. She has captured him. But I, Antoine, I have my own weapon—Emile, he will paddle as the *avant*, the bowman of his own canoe. To lead! Ha, ha! He will not refuse."

Antoine chatted on. His eyes occasionally flicked teasingly toward André, whose heart was hammering like the hooves of a galloping horse.

Finally André could stand it no longer. "Ant … Antoine," he stuttered.

"Goodness, André," Joseph interrupted. "Let him eat your mother's good bread. Do you not see he is famished? Do have another, Antoine."

Antoine took his time and finished yet a third slice. He licked his fingers one by one, then brushed the crumbs from his beard. Smiling, he said, "You have a question, André? What do you wish to say?"

"Will I … will I … am I?" André took a deep breath to steady himself. "Am I to be in your brigade?" he finally blurted.

Antoine stared at him, jolted by the question. "Of course you paddle in my brigade. Why do you worry about such a thing?" he said cheerfully.

André felt like running outside and doing handstands. He thought his heart would burst with joy. *Yes! Antoine wants me. I am a part of the brigade again. I am not too tall.*

"You made friends in the Ojibwe bands—they will want to see you. And who else will keep my records? The *bourgeois*, he gave me a big pat on the back, he did not argue about one little thing. For this he will put extra *livres* in my contract. So much money!"

Antoine, stood, loosening his wide woven sash, then reaching for his *capote*. "But we change this year, new men and different trade goods," he said. He smiled broadly as André showed him to the door. "Berthe, it is a long time since I have tasted coffee, and your bread and gooseberry jam. *Merci*." As he left, Berthe tucked a sandwich into his hand, wrapped in a thin cloth.

André sat, blinked, hoped he wouldn't grow too much. But why worry? He was chosen, going on Antoine's brigade! He reached for his own slice of bread with jam, suddenly hungry.

It was mid-afternoon. André had returned to his bed, to recover from his night terrors. Joseph sat by the fireplace smoking his white clay pipe and Berthe, knitting, when they heard a light tap at the door.

Two children stuck their heads inside and looked anxiously about.

"Isn't he well?" the boy asked.

"André, he means," added the girl. "Is he sick from being in the river?"

"Do come in. Who might you be?" Berthe welcomed them. "And how did you know?"

"I'm Catherine, and my brother is Sam." The girl bobbed her head and looked at her brother.

"When he, I mean André, fell into the river, I called for help," Sam said. "Then I ran to tell Father Goiffon."

At that André appeared.

"You saved me. *Merci. Merci beaucoup.*" He reached out to hold their hands, to strengthen his thanks. "How did you happen to see me?"

Sam lowered his gaze and sighed. "I was playing in the new snow. I was supposed to memorize my English and Latin lessons for Father Goiffon."

"Some days we have our lessons before you, so we know who you are." Catherine reached into a small bag and produced three apples and a stick of cinnamon. "For you, so you get better. Mama said this would help."

"I hope it works." Sam eyed André and added softly, "I want to be like you when I grow up."

André's jaw dropped. *Like me?*

"Sam, where is the booklet Father Goiffon gave us?"

Sam rummaged through his pocket but could not find it. "Oh. I must have left it at the rectory. I'm sorry."

After they left, André wondered that he had never talked to them before today. Now he owed his life to them.

Several hours later, the house was fragrant with their supper of *tourtière*, the pie stuffed with ground pork, spices and onion that was André's favorite, and baked apples.

After a resounding knock, Joseph opened the door to Pretty Mouse, a swaggering voyageur neither pretty nor small. Though his scarred face and twisted nose made him look angry, the man radiated joy. Paired with André in a massive Montreal canoe, he had patiently taught André how to paddle and portage.

Pretty Mouse handed his *capote* and red knitted cap adorned with an ostrich plume to Joseph. "Warm in here. Smells good, too," he said, looking around.

His shirt and trousers had not been washed recently—they were likely his only ones. But he was proud of his new sash—an intricate woven pattern of red, blue, yellow and white, with long fringes. It wrapped twice around his narrow waist before knotting.

From the sash he drew out a paper and unfolded it, pushing it toward André.

"André, I have decided. Me, I will not sign my contract with an 'X' like other voyageurs. *Pas.* They know nothing. *Non.* I, Paul Doyon, will write my name, all by myself, on my contract. Like you taught me at the wintering post."

He pointed to the loopy letters he had written, none in the correct order.

"But it is not quite right. I cannot remember how it goes. You must help me. Me, I will be first to sign my contract. Next week I will do it."

They invited Pretty Mouse to sit at the table while André took his goose quill and ink from the mantel shelf.

"Like this." André demonstrated the way each letter was formed, and then the order to spell his name. Mouse watched impatiently and then scratched away, trying it over and over, leaving blobs of ink, until the letters properly said "Paul Doyon."

"Oho, I have it now," Pretty Mouse said. "This will astound them, don't you think?" He tucked the paper back into his sash.

"Now that you've finished," Berthe said, "would you like to join us for supper?" She set four plates and forks at the table and removed the steaming pork pie from the hearth.

"What a lucky man I am." Mouse savored a large bite of *tourtière*. As the cook for his canoe-mates and at Antoine's wintering post, he had to make do with few supplies. In the village, all his meals were in taverns—a home-cooked meal was a treat.

Over supper he regaled them with his voyageur adventures.

Father Goiffon was the last of their visitors that day. Escorted to their best chair by the fire, he studied André, sitting on a low stool and reading his lesson.

"Nothing amiss, then?"

Joseph shook his head. "An unfortunate moment—with a very fortunate end. All is well."

"André, I received the most interesting letter from my friend in France," Father Goiffon said after a time. "He wrote about this Englishman, Sir Isaac Newton, a mathematician who determined the laws of nature, and sent me a booklet. It is most wonderful. André, we must study Newton. I meant Sam and Catherine to deliver the booklet, but it was on the table when they left."

Late that night, the cottage was quiet after the flurry of their guests.

"Do you think we did enough?" Berthe murmured to Joseph. "That perhaps the accident will not scar André after all?"

Joseph shrugged. "Too early to tell. We must continue to watch."

CHAPTER 3

The rest of the winter André purposely avoided walking near the river's edge while doing errands or on his way to and from his studies with Father Goiffon. He could not summon the courage to look at it—he felt like a fraud. Though the river had frozen over and was covered with snow, he sensed its powerful menacing current beneath the ice. Remembering how his lungs burned and how his brain dimmed—the river terrified him. *Soon I must make peace with this river—or I won't be able to canoe on the brigade. How can I paddle over the waters that I'm afraid of, waters that will so quickly suck me under?*

This tug-of-war—a crippling fear battling against his desire to become a voyageur—took over in his brain.

André was lost in thought one afternoon in late winter when his pathway crossed the village's main road. An ox cart was stalled, a wheel buried in snow up to its axle. Claude and Pierre, his old tormentors, were digging, and Michel pushing.

"Do you need help?" André asked hopefully.

"Not yours," Claude laughed. "You're hardly strong enough to do real work."

"He goes to school with children learning their letters," Pierre sneered.

"Who needs ABCs when you can make things at a forge or build them?" Claude added. He was apprenticed to a blacksmith and Pierre, a carpenter.

"Numbers maybe," Michel said sullenly, "but Latin? What a waste."

"*Bon-à-rien*," Pierre said. "Good-for-nothing. The right name for you."

André had offered sincerely, but their response provoked him. He felt his back stiffening, his anger rising.

"*Je suis voyageur*," he said, throwing back his shoulders. "I am a voyageur."

Two winters ago, when he was twelve, André had been overwhelmed by their meanness, and mired in self-pity. Then a letter had changed his life and given him a goal—to search for a brother he hadn't known. Joseph had found a way for him to live his dream—the adventurous life of a voyageur. To do that, André had needed to keep up with grown men while paddling the canoe and carrying bulky packs over long portages. He was proud of his work. But when he returned, the boys had not sought his friendship.

"At least we have a trade. Voyageurs, they work like pack animals."

"Why do you care?" Stung, André hunched down, on the defensive. Then he took a deep breath and looked at the burly boys, one at a time. Like most of his canoe-mates, they were shorter than he was. "I am a clerk," he said and stood as tall as he could. "I'm going to be a winterer again."

He turned on his heel and walked away as a few snowballs—and more taunts—flew past. It felt better to stand up to them than having them ignore him all these winter months and now ridicule him.

What do they know of the canoe brigades? Of wintering in Indian country? But if I can't look at the river, maybe I will never go again. Then what will I do?

The next day, as he and Joseph carried oaken buckets of water to the cottage, Joseph seemed to read his mind. "You are wanting to go again to the far wilderness, this I see," he said. "But you question yourself?"

"Denis didn't want me to risk voyageur life. He said he would need me in France."

"The road of Denis, it is not your road. No, André, Denis will find how things stand in France. When we know that, then we— you and Berthe and I—we will return. For now we stay."

But over the winter they had not received a letter from Denis.

The days before Denis and Marie-Thérèse had sailed to France had been a whirlwind. A church wedding. And their plain homespun clothing would not do, so fancy garments, a trunk full of colorful silk gowns and fine linen waistcoats and another of warm cloaks for the sea voyage, were purchased in Montreal.

Denis secured their passage before the shipping canal froze for the winter. A voyage in the autumn was unreliable—it might take three weeks or eight, depending on if the winds blew them off course or storms damaged the ship. And Spanish privateers might force them to land elsewhere.

How do they fare? Did they arrive in France? I wish we would receive a letter soon.

Joseph suggested a walk to Lachine. "Berthe needs her spinning wheel to be repaired. The shop is near the waterfront and I cannot carry the wheel myself."

André was glad to help. But when they reached the place where he'd fallen in, he could not glance at the river, his stomach tight with anxiety, though he knew thick ice covered the river and its blanket of snow sparkled in the sun. Instead he shrank away. *I know what a menace the river really is.*

Then he sighed. *Trying to be a voyageur is a mistake if I cannot find some way to master my fear. I don't want to stay here and be like the boys in the village. But how do I overcome it?*

"You are troubled about the river, I see," Joseph said, watching him. "While we wait for the wheelwright to fix the spinning wheel, let us speak with others." He steered them to an inn a few doors away. "I know some men who also have fought a fear of the water."

André was surprised that Joseph understood the problems worming their way into his brain—he had meant to keep it secret.

Inside, grizzly-bearded voyageurs sat in front of the fireplace, smoking and laughing over mugs of ale. From their enthusiasm, André knew they were telling tales of their prowess.

"Men, look—it is the Dancer come to us again. How is with you now, Joseph?" said one with many furrows and scars covering his head. "And is that your André? Growing tall, I see. We heard you were swimming. Voyageurs paddle, André, not swim."

André reddened at the attention. How could they lay bare his deepest secret so quickly?

"*Oui,* this is André. He is going on Antoine's next brigade," Joseph said. "These, André, are my old mates, Louis, and Henri, and Jean-Baptiste."

"Dancer, such a tumble you took near Lac des Chats," Louis continued, barely taking a breath. "Oho, it was spectacular, it was." He told about Joseph tripping over a root at the top of a hill on a portage trail, bloodying his hands and knees all the way down. They all chuckled, having fallen in equally miserable places.

"So it was then," Joseph said smiling. "It's when you named me Dancer. And do you recollect when we came to the Three Kettles?

Our canoe got caught in the whirlpool and a waterfall filled it in less than a second. Was it François who got sucked to the bottom?"

"It was René, my man," corrected Henri, the one with wild spiky hair. "We dragged him to the bank but we could not push all the water out of him. René, he was groggy for days."

"But of course, it was René. I see it now," Joseph replied, and Henri filled in the details.

"And the river—he wouldn't look at the river afterwards." Louis drank from his mug as his friends all nodded in agreement—René had fought hard to win that battle.

"Oho, that *décharge* on the Mattawa, where we all slipped on the rocks pulling the canoe? It was not so deep but we could barely save ourselves. We got drawn into the current—only Antoine and Gerard left to steer the big empty canoe away from the rocks. What treacherous waters they were!"

They told stories of bears and fights and accidents—and of other moments when their canoe-mates had struggled in the rivers but forced themselves to continue as voyageurs. No man was a weakling because he feared the power of the water. Hearing their stories quietly reassured André. He was determined to conquer the fear, as other voyageurs had done.

On the way home, lugging Berthe's spinning wheel between them, Joseph said, "You paddled with René Auger. Did you know he nearly drowned?"

André shook his head. *That René? The gruff and teasing René?*

Later that evening, Joseph sat by the fire, clay pipe in hand. "Show me your map again."

André unfolded his sketch of the route he'd traveled to Antoine's fur post. His rivers were squiggly ink lines, looking tame and not like dark wild rapids filled with boulders. Joseph pointed with his pipe stem to Lac des Chats and the Three Kettles, perilous places the canoe-men at the inn had spoken of.

"Me, I do not remember all the waterfalls and rapids. They were very hard," Joseph said. "But Chute du Blondeau and Point Claire—now they come back to me. The rivers, oh, so beautiful but clear, fast and cold—and dangerous." He smoked for a few minutes. "It was never easy. Our hearts, they were always in our mouths on those dangerous waters, wondering if we would survive. But never would we speak that aloud. It brought bad luck, they said."

Joseph's honesty surprised André. Though the voyageurs spoke with bravado, they weren't foolishly unaware of the perils. *I never realized that he or others had any fears. I only saw Joseph as an enthusiastic voyageur. If René can paddle in a canoe brigade, I can do it.*

"Each of us, we must test ourselves. Will we let our fear take charge of us?" Joseph picked up a stick and poked at the embers in the hearth.

"If you stay here, safe, it changes nothing. You would always wonder, and be angry, not knowing what you could have done. You must persevere, André. Each of us must do this—René, Denis, me, now you. Make your stand. You want to paddle to Lake Superior? To do so, you will have to persist, to force yourself to do things that are hard, to act although you feel fear. Already I know you are good at persistence because of your lessons. You study your problems and attack them a step at a time—and that is what will help you on the brigade."

Then he looked away, tears in his eyes, and he was silent for a time. "At this moment, or another one, a problem may seem impossible, but that only means we must take longer to think it through. We must command ourselves to push past the hard things. We do this for people we care about, or for things that are important, or when it is right. It is how we become adults."

Joseph and Berthe left France many years ago—for me and Denis, at our grandfather's request. It must be hard for them not to know about their families.

André set his jaw, and pulled his shoulders back. *I will do it. Tomorrow I will walk to the waterfront and look at the river. And every day, until it does not scare me any longer.*

CHAPTER 4

Two months later, on a late spring morning, the fur company received word that the ice had finally left the rivers of the far north—canoes from the distant reaches could again travel to the *rendezvous*. Antoine's brigade prepared to embark immediately.

Leaving day was filled with promise—sunny skies, flags fluttering near the painted sterns of over a dozen Montreal canoes, much busyness and efficient purpose, shouting back and forth. Three brigades had picked this day to leave, with more brigades to follow in the next week.

André directly faced the river, taking a deep breath and looking hard at it. In the last weeks, he had made great strides—he was in awe of the river's power but would not let it win over him.

Then he began to help his canoe-mates empty the warehouse of its great pile of trade goods and load them into their brigade's four canoes, floating at the river's edge. The broad-shouldered men—ten *milieux* to paddle in the middle of each canoe—swaggered and strutted, showing off their strength and zest while carrying the ninety-pound canvas-wrapped bales.

Antoine stood by while they carefully placed the cargo—sixty bales, wooden boxes and barrels—in each canoe. He watched while the gunwales of the canoes sank deeper into the river. Their barrels of provisions came next, mostly hard biscuit, dried peas and salt pork. Other canoe supplies and small packs with the voyageurs' personal possessions were tucked in the empty spaces.

Finally the *avants* and *gouvernails*, those men who were responsible to guide and steer, stood in their canoes, rocking them to check for balance—and then demanded that certain bales and kegs be shifted until the load met their complete satisfaction. It gave the men a few minutes to say their goodbyes.

Among the swirling mass of curly-haired, black-bearded men, André, one of the few with reddish gold hair, glanced about to find his friends, the *engagés* he had paddled with before. Antoine was right— nearly all were shorter than he was though he was clearly the youngest.

Some were wiry, others were stoop-shouldered from many years in the fur trade, but they easily handled the ungainly bales they were shifting. Fourteen-hour days of paddling would not faze them.

A few wore woolen *capotes* to stave off the crisp morning air. Many sported feathery plumes in their knitted caps that showed they'd survived long winters deep in the continent's interior.

From André's first crew, he saw Jean and Jacques arguing with joyous enthusiasm, gesturing with their white clay pipes.

He spotted René Auger, standing in the water, reloading the canoe. René wore a new shirt, tied with a long multicolored sash. His canvas trousers were tied at the knees with narrow bands that matched the sash. On the nearby shore, his wife held a baby and huddled with three teary-eyed children to wave their goodbyes. They too wore bright and new clothes, because René—like all voyageurs— had been paid the first third of his wages before he left on the voyage.

The advance money helped many families, who had few coins except when the brigades left, and again when they returned, and received the two-thirds remainder of their wages.

René was one of Antoine's few "pork-eaters," those who only paddled to the *rendezvous* and back to Lachine at the end of the summer, instead of spending the winter inland.

They were called "pork-eaters" because fur trade companies supplied the brigades with food—dried peas and salt pork—for daily meals, to speed their trip to the *rendezvous*. The winterers who had manned dozens of small fur posts struggled to feed themselves along the way with what they could find. So the winterers felt superior in their ability to survive.

René almost did not come back to his family. But he is paddling again. He can, and I can.

Emile was speaking earnestly to a young woman wrapped in a blue shawl. He held her hands in his. *She must be Marguerite Lanfan. So Emile had accepted Antoine's offer of becoming the avant. She looks sorrowful, but I'm glad he is in the brigade. I hope I'm in his canoe.*

Finally he located Pretty Mouse, his beard scraggly, but his clothes no longer stained and disheveled. Like René, he had used part of his pay to buy a new shirt and pair of trousers. His grin was infectious— he turned from the work of loading to engulf André in a bear hug.

"André! Oho, you are here!"

Besides the bustle of the voyageurs, it seemed the entire community had come to see off the brigade. Joseph and Berthe watched from the shore. On his first trip they had been nervous about being noticed by Basile Roche, but that was past.

Berthe patted the knot on André's red and blue sash, which she had woven. "You look so fine today." She admired him in the red *tuque* cap she had knitted and the creamy linen shirt she had woven and sewed.

Joseph's eyes shone, proud of his foster son. "One more thing—trust your mates. Friends can help to overcome whatever stands in your path. And Antoine's men, they are specially chosen, not just for their canoe skills." Then he slipped André a knife with a bone handle he had polished.

André tested its balance and was delighted. And surprised that he had not noticed Joseph working on it over the winter. He grinned as he slid it into its leather sheath and inside his sash.

"Merci," André said. "My thanks. This will be handy every day." *Using it will remind me of you—and what you have said will help control my fears.*

Berthe handed him packets of her dried herbal medicines for pain, swelling and stomach ache.

"I hope you will not need them," she said, dabbing her eyes.

André placed them in the small bag around his neck which contained coins, a broken pipe of Joseph's, though he did not smoke—holding it in his hand reminded him of family—and a twist of tobacco to appease the spirits of the waters they were about to traverse, a suggestion of Joseph's.

"We will save your wages," Joseph said.

"But you must use what you need," André said. "At Antoine's post, I won't be buying tobacco or high wines on credit, like the others, though I may have to replace shirts. So when I am paid the remainder at our return to Lachine, I will still have a very good sum."

Father Goiffon handed him an oiled canvas parcel, tied with string. "It's the booklet by Sir Isaac Newton. Take it with you," he said. "We didn't finish discussing the laws of nature. You shall read it and explain it to me. I do like history better."

André nodded at the nearly-loaded canoe. "Well, Newton said that a body stays at rest unless it is acted upon. So I am 'at rest' for a few more moments, until Antoine orders us to paddle. Then we 'act upon it' and will be on our way to the *rendezvous*."

"You will make sense of it. Now go with God, you and your mates."

While Father Goiffon stepped away to bless the other canoes, André tucked the parcel into his small personal bag.

A little black-haired girl dashed out holding a brightly-colored braided string in her hand. It was Catherine. Suddenly unsure of herself, her voice faltered as she pressed it toward André.

"For you," she squeaked. "To remember me. I ... I mean us."

When André turned around, Sam stepped next to her.

"I asked her to make that for you." He slid a wooden button on the colorful string and tied it around André's wrist. "I carved this part. For good luck."

"*Merci*." André examined the disk—one paddler standing in a canoe, in a river flanked by tall spruce trees.

"See, you are steering. And there is the sun, shining on you." Like his eyes were shining when he looked at André and softly, very softly, added, "I want to be like you." He looked at his sister. "So does she."

Their gift, and Sam's comment, choked up André. Surprised, he tried to thank them, but they had already slipped back into the crowd.

He looked across the fast-moving waters, where he had recently fought for his life, and took a deep breath. *I can do this—I can master this fear.*

Father Goiffon paused by the ready canoes of Antoine's brigade and raised his silver crucifix. The voyageurs bowed their heads, their boisterous cheer momentarily quieted. Then he offered a Latin benediction, with prayers for their safe travel in French. The voyageurs slipped into position, each holding the paddles they'd spent the winter crafting, ready for the signal to take off.

Antoine nodded to a gray-bearded canoe-man who had observed the loading. The old canoe-man nodded in return. Antoine waved and shouted "*Au revoir!*" and stepped into the bow of his No. 1 canoe. He yelled, "*Allons!* To the *rendezvous!*" and his men echoed, "Let's go!"

Church bells rang, people cried and laughed, held babies high, shouted goodbyes, and waved them off.

Seconds later, Antoine's four canoes sped up the St. Lawrence River. Dozens of paddles churned the waters, each dipping into the river at exactly the same moment. The men sang "*Le Bâtiment Merveilleux,*" teasing about "The Wonderful Boat" and themselves, with vigor and humor—a glorious leave-taking.

They kept up the speed and bravado until the canoes rounded the point and those on shore could no longer see them.

But instead of slowing, Antoine called for extra speed—he wanted as usual to be first at this night's campsite, and first at the *rendezvous*, though this year his brigades had more new men than usual.

At Ste. Anne's chapel, a small stone church some miles upstream, they pulled ashore to say their own prayers for a successful voyage.

"Ste. Anne, she especially protects us," Pretty Mouse said, as he added his coin to the offering box and made the sign of the cross.

Help me do this, Ste. Anne. Help me to persist, André prayed. *Don't let fear defeat me.*

CHAPTER 5

Paddling hard against the current, the brigade left the St. Lawrence and entered the Ottawa River. Singing heartily as he dipped his paddle, André glowed with happiness. Like Joseph, he exulted in the magnificent wilderness he was entering.

Of course Antoine led the first canoe, their guide and *avant*. He had dispersed the veterans and winterers throughout his brigade to ensure each canoe had power and skill.

Emile had become an *avant*, captaining canoe No. 2. André, with nine other *milieux*, or middlemen, paddled in canoe No. 3, while Pretty Mouse was a *milieu* in the fourth canoe. André felt dismayed not be closer to any of them.

Less than a week into their journey, he paddled stroke-for-stroke with the older voyageurs, helping propel their heavily loaded canoes up the rivers. On portages, he carried two ninety-pound packs. He was not a weak link in the chain—so different from the first trip, when André had struggled to paddle smoothly and carry the ungainly bales over portages. This year, he wasn't totally spent.

Well, except for the first days when all the men ached, getting used to forcing their shoulders into fourteen-hour days of paddling one stroke every second against the current. André was making an equal contribution to the brigade. And his fear of drowning did not plague him while he was paddling.

Nights he fell asleep listening to the calls of loons and owls, wolves and lynx. *Once those sounds scared me, especially the lynx the first time I heard it. How my canoe-mates teased me. Now those sounds are voices that I know in the forest.*

But André felt like an outsider. Most of his canoe-mates were from the same village northeast of Lachine. Two were named Jean-Baptiste, nicknamed Butterfly and Bull, the opposite of how they moved. Three were named Louis. Old Louis, who paddled shoulder-to-shoulder with André, was the youngest, Big Louis was the shortest, though his shoulders were massive, and Baldy had the bushiest, blackest beard. They had grown up together, and worked together at home and as voyageurs. Instinctively they knew what the others would do next. So they spoke little and usually left André out.

Though on the first trip he had been constantly exhausted, at least he had been with friends.

When we were in the same canoe—me with Antoine, Emile and Pretty Mouse—it was lively, friendly. We laughed, we sang all the time. I know Antoine said we'd be paddling in different canoes, but I'm disappointed not being with Emile and Mouse. Most nights this year we've camped apart.

So far this trip was not much fun.

The man who led the songs in André's canoe was Baldy. His voice carried and he knew many songs to keep their paddling in time, but the songs didn't seem to ease their load, as Emile's had.

When André met Emile along a portage, Emile had said, "To lead the singing, it is harder than you think. Me, I can't start a song any more—I'm too busy as *avant*. I watch the river every minute. When my singer starts, I pitch in. No, don't tell Baldy what to sing."

Nor was supper much to look forward to. Big Louis, who cooked for their canoe, apportioned the pea soup fairly, but it was tasteless.

How had Pretty Mouse managed to make supper appealing? At least we'll be together at the rendezvous. It takes about six weeks to reach the New Fort. Can I make it that long without friends?

Eustache, the bowman of canoe No. 3, yelled, "Big rock ahead, under the surface," his long steering pole altering their course.

That jerked André's mind back to the river.

Standing in the stern, the steersman, Ignace, shouted, "I see it."

Eustache called the orders. "Pull all. Now—left dig! Right side—lift."

André and his canoe-mates pulled and dug and lifted, their arms burning with the exertion.

Their canoe curved around the rock and shot past easily. Ignace deftly planted his setting pole and shifted their direction enough so their long birch bark canoe slid past yet another boulder. André and his mates breathed a quick sigh of relief.

Facing the next low rapids, the *milieux* urged Ignace and Eustache, "Run it! We paddle double-fast, we slip over the top. Nothing to it."

But Eustache, the *avant*, spotted a rugged line of rocks churning the current. He called for a *décharge*.

Seconds later all the *milieux* leapt in the icy water to shoulder the fully-loaded canoe upstream with sixty-foot ropes, while Eustache and Ignace poled the three-ton cargo, until it could be paddled again.

André felt anxious at the *décharges*, when he had to wade in the river to help haul the canoe. He shuddered, his stomach in a roil, his feet numb. *Will I slip and get swept back into the river?* Then, recalling Joseph's words, he pushed himself to act. *I will not let myself think of fear. I am doing the best I can.* He heaved and grunted with the others until their canoe reached deeper waters.

For André, a *décharge* in shallower waters was easier, though he and his canoe-mates had to unload the entire canoe before hauling it upstream with ropes, all the while treading rock-to-rock in chilly waters. Or half the cargo—thirty pieces—pulling the canoe over a rapids. The *milieux* stacked that half-load on the shore, and returned the emptied canoe to haul the rest of the trade goods. Afterwards their wet clothes made their teeth chatter.

Once his feet slid out from under him—and he took a spill, splashing water high in the air. For a moment he panicked, thrashing to keep his head above the surface. His canoe-mates, who knew nothing of last autumn's near-drowning, teased him.

"You are playing while we work. Come, Scarface."

"We all need a bath. But not now."

"Are you trying to swim? Give up."

"He can't do anything right. A good-for-nothing, I say."

Scarface was their nickname for him, because he had no scars on his youthful skin. That name didn't bother him. But Good-for-nothing—*Bon-à-rien*—had been André's name the first year and those words stung. *I may look foolish to them, but I am doing this work the same as they are. This river won't get the best of me.*

Sputtering, he dragged himself out of the water and stepped back to the towline to help haul.

He was surprised to notice that others slipped, and were teased as mercilessly. While the jokes were in fun, André decided not to use their nicknames that mocked.

When the rapids were too high, too rocky or too dangerous, they could not paddle or *décharge*. Instead they had to portage.

Every man groaned at the thought of the back-breaking carries. Anything to avoid it!

At portages, the *avant*, Eustache, leapt into the rushing water, steadying the thin hull. Ignace followed in an instant, holding the stern. The *milieux* slipped out quickly on both sides. The entire load—trade goods, provisions, canoe supplies and personal gear—was taken out and carried over a rocky footpath.

The *avants* and *gouvernails* were responsible for carrying the huge Montreal canoes. At close to four hundred pounds, each one needed four men to hoist and haul it.

Some portages were a half-mile or less, a ten-minute trek for a *bourgeois* who did not have to carry anything. Because Antoine's brigade left early, he rarely carried one of these high-ranking wintering partners, or their clerks. For that, his brigades were thankful.

That same half-mile portage took much longer for voyageurs because each man was responsible for at least six pieces of cargo. André and the *milieux* hefted two packs and one irregularly-shaped piece—iron soup kettle, basket of pine pitch—and dog-trotted up a steep rocky trail. If a portage was a mile or more, after a half-mile they dropped their burdens and headed back for a second carry, and a third. Then they went on to the next half-mile, two bales at a time, until everything had crossed the portage.

Voyageurs are like pack animals. Maybe Michel from the village was right.

But his canoe-mates never complained.

Once they camped at the end of a portage that had taken the entire day. Every muscle in André's body screamed.

"This was a hard portage," he began, squeezing his sore arms.

"Je suis voyageur," answered Old Louis, next to him, squaring his shoulders in pride. "I am a voyageur. No carry is too long for me, no pack too heavy. This is nothing."

"Barrels and wooden gun boxes, they are harder to carry than the bales," Big Louis added.

André nodded, grateful that he had not been given the bulkiest, heaviest pieces to portage. They would brook no whining. And he knew there would be harder work ahead.

Chapter 6

While on most days the brigade was well-spaced in the water and on the portages, on one day all four canoes collected in a small bay while Antoine discussed with the *avants* and *gouvernails* the boulder-filled watercourse they were about to navigate.

The *milieux* waited impatiently, watching white foam smash on dark glistening rocks, and held onto the gunwales of each other's canoes to keep them in position.

How do the bowmen pick the safest way among the rocks that lurk in twisting currents and narrow chutes? What do the steersmen see?

"Gerard, what helps you to steer?" André asked the *gouvernail*, the steersman who had returned to Emile's No. 2 canoe.

"I cannot speak now, son," Gerard answered, analyzing the current. "If I talk, I cannot hear the waters."

I should have known that. Gerard envisions how water dashes against each rock, altering its course, and our canoe skimming past. We paddle hard against the current, but Gerard's long setting pole makes the last-second course corrections to ensure us safe passage. His angles have to be perfect—with little time to correct our errors.

In that moment, André wanted Gerard's knowledge of the rapids and chutes. He studied Gerard who stood in the stern of his canoe, his focus intent.

His skill keeps us all from drowning, a death that almost took me. André grimly imagined a rock slicing open their frail canoe and stiffened at the thought.

After the *avants* and *gouvernails* had decided their routes, Antoine directed canoe No. 1 up and through the chute. Long minutes later, André and the others heard a faint but joyous cheer—they had made it! Over the roar of the rapids, Antoine shouted additional instructions for the remaining canoes.

"Ready?" Emile asked Gerard, his steersman.

"*Oui*," yelled Gerard. "Let's go, men. *Allons!*"

In a flash, the No. 2 canoe slipped into the current and disappeared from view around the bend.

Waiting his canoe's turn, André's stomach soured with worry. *Will we make it? Can Eustache and Ignace guide us safely through? One false move will smash our canoe and suck us under.* Then he stopped. *Joseph said not to focus on fear. Thinking like that won't help me.*

They waited until they heard the joyful shouting to announce their safe arrival. The third canoe slid in place, its gunwales mere inches above the water. The men's eyes were darting and alert, every muscle poised for action.

Eustache leaned forward and dug his setting pole deep. They were off, lunging against the rushing current. He switched sides and shouted, "Boulder! On the right."

Ignace jammed his pole and swung them barely enough to miss it.

André and the other *milieux* paddled with precision, and double-time, to allow Eustache and Ignace better control.

The rocky canyon wall sped past at an alarming rate, but André kept his eyes on Eustache, in the bow.

Eustache shifted his balance.

A rock underwater?

A second later, Eustache recoiled, bending his knees. He tapped his pole against a dark rock shelf a foot below the surface.

André felt the canoe scrape against it. His eyes widened. His paddle stopped.

Our canoe will split. We will all go down.

"Paddle, Scarface," growled Old Louis.

Jolted back to the moment, André matched his stroke to the others, relieved that the canoe had not veered because of his lapse. And he remembered Joseph's words, to act even though he felt fearful—and was encouraged.

Another bend through the sheer rock walls and suddenly they saw the first two canoes waiting for them at a curve of the river. Another cheer rose up.

Though the chute took hardly a minute to run, it felt like hours to him. His heart thudded and he gasped—he had forgotten to breathe. He wanted to cry, but would not allow his eyes to mist.

Finally the last canoe traversed the chasm. All safely through!

Again André released his pent-up breath. *This is why voyageurs brag at home. Who would believe how hard it is? They fight each stretch of rapids. They—no, we—we do it for each other.*

After they had made camp, André noticed Gerard sitting alone on a flat rock, listening to the chorus of frogs. Like Antoine, Gerard's knowledge of the personalities of the rivers was legendary. André handed him his supper and perched beside him on the ground. "How many years have you been a voyageur?"

Gerard thanked him for the pea soup. "*Merci*. Many years I am voyageur. Too many, I do not count them." He turned to his thick porridge.

"You know these rivers like your own front yard. You see the current, even under the water. How can I learn this?"

Gerard looked off into the distance. He shook his head. "Alas, it cannot be taught. You must learn to feel the river and the rocks. You must be like the water. If you were this water, where would you want to go? How would you curl around the banks? How would you push against big boulders blocking your way? Which ones could you tumble along, and which could you not? A river may look quiet on its surface, but below it, the current dances, and cuts away at the bank." He sighed and attempted to eat his porridge before it got cold.

André wanted to ask more questions. But he ate his own supper in silence. *Father Goiffon's lessons in geometry have answers that I write on my slate. But the problems of the wild answer in real life—like our canoe slipping through the rapids.*

He vowed to study the steersmen as often as he could. From now on, he would observe how each man selected a course for his canoe.

After a surprisingly bitter night, they awoke to a thin coating of ice on the waters.

"This ice, it is like knives that slice through our canoes. So we give the sun a little time to melt those knives," Antoine decided. "Breakfast first. Then we load and leave."

That gave André the opportunity to ply the *avants* and *gouvernails* with his questions.

When they left, Antoine was relieved that only a half-day was lost—they were yet in the lead.

Following an arduous stretch of rapids and fast waters where they had made several *décharges*, his paddling partner, Old Louis, said, "Ah, next we come to des Chaudières. Do you know it?"

André shook his head. "Tell me." This new land excited him. He paid close attention.

"The rapids, it is one big fall," Old Louis said, paddling today on André's left. "But the river, she twists around all these rocky islands, and makes so many little falls I cannot count them. The river, I think she is angry with the rocks. She fights them, each one."

The beauty of the falls at des Chaudières—a deep gorge sided with limestone and another river converging—amazed André. It looked like the boiling cauldron it was named for.

"But the portage—next time you will not forget." Old Louis pointed to it. "So steep we all must help the canoe over. The whole portage, it will take us two days."

Eustache directed them to a landing impossibly close to the falls at the head of the gorge. They were instantly soaked by its spray. As Old Louis had said, every man was needed to maneuver the canoe up the nearly-vertical trail.

Then they portaged the trade goods and gear—oiled canvas to cover the cargo in bad weather, kegs of liquor, barrels of dried peas and salt pork, wooden cases holding the long guns, iron cooking pots, spare birch bark rolls for repairs, extra setting poles and paddles, blankets and personal gear. Old Louis was right—they needed most of two days to cross it.

The New Fort seems a long ways off. I've lost track of how long we've been gone, how far we are, or what day it is. Probably three more weeks to get to Lake Huron. Then it will take two weeks to cross the big lakes. At least it's coming into summer.

One portage seemed to have steps cut into the stone bluffs.

"Probably by Indians long ago," Old Louis said, as he hastily spooned breakfast—pea soup—into his mouth. This morning, they ate before the portage so they would have less to carry across.

Another mile, another series of rapids.

Will these rapids never stop?

At a beach they rested to get ready for the next rapids, while their steersmen studied the river.

"Oho, we are near the Deschênes. I do not like it—no, this year the water is too much," Ignace said, thinking out loud. "I think the men must pull the canoe. But what do you say, Eustache?"

"*Oui, décharge* it is." Eustache slid out of the canoe's bow.

To André's dismay were four miles of turbulent rapids before he would see the lake with the great oaks, the Deschênes.

Each time I force myself to go into the river, I conquer a little more of my fear.

The lines tied to their canoe ripped into the middlemen's shoulders as they pulled, grunting with every ounce of strength against the raging river. After reloading the canoes, they met more torrents and made more portages and more *décharges*.

Watching Eustache and Ignace steer while they stood in the canoe, André realized how much deeper they could see into the water. *Then the river cannot trick them—they can react faster to the changes in the current.*

After supper, André wanted to ask them about the next section of the river, but both were snoring, rolled in their blankets near the canoe.

He crept away. *They get paid double what we do, and worth every bit. Steersmen aren't the ones who talk big in the taverns. But it takes all of us to get to the rendezvous.*

Je suis voyageur—yes, I am a voyageur, too.

Though the river challenged them—with menacing boulders and narrow chutes that seemed impassable—André took in the beauty, the scented forests of pine and cedar, the craggy pale cliffs, the clusters of islands, the buffeting winds, and imprinted them all on his heart.

He flourished in the budding spring, the greening of the countryside and the fragrance of unseen wildflowers. *It's why Joseph loved this land and wanted me to know it.*

But he also knew why his fellow voyageurs met it like a battle with an opposing warrior to be bested. *I will face it, and not let it get the better of me.*

CHAPTER 7

At their campsite one night, André asked his *gouvernail*, "Ignace, how fast does the river flow here?"

Ignace half-closed his eyes, seeing the river in his mind. "Many speeds, son, many many. Listen. Zee river she sings. Like our songs, many verses. Each one changes a bit. Higher—it is faster. Swirling around a rock, it bubbles. With deep water, it rumbles. Zee sounds tell you how fast zee water goes."

André tilted his head and listened. He heard the singing water change tones when it struck rocks, swirled around a deadhead or washed up on a sandbar.

Gaining information about the rivers had become his obsession. He peppered men of the brigade with questions at every opportunity.

To the *gouvernails*, scrutinizing the ends of their setting poles, he asked, "How can you feel anything in the water with an iron tip on a long pole?"

"Oho, son," said Ignace. "This setting pole, it is like a part of my body."

"*Oui*, 'tis true," Gerard grinned. "This long arm, it has long fingers, too. The fingers, they squeeze between each rock. They know if this rock, it is my friend or my enemy."

André tested this new mystery, standing on a nearby boulder, placing a setting pole—fast, deep, at long or shallow angles. It did not feel like fingers to him.

If other *milieux* smirked at his questions, they hooted at his play-acting as steersman.

"Such a big load. Don't lose it in these rapids."

"Pole around the rock, Scarface. Don't stand on it."

Occasionally André joked back with his canoe-mates. "I don't seem to be getting past this boulder. I must learn to pole faster. Oh, but by then it will be a different boulder. Tsk."

He grinned and let them jeer—teasing was their way. He wanted to know how to move a loaded canoe against fast-moving water, and could only learn by asking those who knew, and trying it out. What they thought about him did not matter.

While they portaged, he mumbled the scientific terms he had studied with Father Goiffon and worked out their meanings.

"'Mass'—for us, it's our loaded canoes. 'Force' is how hard we have to paddle. Exerting more force makes us move faster. When we need more force against the current, we paddle double-time. There's a formula to calculate it, in Father Goiffon's booklet—one of these nights I will have time to read."

His words were incomprehensible to the other *milieux*, who rolled their eyes and shook their heads—but smiled.

At night, while the steersmen repaired the canoes' laced seams, André held their pitch pots and spruce roots. He used the opportunity to ply them with questions.

"When little streams feed into the Ottawa, how do they shape the river?"

"If the water is colder, does that change the way it moves?"

"Why does the current dash on that side of the river, but slows here and curls around?"

He hung on their every word, learning and remembering.

The Grand Calumet portage loomed—the longest carry on the rivers.

Old Louis grumbled. "More than a mile, it is, the Grand Calumet."

André quickly multiplied. "That's over three thousand paces," he said, aghast.

"Who counts when we must watch our feet?" Old Louis said. "It's another portage that takes two, three days to get everything over."

"Would you rather cross the two ravines?" Baldy poked back, and André realized, though long and hard, three thousand paces was the easiest place to portage.

They grunted and lifted and carried and forged ahead with sore feet and aching backs, until they were finally on the other side. There, they were greeted with a sudden driving rain. Though exhausted, they dashed to cover the cargo with oiled canvas to prevent the bales from absorbing water. No sense in paddling that extra weight. And they might not lose time to dry the bales, which pleased Antoine.

Every day André noticed the diversity of animals—great flocks of birds returning to nest, moose and bear searching for food in the distance—and spectacular land features in the great wilderness. They paddled through narrow box canyons, the shores only a stone's throw apart. He guessed one majestic passage was a hundred feet up, using a formula Father Goiffon had taught him.

He gazed on many marshes, one clear sand beach curved like the moon, a string of narrow lakes surrounded by dark pines, a chain of mountains visible in the distance. This year his brain marked them all, though he had remembered none from his first trip.

However, he realized Antoine and the *avants* and *gouvernails* knew every one of those places. Besides that, they noted new beaver dams, burnt areas and changed water levels.

About each spot, André asked his barrage of questions, making maps in his brain.

"What comes next?" he wanted to know.

"First we must find the best channel of the Allumets. Then we paddle the Lac des Allumets, shallow and filled with shoals," Ignace told him.

More *décharges* and portages.

"After that, Des Joachims," Gerard said. "The river, she makes a big curl and around again. The rapids, they are like thunder. Our Montreals go the long way around—two bays and a lake—in order to portage less. But such a pretty falls."

Above many rapids, they came upon broken canoe paddles lashed together to form crosses and stuck into the ground to show where, in previous years, voyageurs had drowned. The men removed their caps and whispered prayers, for some had been their friends.

Bone-weary, André saw that his canoe-mates also felt the strain. They sang less while paddling, swore more on portages, grumbled more at *décharges*.

While paddling and carrying, they pushed their bodies to the limit, swearing, grumbling, looking somehow to ease their work. There was never enough supper nor sleep.

Nor rum. Though they often called for alcohol to ease their tiredness, Antoine held them off, by insulting their manhood and their pride.

"What? You are tired? My sister, if I had a sister, she could carry this load. My mother could pull this canoe up the *décharge*. Maybe you wish to be a farmer instead? Besides, you drank half of our allotment of high wines the first night."

"Tomorrow we come to la Roche Capitaine," Old Louis said at a pipe break. "La Roche, she is a towering rock that rises in the midst of the waters."

"With many crosses," added Baldy. "Nearly one every year."

When André stiffened, Old Louis glanced at him. *He doesn't know there might have been a cross for me before we left Lachine.*

After that, André eyed the banks for the crosses, wondering who the drowned men were. His stomach tightened as he thought about them falling into the water, flailing, being sucked by currents too powerful to fight. Images and emotions from his own near-drowning rushed into his brain. With great effort, he tried to disregard them.

Joseph said to force myself to do things, not to let fear control me. I can do this—but it is getting harder.

More and more often, he battled to release his own terrifying accident.

They struggled crossing the turbulent waters at la Roche Capitaine. Wet, sore and deeply tired, everyone grew increasingly cranky. Finally they reached its end.

"Men, we have passed la Roche," Antoine announced while they ate their portions of pea soup, "and we have lost but a half-day, and that to weather. Only one express canoe, carrying important passengers, is ahead of us. Not even two more weeks on the rivers, before we paddle the big lakes. So tonight we celebrate. Pretty Mouse, open a cask of high wines. The men have earned it."

They cheered. It would numb their weary bodies and soften the reminders of family they had left in Lachine and mates they had lost in past years.

Mouse chose a large cask of liquor and passed it around to the whole brigade. The men grinned, some downing cups recklessly.

André took a sip—it was not to his liking. He had not minded the wine served after the wedding of Denis and Marie-Thérèse. That was tastier than the harsh rum of the fur trade.

But others filled and refilled their cups. Their songs grew louder and jokes rowdier. When René and Baldy tripped while dancing, the men roared. Gerard's leg wrestling challenge to Ignace ended in a tie because neither could master their coordination. Louis took Charles to task because he had not carried his share on a portage. Paul and Matthieu dared each other, throwing their knives at each other's feet, but when they drew blood—to the loud laughter of their mates—they switched to throwing at a tree.

Antoine did not join them. Instead he patrolled their camp, watching each man with an eagle eye. He deemed the celebration not excessive, and did not curb their fun.

Still an hour of daylight. Other nights we stop at sunset and it's twilight when we make camp. But now I can read Father Goiffon's booklet.

Deep in his pack, André located the wristlet that Catherine had braided. He looked closely at its colors and the wooden disk carved by Sam. *It's for good luck, they said. And he said I was the steersman. But then again, I'm the only one in the canoe.* He fingered it gratefully, remembering their role in his rescue. He would have liked to wear the colorful wristlet, but it would been spoiled quickly with constant contact with the water.

He dug until he found the oilcloth-wrapped packet. He untied its string and unfolded the papers and booklet inside. The booklet, "Some Practical Applications of Newton's Principles of Natural Philosophy," was written in French. André grinned. Translating from Latin would have gone slowly.

The loose papers told of Newton's life. André found similarities—their fathers had died when they were young. Newton, born in 1642, had been educated, but his mother had wished him to take over their family lands and become a farmer. *If I hadn't found Denis, I might have to run the family estates in France.*

Newton became a top student to get revenge against a school-yard bully. André remembered the taunts of Claude and Michel. *I wish I could be their friends, but they don't want me.*

With Father Goiffon, André had studied Newton's first law of motion—"An object won't change its speed unless an unbalanced force affects it." *That's how the steersmen's setting poles change our speed and direction.*

Father Goiffon and André had briefly discussed the second law, so he read it more slowly, reminding himself about the less familiar terms. "Multiplying mass and acceleration equals force." *Our cargo and canoe weigh nearly four tons with us inside. Acceleration has to take into account the different speeds of the current that we paddle against, sometimes double-time. Could I measure it and calculate it?* "Inertia." *That's how I felt after paddling and portaging over la Roche Capitaine.*

André barely heard his canoe-mates' laughter at their amusements. Nor did he notice the voices of the forest, the hooting owls or the calling loons.

"An equal and opposite reaction." He marveled at how the ideas dovetailed with his voyageur life.

Stimulated, he read until the day's last light failed. Finally, though he squinted to make out the words, darkness had come. Many of his fellow paddlers continued to make merry.

André slid the wristlet into the booklet as a marker. *Tomorrow I'll rise before the others and read again. They will need more sleep.*

CHAPTER 8

Instead Antoine had plans for an early departure.

"Get up, men, get up!" He banged on the iron kettle filled with their day's allotment of pea porridge. "On to the Mattawa River."

Groaning, the men rose, stumbling and slow, and splashed their faces with the cold water to clear their minds. They had emptied only one cask, but the thirstiest had often refilled their cups.

André hastily rolled up his blanket and stuck the booklet and letter inside. *Tonight I will study it again.*

Then the brigade shoved off into fast-moving waters. Great jagged boulders lined the river, and the torrent was fierce. The men strained to propel the canoe up the river, paddling furiously, but this day their effort was less coordinated.

At a wide rapids, André's canoe caught up with the No. 2 canoe and, for some moments, he watched Emile and Gerard navigating. Rocks studded the near shore. Up ahead, a tree trunk sped toward them, its broken branches and roots ready to trap the canoe. They poled against it like a boulder.

Tense and anxious, André stopped breathing. *That tree, with its branches sticking up—it looks like when I was drowning.* Immobilized by the memory of his own brush with watery death, his arms stopped.

"Paddle, Scarface," Old Louis scolded. "Keep up."

The tree shot past, so close that a long-fingered branch nearly snagged Baldy's red *tuque* hat.

They all watched as Emile and Gerard stood balancing canoe No. 2, their knees flexing and legs spread wide as the canoe charged around boulder after boulder. The *milieux* paddled hard, following Emile's directions. "Pull, left up. Now both pull, pull double. Rock on the right. Pull, pull. Left up!"

André watched the setting poles of the *avants* and *gouvernails* in near-constant motion, on the same side, on opposite sides, a light tap here, a deep pry there.

Emile spied a submerged boulder swiftly approaching and planted his pole to prevent them from hitting it. Judging the hazard, Gerard leaned left, and jammed his pole to lever them away. Again and again. The canoe skimmed past—or over—the dangers.

Then Gerard's pole stuck, wedged deep into a cleft between boulders. Gerard swore.

He tried to pull it out as the canoe kept moving. He leaned out to grasp it. Too far. He angled on one leg, his eyes on the pole instead of the river.

Emile jabbed his setting pole at a submerged rock to veer them away. The canoe suddenly swerved and Gerard was catapulted out.

"Eeyaah," he yelled.

He was heaved head first into the river. He rose, arms clawing at empty air, but his body was sucked below the surface. In an instant, his canoe shot yards ahead of where he had disappeared.

"Gerard!" André screamed.

There was no Gerard, a second later.

Trailing twenty yards behind, André and his canoe-mates saw it all happen. Saw Gerard flipped into the foaming waters of the rapids. Saw him go under where they could not paddle.

André tried to keep Gerard's location in sight in the angry river, his eyes white in fear of the current. *He is under! My friend! I must help him! But the river ...*

"One man in," bellowed Eustache. "Antoine! Stop!"

Immediately Eustache and Ignace angled canoe No. 3 to pull up along the river's rocky edge.

As soon as their canoe slid near enough to shore, momentarily forgetting his own fear, André leaped toward where his friend had gone under. "Gerard, I'm coming!"

Several middlemen jumped out at the same time—all on the same side.

Canoe No. 3 no longer balanced. It tipped, and filled in a flash.

Some of their trade goods and kegs, loose packs and supplies floated downstream. Heavier bales sank, their canoe under them. A keg tumbled over André, smashing into his back. He fell, the fast current dragging him under the waters.

"Two men in," Ignace yelled hoarsely, his face white with anger.

Big Louis clutched André's arm and pulled his head up, thumping him on the back. When André spluttered water, a cheer rose up from the rest of his canoe. Big Louis waded to shore and deposited him, coughing and wheezing.

"The cargo," shouted Emile, his canoe No. 2 now safely beached. His men formed a line to grab some of the floating bales from canoe No. 3 and pass them to shore to be stowed.

"There … I see him," shouted Bull, pointing to a place in the river where something had risen.

Baldy grabbed a rope and tied it to Bull's waist. Then Bull waded toward Gerard's setting pole in hopes of finding the steersman, but struggled against the current.

Though woozy, André grabbed hold of the rope to help haul Bull—and Gerard—in.

If I can't go get Gerard, I can at least help them.

But there was no Gerard.

"Pull the Bull back to shore."

After that, they hauled the sodden bales to the bank.

Other bales had floated beyond their grasp. Antoine signaled to the No. 4 canoe. "Stay downstream. Watch for Gerard. Retrieve what cargo you can."

Four men joined hands to form a chain to retrieve the heaviest pieces that were underwater—wooden cases of guns and kegs of powder and shot. That cargo weighed the canoe down in the riverbed and the pieces were carefully lifted out.

Once their submerged canoe was empty, the *milieux* carefully raised its frail hull, anxious that the pressure of the water not split its seams. The men supported the canoe, turning it gently and floated it to the bank.

"Tonight check every seam," Antoine shouted to Ignace, who nodded. "When it's dry enough, re-gum it." Though it ensured their safety, the order sounded like a punishment.

In mere seconds their lives had been seriously threatened. All had been changed forever.

And Gerard?

André looked back at the rushing river for any sign of him. His eyes misted, and a tear slid down his cheek. *Oh, Gerard. we couldn't save you.*

The men from No. 4 canoe shook their heads sadly—they had retrieved floating pieces of cargo, but had seen no sign of Gerard. Men from the brigade gazed soberly toward Gerard's setting pole, held fast by rocks beneath the waters.

The other canoes landed safely at the portage site. Once their cargoes were unloaded, the entire brigade turned to the search.

"Canoes No. 3 and 4 on the far bank," Antoine directed. "My men and Emile's will see to this side. Look for Gerard, or his red *tuque* hat, or anything we can bury in his name."

Hours later they straggled in with no success. They looked grimly at each other, the men of his hamlet wondering how they would tell Gerard's wife. They prayed a later brigade might find his body.

"Now we portage, men," Emile said, "and make camp on the far side of the portage. Leave room for the next brigade coming through—pile our goods higher here. I must count to see what was lost."

"These bales, they are soaked," Antoine said. "Open them so they dry tonight. Or you'll be paddling extra weight. Get to it, men."

After seeing to the remaining concerns of the brigade, Antoine, decisive and rigid, turned to André, and pointed to a tree some distance away.

"I speak with you. Over there."

André rose and pulled his shoulders back. He expected a tongue-lashing.

Antoine surprised him. "What did you learn?"

It was a short recital for André, who could barely speak, his guilt a heavy yoke on his shoulders. "To follow directions. To pay attention."

"Each man carries blame," Antoine said. "I hurry to be first at the *rendezvous*. Last night I gave high wines and some drank too much. Others, like you today, didn't wait for orders."

He looked away and cleared his throat. "But Gerard, he is only the second man I have lost in all my years."

Full of remorse, André could not meet Antoine's eyes. Nor did he see Emile and the others standing about, shame-faced and waiting their turns in front of Antoine.

CHAPTER 9

In contrast with a glorious sunset, the mood at their campsite was of deep sadness. Gerard's death jolted the men and they had portaged in silence. None of the usual daredevils would be willing to shoot any further rapids. Antoine paced the shorelines, giving only the tersest of responses to their questions.

André vibrated with anxiety and guilt. He vividly saw the tree trunk careening wildly toward them a few hours before. His own body thrashing in the St. Lawrence River. Basile Roche's arms flailing in a too-fast current. His mind raced, berating himself. *First I was scared. I jumped out of the canoe without thinking. I forgot about the canoe and the others. I failed my friend and my canoe-mates. Because of that, Gerard is lost.* Then the circle of hot shame repeated itself.

Gerard's setting pole remained stuck upright between rocks in the river. With that too-sharp reminder of their pain, a few men offered to paddle to get the pole, but Antoine's refusal was gruff and final—the pole would not be retrieved.

"The current here, it is wicked." He rubbed his eye and looked away, and added in a low voice, "We cannot lose another man, nor a canoe."

"But the iron tip of the setting pole—we need it, *non*?"

"Not that one."

Instead of using Gerard's personal paddle to form the cross that marked his passing, Amable and Urbain, Gerard's closest friends, sat and solemnly carved branches in the shape of a blade and a shaft. They would save his paddle, with its narrow blade and the lopsided grip that Gerard favored, to return to his wife.

Nobody spoke, waiting for the kettle of pea porridge to be ready.

The bales of canoe No. 3 had been opened to dry. Usually the contents might be strewn wherever there was space. Tonight, as a small way to acknowledge losing Gerard, the men kept the campsite organized and tidy.

Nobody mentioned celebrating with high wines, but they knew they had been slow to react and had weakened judgment. Had they paid close attention to their *avant* and *gouvernail* at the moment of peril, they wouldn't have tipped their canoe. Their eyes looked haunted.

Emile reported that, in addition to trade goods, a keg of peas and another of hard biscuit had tumbled downstream. So this meal might be the last large portion for some time.

Of the cargo, three barrels of high wines and one bale of trade goods had not been retrieved. They had also lost canoe supplies—a spare roll of bark for patching, the long spruce root, called *wattap*, used to repair the canoe lacings and one basket of pine pitch for sealing the holes. Those things could be shared across the brigade. But the voyageurs' personal packs were lost forever.

Including André's, with his packet from Father Goiffon tucked inside, and the wristlet from Catherine and Sam. Gone. Those losses hurt, but worse was his dull feeling since Gerard's death. He had sought Gerard's friendship—among the *milieux*, he had few others.

Antoine met with the *avants* and *gouvernails*. Though Eustache and Ignace had reported no breaks in the canoe hull, they were reinforcing every seam. When Eustache reached for the pot of pine pitch to apply the sticky goo to a lacing, Antoine motioned André, who was helping them, to his side.

In a quiet voice, he said, "It has been a hard day, losing Gerard, my longtime friend." He looked away and was silent. "For you, getting hit by the keg as you tried to help Gerard. I know you struggle since your fall in the St. Lawrence." He glanced briefly at André, judging his resilience. "Ignace, he said your blankets and spare clothes were lost. And your book."

André shrugged. "Father Goiffon will understand about the book. It is not important, compared to ... to ..."

Antoine took a deep breath, staring across the river for a long time. "There is something else. Tonight, I am asking a big thing of you, André. After Urbain and Amable finish lashing together their cross for Gerard, we will walk back to the rapids. We will pound his cross in the ground. That we know how to do." Antoine was silent for some time. Then he turned to face André, his voice thick with pain. "But no one knows the words a priest would say. Except you."

André was startled. He had not expected that. But the brigade carried no *bourgeois*, or anyone who could preside at a funeral.

"You must be that one, André, to say the priest's words. You are the only schooled person among us. Think of Gerard—he was your friend. Tell us words to remember Gerard. You can do this?"

He wanted to refuse. *Speak in front of them? And me the youngest?* His knees weakened at the thought of leading them. But in his lessons with Father Goiffon, he had read and discussed the Scriptures. None of the men could read and no one had a Bible. *A hard thing. I must force myself to do it. But for Gerard I will.*

He nodded, numbly.

"*Merci.* Go now, to be ready." Antoine turned towards the canoe.

While walking back, André was unsettled. He wondered what verses would offer a worthy tribute to the steersman. *What does Father Goiffon say at funerals?*

⌣∶∾

After a melancholy supper, the brigade silently hiked the rocky riverbank overlooking the rapids. They doffed their knitted *tuques* and a few pulled silver crosses strung on cords hidden under their shirts. They stood quietly while Amable and Urbain erected their makeshift cross. Pounding it straighter than the other memorials to show respect for their friend and *gouvernail*, the hammering hushed them all, echoing like final heartbeats across the glade.

After Urbain finished, Antoine said, "André?" The men shuffled their feet and turned their surprised eyes to André.

He took a deep breath, his voice filled with emotion as he broke the silence, and began shakily. "In the Bible are words about the kind of people God wants us to be." He paused to still the trembling of his voice. "It says, 'And what does the Lord require of you, but to do justly, and to love mercy, and to walk humbly with your God?'"

They stared at him when his voice quaked, but he continued. "Gerard LeMoine was like that. He was just, and merciful, and humble, as these words say. He was a good man—and kind to me."

At these words they nodded. André was speaking true.

"Gerard became a voyageur, but he missed his family, like you miss yours. We became family for each other. Now he will not return to them. Nor to us, for we are, uh, … we were also his family."

His voice cracked, and he was silent for a dozen heartbeats. "What were the best moments of your days with Gerard? Please tell us what you will remember of him."

He paused while the emotions shuddered through all of them. He saw gratefulness in their eyes.

In the silence, they heard an owl hooting.

Antoine spoke first. "What a steersman. I trusted him with our lives."

One by one, somber voices added memories.

"Gerard, he taught me to be the *avant*. Every day he helped me," Emile said shakily. "I will always think of what he told me."

"He grew up on zee farm next to us. Gerard, he helped my uncle find and dig a well—it has zee best water."

"Gerard and I, we paddled shoulder-to-shoulder almost twelve years. Until he became steersman."

"No one could whittle or carve things like he could. This whistle, tools, toys for my boys."

"He read zee rivers like zee priest reads a book. He see what is under zee water. Gerard remembered it all, year after year."

"Like a brother to me."

"Gerard, he helped me to laugh," Pretty Mouse said, his voice choking. "Without him I am sad. We are all sad—but he would not want us to remember this black night. Instead he would think of the bright days before he left us."

When it finally became quiet again, André thanked them. "One more verse may help us remember Gerard. God said about Jesus, 'This is my beloved son, in whom I am well pleased.' I think God is also pleased with our friend Gerard."

As he began to recite the funeral prayers, others chimed in. They knew the words when he forgot or he faltered. Afterwards some men bowed their heads, whispered their own prayers and made the sign of the cross, while others looked deep into the starry sky or across the rapids where Gerard's setting pole stood sentinel.

The next brigades arriving here would see this new cross near the portage and pay tribute to yet another man who would not come back.

Though it was dark on the return to the campsite, they watched as birds swooped over the water. The intense weight had lifted and for that André was glad. *But tomorrow, we are minus one man, minus a steersman, minus rations, minus cargo and supplies. What will the next part of this voyage be like?*

CHAPTER 10

A pearly mist rose like a veil over the waters the next morning as Antoine stood in front of the long-faced voyageurs reloading the canoes. "I have two things to say. First, you know we lost provisions—it is ten days' worth. All canoes will have less to eat, not only canoe No. 3. Every man's supper will be smaller. When we reach Sault Ste. Marie I will trade for more. Which you know."

Less food meant less energy and less distance each day. That would push their stamina and their tempers to the limit. The men eyed each other grumpily, not pleased to suffer because of the mistakes of the *milieux* of canoe No. 3.

"Second, we cannot hire another steersman. The few people who live along these waters are farmers, not voyageurs. They do not know these river currents like we do," Antoine continued. He took a deep breath. "Our new *gouvernail*, he must be one of us. The *avants* and *gouvernails*, we have discussed this."

He gestured towards Louis Dutremble, a wiry short man with broad shoulders and a trimmed beard. "Today, Louis will be *gouvernail* in canoe No. 2."

With a swagger, Louis picked up a setting pole and confidently fitted a metal tip to one end. Louis had been a voyageur many years in Antoine's brigade—this year he had paddled *milieu* in the fourth canoe. He threw back his chest, proud to take on the new task.

The men murmured. "But does he know steering?" one voice said.

Antoine planted his feet and looked directly at the questioner. "He is ready to meet this challenge. *Merci*, Louis. Thank you."

Antoine turned his attention to re-balancing the load in the fourth canoe. Its *avant* and *gouvernail* would have to make up for one fewer man in their canoe and it would be harder to stay on course.

Along the banks that day, the men glanced sharply at other crosses lashed from broken paddles. They did not speak Gerard's name. Though they sang, the spark which animated them was dull.

André continued to berate himself. *I should have done something. But I was afraid. Now I have lost a companion, my teacher, my friend. He is gone forever.*

The rocks in that part of the river were like jagged teeth, and Louis became exhausted reacting to each one, as well as the currents that smacked against them and twisted the course of the canoe.

At sundown when they stopped for the day, Louis shook his head, humbled by the difficulty of the new task. "One day I am *gouvernail*. This was one day too many. Someone else must steer." He laid the setting pole on the ground and walked away.

Antoine quietly conferred with the *avants* and *gouvernails*. Next they approached Prisque Peloquin, quick and strong and spirited, and called the Stick.

"Stick, how about you? Can you do this?"

Prisque lifted his head, laughed. "Of course. I am a voyageur."

That day the canoe scraped many times against submerged boulders, each man wincing to feel it. Beneath the surface they imagined seeing shreds of their own birch bark hull.

At the campsite that night, Prisque shook his head. "I did not know it would be like this. Too hard. I cannot sing and steer—not another day." He leaned the pole against the canoe and slumped down. "Me, I am better as our singer. And I like my little paddle better than the long pole."

The next day, Matthieu Neveux volunteered. "I know this Mattawa River. She is jealous and wants to make us turn around, go home. She shows her ugly teeth every day—rocks everywhere. At least eleven carries here, I know them all. And the waters even better."

André remembered Gerard naming the unique portages: Hell's Gate, Great Rock, Lazy Portage, Prairie Portage, Cave Portage, Talon Portage, Music and Bad Music Portages, Rocky Portage, Turtle Portage among them.

With bravado, Matthieu said, "Hell's Gate, it is not so hard. Me, I can bring us through."

While the canoe made it without a scratch, Emile, as the *avant*, was white-faced—Matthieu had argued with his commands. They did not work well as a team.

Antoine continued testing a different steersman each day. None consented to a second ordeal of split-second life-threatening decisions. To a man, they preferred paddling in the middle of the canoe. The rugged trials of their endurance—paddling against the raging river, a *décharge* over slippery rocks, carrying the cargo over muddy and nearly-perpendicular portages—were already too daunting.

In each rapids, André saw again the waters swallowing up Gerard. He wished the other voyageurs would speak again of their friend, because his death was a heavy burden they shared. But talking was not their way—joking and teasing was. *I will have to find my own way to keep his memory fresh.*

The brigade traveled slower now, with inexperienced steersmen and one fewer paddler. Other brigades and express canoes passed them. They would not be first at the *rendezvous* this year.

CHAPTER 11

Late one night, a week after Gerard had disappeared, Antoine stepped softly near where André lay sleeping, and cleared his throat. "André, come here. I must speak to you."

André shook himself and rolled out of his blanket. Antoine had already walked away. André followed, mystified.

A dozen steps beyond the camping area, Antoine turned. "André, tomorrow you will be canoe No. 2's *gouvernail.*"

André swallowed hard. *Gouvernail?* He started to protest, but Antoine held up his hand.

"You are too young—this I know. You have not been a voyageur long enough—this I know. The rivers are not familiar—this I know. But when you asked Gerard and Ignace about how they steered, you showed me who you are—one who watches, one who wants to know, one who is not afraid to ask when he needs to. The others, they teased when you tried to paddle a boulder—you did not respond in anger, in spite or meanness. But you keep trying to learn, and you have learned from your mistakes. All those things are important to me."

"But the men—will they accept me?" André protested. "To be steersman is an honor, but I have not ...."

"I do not ask you to honor you. This is a great responsibility, a heavy load, as you have seen from the others. Your talk—about force and angle and pressure—we don't understand it. Somehow your schooling, it has taught you another way to think about our work. We do not have learning from books. Maybe now we will discover what we missed by not having lessons. The others, they saw how you helped to say goodbye to Gerard. They were impressed. And they will accept you because I ask. They will do what you ask, if you are fair. We shall see tomorrow."

He paused, listening to the crashing waters of the rapids. A cool mist blew over them.

"If this task is not for you, I will ask others to take that yoke for a day. But I think it will become your task. *Non*, I know it will be."

Late into the night, André tossed and turned, recalling how Gerard had described the river's challenges. *Tomorrow we face the Cave Portage. Then the Talon, a waterfall of forty feet, in two cascades. That portage is dangerous—a day's work to get through. Then both of Les Musiques, one which is up and down among broken rocks. Somewhere is the height-of-land, where the setting poles will be tossed out and the long paddles are used instead. And after that, the canoes travel downstream.*

But perhaps someone else would be steersman then.

I let my thoughts wander on the early days, when we passed the Long Sault, the Chaudières and the Grand Calumet. Someone else made the decisions. That time is over. Now every minute I will have to watch the current in the river. But I can do this for one day, because Antoine asked me. It will be hard, but it is the right thing to do. Help me, Gerard. Tell me what I need to know tomorrow. Help us all, Ste. Anne.

In the morning, Antoine announced André as the steersman of Emile's canoe. It raised a few eyebrows, and a guffaw.

"Scarface?"

"How old are you, boy?"

"Antoine, you jest."

"Tomorrow it may be you." Antoine looked pointedly at them, and they closed their mouths.

Emile grinned as he handed André a setting pole.

Uncertain, André took a deep breath, nodded and looked around. His late-night thoughts steadied him and, though he didn't feel confident, he would test himself. Their lives depended on him.

As the canoes set out, André kept his eyes on Emile. Sensing Emile's body language—his every muscle tightening or leaning—gave him information on what was ahead on the river and its shifting currents. Recalling Gerard's words, he listened to the sounds of the water to feel its moods and whims. Using the setting pole as fingers, he felt between the rocks, pried loose ones, slid the canoe past immovable others. He looked deep under the water's surface and steered between rugged boulders and through narrow whirling channels.

The waters rushed and swirled and the submerged rocky ledges threatened—but under Emile's leadership, the *milieux* reacted with precision and strength, even during the day's last miserable *décharge*. It was almost as if Gerard were steering instead of him.

At nightfall, André handed his pole to Emile. "*Merci*, you made it easier. I was lucky today."

Emile smiled. "I knew you could do it."

"Good, my man. I watched you." Eustache clapped André on the back.

Prisque and Louis followed, shaking his hand. "And tomorrow—you will be *gouvernail* again?"

Others punched his shoulder. "The balancing—you were born to it."

But a few, including two who had failed at steering, did not look at him. "Too easy," they sneered. "Not a fair test. But that will come."

Though André fell asleep quickly, the distant baying of a wolf woke him. He checked the moon to judge the time. In a few hours, the brigade would decamp. When a return to his slumbers did not come, he reviewed the day's work, the rapids he'd wished he'd done differently. *Others have had harder waters. Matthieu was right—my day as gouvernail was not a fair trial. But surely Antoine will have another man steer tomorrow.*

The next morning, André returned to his seat as a *milieu* of canoe No. 3, but Emile and Antoine shook their heads.

"Of course you steer today," Emile said. "Now, my friend, this day we will come to several hard rapids—at some we *décharge*, others we portage. You can do it."

Numbly, André took his place at the stern, watching Emile's every movement. They guided their canoe a second day past rugged ridges and eddying currents with no mishaps. The rapids Emile mentioned were not as difficult as ones they had previously tackled.

His legs were stiff as he slipped out of the canoe and waded ashore, steadying it. *This cold water feels good today. Maybe we have gotten past the worst. What do you think, Gerard? Merci, my friend, for helping me today.*

Exhausted at the end of the day, he mechanically examined the canoe seams and ate his supper—and dropped off to deep sleep.

When the brigade reached the height-of-land, the *avants* and *gouvernails* marked it in the traditional way—by noisily heaving the setting poles, no longer needed, into the rushing waters. The rest of the journey was downstream and they would use long paddles, not poles.

"Here we always have a dram of high wine to celebrate," Pretty Mouse said hopefully.

Antoine lowered his eyebrows and looked sharply. "Then we start a new tradition."

Pretty Mouse sighed—and nodded.

"I traded for smoked fish to add to our supper tonight," Antoine said. Then he stirred cocoa, nutmeg and sugar from his special rations to the teakettle—treats they had not tasted since Lachine, to make up for the scantier suppers and lack of rum.

"Me, I will dance." Pretty Mouse held up his paddle. He had tied a cedar bough around its blade, and slid his red *tuque* onto the handle. "My partner, she has stolen my hat. See her skirt, it swishes. And she wants to dance, but only with the Mouse. Sing the Kettle Song."

Big Louis, one of the cooks, hurried over with his iron pot and a wooden spoon, wet from being rinsed at the water's edge. "Antoine, next year hire someone who plays the fiddle." He kept time for the singers who had gathered by the fire.

"Now sing 'There was an Old Grandmother,'" Pretty Mouse said.

They did while Mouse whirled his "partner" around the campsite. After "I Know a Thing or Two" and a few more songs, Mouse was spent.

Urbain, Matthieu, Old Louis and Baldy surprised them with a dance of energetic high kicks. Emile borrowed Pretty Mouse's paddle and danced gracefully, as if he were with Marguerite Lanfan, while they sang "I'm Not Quite of the Peasantry." Others followed, including André who challenged Alfred, one of the most athletic, to a mock sword duel.

Games of agility and strength followed—leaping the fire, tossing knives, leg and arm wrestling, a tug of war. Laughing washed over the sadness of losing Gerard and the tension created by paddling with fewer men. Celebrating at the height-of-land began to bind them into a brotherhood, again.

"André, use Gerard's paddle now," Emile said the next morning, handing him a long-shafted narrow-bladed paddle with an offset grip. "Your *milieu* paddle, it is too short for a steersman. We don't have time for you to carve one. And Gerard, I think he would like you to use it."

André took the paddle hesitantly. The wood was polished, and dark brown where Gerard's hands had held it. *Be with me, Gerard. Help me see into these waters. With you guiding me, I can help the brigade.*

With slightly more confidence, he continued steering, through a small lake, then a narrow passageway in a swamp, barely the width of a canoe. He kept his focus constant at each change in the current, as they neared Lake Nipissing. *Steering takes less skill here than against the rapids. Tomorrow they will choose someone else, because the more experienced men can do this.*

At night Antoine beckoned him to sit. "Join us. What did Gerard say of the route after Trout Lake?"

Holding the borrowed paddle, André recounted the challenges Gerard had described. That night, he fell asleep while eating supper.

Antoine looked over at him and shook his head. "Maybe it is too much."

CHAPTER 12

André piloted canoe No. 2 through a winding boggy tributary that beavers had dammed. He knew the whole brigade was traveling slower than usual. He did not feel their criticism, but instead their gratitude at not having to steer.

Navigating through these watery meadows is not so hard as the rapids. If the river is like this, I can probably steer all the way to Lake Nipissing.

As their canoes slipped along, Prisque began "*À la claire fontaine,*" a love song, and the men joined in, though not as lustily as they once had. When they came to Lake Nipissing, a high wind rolled choppy waves at them, and their canoes rose and fell.

During a pipe break, Hercule beckoned to a group of crosses on a small island in the center of the lake. "A rock, it found their canoe."

André wished he would say Gerard's name. *But I must be vigilant so that is not our fate as well. Gerard, can you help us?*

Antoine had been unusually quiet since Gerard's drowning. He decided the waves were too high for them to cross safely, so the brigade laid over for a day, waiting for the wind to drop before their final days on the rivers.

Men with fishing or hunting skills supplemented the cooks' suppers. The rest repaired their shirts and moccasins, which had taken a beating over the portage trails.

The *avants* and *gouvernails* discussed the last section of the route leading to Lake Huron, a breakneck series of chutes over seventy miles long—the French River.

Antoine motioned for André to join them. "Come. They speak of navigating the French. Their secrets you need to know."

"I … am to steer downstream? Not someone with experience? I am ready to hand this yoke to another."

"*Oui*, André, you are now our *gouvernail*. You have questions?" He patted André's shoulder.

The steersmen considered the water levels, how that affected the most difficult or hidden perils, the condition of the short portages, and André imprinted their advice:

"Follow the south shore. Look for a flat rock in the bay. Where you can see still waters, that is the start of the French."

"The first portage is at Recollet Falls. The one at Petite Faucille—not thirty paces to the end."

"The French River, she has four mouths into Lake Huron—take the channel to the west. It protects our canoes the most from the great open waters of the lake."

"Remember the headwinds two years ago? As soon as we saw Huron, the wind spun us around. I nearly swamped my canoe."

When they were by themselves, Antoine asked, "Are you ready?"

"I will do my best, but it scares me."

"To be scared, that is normal, though most voyageurs would not speak the words. Few run the French River without planning. Take as much time as you need to get a good look downstream—then you will find the clear channel."

The responsibility terrified André. Without a memory of the route, he could only apply his geometry and physics to steering downstream. He hardly slept. What helped was Antoine's echo of Joseph's wisdom—to take plenty of time to prepare. *I can only ready my mind, because once we are on the river, I have but split seconds to find the best route. Help us all, Ste. Anne.*

By the next morning the wind had abated. With uncertainty, André said his daily prayer, took up Gerard's long paddle in the stern and traversed the canoe across the lake to the French River. At the last tranquil waters of its outlet, boulders loomed everywhere, hiding beneath the glassy surface and ready to punch holes in the thin birch bark. Ahead of them, the river swirled foamy, its roar deafening.

After the *milieux* prayed to Ste. Anne for safety and then tossed tobacco offerings to the water, André steadied himself with thoughts of Gerard's wisdom and his paddle. *Gerard would think ahead of the current. He'd listen to the water. Be with me, Gerard. I need you today.*

The canoes carefully separated themselves—they did not want to crowd each other on the narrow passages. André and Emile studied the raging white waters.

"*Allons!* Let's go, men!" They called to each other as they navigated.

"Double-time," Emile yelled, then, "Triple" and they sluiced a small rapids, hurtling through a tight spillway.

André intuitively finessed the waters, tapping against boulders to get better angles. At the top of a rapids, he levered them away from a rock ledge before they plummeted over the falls, flying through the air. For a few terrible seconds there was no river beneath them.

A moment later, they plunged into the water, a giant spray flying around them. They rocketed through the frothing waters and around tight bends.

Another tapering curve, another current speeding through the rocks, another dizzying falls.

Finally they pulled up at the portage, the *milieux* grinning as they unloaded, carried and reloaded the bales. The first canoe had already left for the next section.

André's heart thudded. "We did it." He felt giddy. *Thank you, Gerard. Merci beaucoup.*

"But of course. We are voyageurs."

"Ste. Anne, she was with us."

"That was the fastest we ever shot through."

"Water is high this year."

"We only skimmed that boulder—it didn't sink us."

"Good work, André. Learning to pole while standing on that rock back on the Ottawa—it must have helped."

Readying themselves for the upcoming section, Emile said, "The second part of the river is like a gut—long, narrow, twisting." They discussed its most difficult features, and what they would do.

"*Allons!* Let's go." André took a deep breath and smiled. His hands caressed Gerard's paddle. *You're coming along again?*

The pipe break over, they set off for the next cascades and bends. The river tapered dramatically, and dropped, and sped up. Their canoe catapulted and lurched.

André's skills and focus were tested constantly. In a gorge, he poled off the walls with his long paddle. He steered through one chute so narrow the *milieux* had to hold their paddles close to the canoe instead of paddling. They fought the current—rode it—used it. The water had a mind of its own.

The river widened briefly, then turned straight into rocks.

"Left channel."

"Swing. Rock ahead."

"Dig men."

"Triple-time."

"Right side, up."

When they had passed through the worst of the treacherous waters, André maneuvered them along the edge of the river where the current slowed. To steady the canoe while they rested, the *milieux* grabbed at overhanging branches. Then they found the portage.

The men, laughed, relieving their tension, as they toted the bales overland.

"My heart was in my mouth the whole time."

Mine too. Exhausted, André needed rest. *Did I breathe? My back and shoulders sting, they are so tight. Is that how it was for you too, Gerard?*

"Hoorah! I want to dance."

"But not now, Bear. Wait until we camp."

"This makes up for all the slow days at the Long Sault."

Emile grinned at André. "That was the famous Little Sickle. One more rush of roaring current to come. You can do it."

André nodded.

"The last section of whitewater is long. The river races through to get to Huron," Emile said. "She will try to suck us into the channel straight ahead—look for the old fort. But we veer to the right. More rocks and rapids before we find the mouth. After today you will not forget this river."

The last of the whitewater. I can do it. Gerard, guide me over the last section. Please.

André scooped water from the river to splash his face and to drink. He took a deep breath. "I'm ready."

"Here we go, men!"

They crossed fast narrow passages, one after another. Finally Emile and André spotted the Voyageur's Channel, a wide mouth into Lake Huron. Suddenly, as they entered it, the river slowed toward the Georgian Bay, and the horizon opened up and stretched for miles.

Exhilarated, the men yelled and hooted at their speedy traverse of the French River. They tossed triumphant pinches of tobacco into the great lake.

Deeply relieved, André thanked Ste. Anne for their successful passage, especially on the Mattawa and French Rivers. He had felt Gerard's gentle words in his ear to guide him and his hands on the long paddle.

"A song, Stick."

Prisque began *"Alouette,"* and they paddled with renewed energy, their voices full of glee. As they came in sight of the rest of the brigade, all of Antoine's men picked up the refrain. Never was there more joy in singing. They improvised on the verses, laughing, and it powered their strokes.

And for the first time on this trip, André was happy. They had made it! He had made it! His heart soared. *Merci, mon Dieu.*

When the song ended, Emile shouted, "We camp tonight on the grassy meadow, La Prairie des Français. Big enough for the whole brigade. Antoine will be there soon."

That night André spent extra time with his canoe, finding scrapes and loose lacings, repairing them with great care. Glancing at Antoine, who winked at him, he gave special thanks to Gerard. And Joseph. He had proved himself—with their help.

We've been gone more than six weeks. In maybe only two more, if we are lucky with weather, we will be in Grand Portage. No, it's the New Fort. One day nearer. Good.

He listened intently as the *avants* and *gouvernails* recounted the day's adventure and planned the final leg of their journey—the vast inland oceans of Huron and Superior would tax them differently than the rivers had.

"Hug the mainland. Then the small islands, they screen us from big winds."

"*Oui*, but be wary of the rocks on the lee shore. They bite."

"Too bad we cannot cross the bays—this way is much longer."

"Speed is not all."

"Hear that, Antoine?"

André, exhausted from the exhilarating day, was relieved the next part of the route had no more rapids to complicate things. *Paddling over a great lake for hours, stopping only for short pipe breaks—that's the picture I have of voyageurs. No portages, no tricky currents, no hidden rocks, no deciding which side of the river is safer—I should be able to handle this.*

Chapter 13

It was not yet dawn, most of the men sleeping hard, when Antoine banged on the kettle to announce the final changes in the brigade. They jolted to attention.

"Canoe No. 1, we leave now for Sault Ste. Marie so I can trade for extra food. Other canoes, you travel as a brigade. Together." He stared at each of them to drive home his point, his eyes no longer sparkling with joyful energy.

"Canoe No. 2 will have nine *milieux* and the rest of the brigade, ten each. Emile and André, your canoe-men are younger—you have more strength and stamina. I have faith in you."

With one fewer paddler, and me a new steersman, our canoe will be hard pressed to keep up. How can Gerard help me here?

Antoine's canoe left with a loud cheer. With good weather, he would arrive at Sault Ste. Marie in six days, and at the *rendezvous* in less than two weeks. Longer for the rest of the brigade.

"At the Sault—food will be there for you."

"Soon we see you. My stomach, it wants *rubbaboo*."

They were all hungry for *rubbaboo*, the hearty stew made from dried corn and bison *pemmican*, foods produced by tribes in the interior. Last night's pea soup had been watery.

Their first night on the great lake had refreshed all the men, who liked seeing wide beckoning expanses of water instead of feeling hemmed in by dark pines lining the river canyons. In the weeks since they left Lachine, they had hauled three tons of cargo over thirty-six muddy portages and dragged it through thirty-six wet *décharges*. They were unspeakably relieved to be past that drudgery.

The other three canoes would travel slower, especially André's canoe No. 2, shorthanded and with his limited experience as steersman. To keep up, their days would be rigorous—rising earlier, paddling longer, finding a campsite later.

An hour after Antoine, they launched the rest of the brigade. Their hearts were light and they sang long and loud, hoping to make up lost time.

With an uneven number of *milieux*, André found it difficult to steer the canoe straight. Veering crookedly across the lake wasted the men's energy, so he and Emile rearranged the men and re-balanced the loads.

Paddling in the crystal-clear water of the big lake, with a high range of coastal hills visible on the north, André's canoe-mates eagerly pointed out familiar sights.

Like the Grondine, where the waves surged among large rocks. André remembered it because it sounded like moaning. *It's how I felt then—every muscle ached.* But this year was different—he heard its surf crashing, calling him to appreciate this north country, its waters mirroring the sky.

"The Bell, it is not so far," said Prisque. "We stop there for a pipe, a narrow strait—between two islands."

"Ahh, *oui*," Hercule said. "When you pitch a stone against that great dark rock, you hear the low clear ring of a bell, not a clunk."

Soon they paddled past the massive black boulder that was a source of amazement. At the pipe-break, André was surprised that two men had brought their own pebbles to hear its bell sound.

And on they paddled and sang.

Paddling on the Ottawa and Mattawa was like fighting a wild beast. Paddling the great lakes is easier than the rivers. Others say the lakes are fearsome and can rise up to destroy us, like slipping past a sleeping dragon. But dragons are for storybooks. I'm not that superstitious—this will not be as treacherous as rapids.

Suddenly his muscles tensed as he thought of the wild beast of water that had almost drowned him at Lachine, and then flashes of Gerard disappearing. And Basile Roche. *Maybe ... maybe there are dragons.* He pushed the thoughts away, paddling harder.

André searched the sky and waters for clues. He discovered that each color of water—from icy gray and slate blue to pale blue and brilliant blue—meant different depths or weather conditions. The wind affected the waves, sometimes frothing its tips, other times rolling along looking hardly dangerous at all.

"See that point, Emile? So much shorter if we cut across this big bay. What do you think?" asked Urbain.

"We could catch up to the others," Alfred said hopefully, seeing canoes No. 3 and 4 already far in the distance.

"*Non,* this wind, it can whip the waves into dangerous crests. We follow the shoreline. Or did you not hear Antoine?"

But traveling closer to land, with all its inlets, meant André needed to stay vigilant for submerged rocks and deadheads. *I can't relax for a second. I dare not take my eyes from this water.*

The next morning, Pretty Mouse, representing canoes No. 3 and 4, came with his *tuque* in hand and head meek, asking to speak to Emile and André. "I know Antoine said to stay close together but it is hard to paddle so slow. We are sorry. Can we go ahead?"

Emile glanced at André, who shrugged. They both knew how restrictive their slower pace felt to the rest of the brigade. "But of course," Emile said. "We'll look for you at the campsites. And when we find our rhythm, then we'll charge ahead of you, before the New Fort."

As the two canoes sped away, Mouse called back, "Don't forget. Stay close to the shoreline."

By mid-day, André could no longer see their canoes across the waters—canoe No. 2 was alone.

Like an ocean, Lake Huron could be unpredictable—weather changed hourly. After crisp mornings, the afternoons grew hot enough to take off their shirts. An hour later, a blustery wind might chill them, or rain might pelt them.

With rapidly depleting provisions, their empty stomachs gurgled. The men said nothing, but tightened their sashes over shrinking bellies. Their faces became pinched and their tempers got shorter. Even paddling longer days, they did not catch up to the other canoes of the brigade.

During the day, singing helped them forget. At night, sleeping renewed them, until swarms of buzzing, biting mosquitoes arrived, cutting short their precious sleep.

On the sixth morning André arose to fog so dense he could not tell if it was day or night. *Finally the lake is smooth, but how can we pick our way through the rocky reefs and islands of this shore when we can't see anything? I could point us the wrong way and not know it.*

Emile prowled around the campfire, peering into the mist. "The 'old woman' wants us to wait here."

"The old woman?" André looked puzzled.

"Have you forgotten? This big lake, it is like an old woman, *la Vieille,* who changes her mind often—she helps us, then she is angry with us. Today she has made the waters calm but filled the air with her blanket of clouds. To trick her, one year we paddled at night. But we had a moon to guide us."

"In this fog, skirting the shore will be risky," André said.

"So we let the men sleep. Until the mist burns off."

A few woke anyway, their bodies naturally ready for the day, but they were restless in the fog, feeling caged on the rocky beach. Suddenly Prisque pointed to a huge pair of horns moving toward them. André froze at the apparition.

"A moose," Prisque said. "You can't see its head or legs in this fog. Make some noise so it doesn't head this way. Moose, they don't like us."

They hooted—and the moose paused, gazed at them for several seconds, and turned back the way it had come.

Two men edged near André and Emile.

"Our grandmother grew up in the woods," the one called Trumpet said, gesturing to the pine forests mere steps away from the rocky shore. "She taught us what plants to eat."

"We look for roots. Now, until the fog breaks up," the other one, Porcupine, added. "At night it is too dark to find them." He looked at the sky. "About an hour, I think."

"Good, one hour," Emile nodded. "Then I hope we can leave."

As they slipped into the forest, André studied them. *Straight dark hair, not curly like most of the voyageurs. No beards, a dark cast to their skin. So they have native blood. I wonder how they became part of Antoine's brigade in Lachine.*

André realized he hardly knew the men in his canoe, except for Emile. There had been little time, with his constant attention on steering. His *milieux* had graciously accepted him instead of humiliating his limited steering skills. In most brigades, mistakes were met with mocking. *These milieux are kind. I want to know them better.*

Because the two men had the same grandmother, André reasoned that they were cousins. Pierre was called Trumpet because he was quiet and Toussaint was called Porcupine, because he easily slipped through the woods. Neither name fit. *I wonder what their tribal names are.*

He considered what he knew of the others in his canoe. Prisque, called Stick, and Alfred, called Bear, were brothers, Prisque the older by eight years.

Hercule's name already had teasing built in. Hercule and Urbain and Amable had wintered together for years with Gerard. Urbain was known as Weakling, and Amable, Clumsy. Louis the Lemon and Jean the Rabbit made up the rest of the close-knit group.

I don't like being called Scarface, though it sometimes shows I am one of them. But from now on I will use my canoe-mates' real names.

"Emile," André asked while they waited for the fog to lift. "Why don't we use fish hooks to catch fish while we paddle? Wouldn't that help us get more food?"

"Who knows? Maybe we travel too fast for the lake fish. Or maybe they swim so deep in the bottom of the lake that our line does not go far enough down. Maybe our hooks are too small for the big ones."

"While we paddle, we don't have time to haul fish in, nor a place to put them," Alfred added.

Emile looked out at the fog hovering over the vast waters. "Instead hope for rabbit or squirrel. If anyone can snare some, it would be the cousins."

Within the allotted time, the cousins returned, their small kettle filled with an assortment of green leaves and muddy roots, but no rabbit.

As they named the mysterious lumps in Ojibwe, the other men looked dismayed.

"Won't they make us sick?"

"We eat these. Watch us," Toussaint said. "You will see if we get sick—or not."

"Besides, when we eat the roots," Pierre pointed out, "your share of pea soup, it is bigger."

"Look, men. The mist, it burns away," Emile said.

Though the sky was heavy with low clouds, they reloaded the canoe and pushed off, paddling alone on the lake. André missed the brigade and wondered how far away they were. *When we heard their songs, we knew their location. Now it's up to Emile and me to find the way.*

Paddling in the light fog, André noticed birds chirping, the sound of waves lapping on rocks, the smell of pines that lined the shore like a dark curtain. Each gave him a sense of how close they were to the land.

He wondered which direction they were headed. *I wish I had a compass. Or a map of this shore with all its inlets and islands.*

Eventually the fog lifted, and by the third pipe-break, the sky was clear. Cheered, the men sang. Another hot day.

They paddled longer, until nearly dusk, to make up for the late start.

While Hercule tended the soup pot, Pierre and Toussaint scrubbed their brown roots by the shore, peeling, chopping, then dumping them into a small kettle of water. It drew skepticism.

"Are you sure it can be eaten?"

"Do I smell onion?"

The cousins shrugged. While their kettle boiled, they returned to the woods following a stream that fed into Lake Huron. In an hour they returned with a few more greens and two fish which they cleaned and tossed into their bubbling stew.

Soon the smells became mouth-watering, aromas that André couldn't identify. *Berthe would know. I should have gone with her when she gathered herbs.*

"What are those brown things you added last?" Hercule, who cooked for this canoe, was the most curious.

Toussaint offered its Ojibwe name, but André could not pronounce it. Nor could the others.

The men, snugging their sashes more tightly around their unsatisfied stomachs, watched silently as the pair downed their soup.

CHAPTER 14

Again the next morning, the seventh day on Lake Huron, a dense fog blanketed everything, thicker than before. The hungry men became testy, with strong opinions as to when to leave.

"We are voyageurs, we paddle. This fog is nothing."

"Five years ago, the fog was so heavy we waited three days—on an island."

The subject turned to food.

"One year in the far north," Prisque said, "we had so little that we ate the moss on the rocks, same as the caribou. Our stomachs always hurt. Do you remember, Hercule?"

That quieted them, pondering how hungry they would have to be to eat moss.

"What did it taste like?" André wanted to know.

Prisque shook his head. "Bitter. But it was food."

"Mostly we ate what the tribes ate—berries and fish in summer," Hercule said. "Nuts and wild rice in the fall. Meat when they hunted. Sometimes nothing at all."

"We can eat what bears eat," Toussaint said, "but you may not like it. Like grubs, beetles, frogs and snails, earthworms, snakes." He saw they were shocked and would not eat such low food. If their hunger got worse, they could talk about it again. But not now.

"What about in the spring? Not much is growing yet."

Pierre lifted out a whitish lump from his soup. "Cattail. You can always find roots."

"In a few weeks we can eat the green cattail spikes," said Toussaint, the older of the two. "Even the pollen, later in the summer."

Hercule was curious—the canoe's sack of provisions was almost empty. "Enough food to feed the whole canoe?"

Urbain resisted. "Me, I will not chance it. I need all my strength." He did not say they were short one paddler and moving slowly.

Nor were the other men ready to try something unusual. Toussaint and Pierre disappeared back into the forest.

"*Rubbaboo*, soon it will fill us," said Prisque, thinking ahead to the food they would get at Sault Ste. Marie. *Rubbaboo*, prized by natives and voyageurs alike, would easily sustain them for the rest of the journey. They looked at each other, licking their lips.

"To the Sault, most years it is four hard paddling days," Louis argued. "Already we paddle five days but we are not there. Each day we wait in the fog, that is another day without provisions."

By mid-morning the sky lightened enough to relaunch the canoe. The breeze was light, darting off and on—turning into a nice day. But then the wind freshened.

André and Emile quartered into the waves, to keep water from sloshing into the canoe. A rogue wave crashing over the bow could sink them. And *Gerard said he had to be as vigilant for wave crests over the stern, because they travel faster than the canoe.*

Suddenly, when they were nearly a mile from shore, a strong wind gusted. The once-clear sky darkened. Clouds sped past, changing from wispy white to heavy gray to near purple.

Rain? He checked the horizon. *Yes. Can we make it to land before the rain hits? No.*

"Double-time," Emile shouted. André pointed the canoe towards shore.

The men responded immediately, and Prisque chose a lively tune to spur them on.

With this headwind could come a storm. But we're too far out. How long will it take to get to a safe place?

As their canoe tilted downward into a wave trough, water poured over the bow. Jean grabbed a sponge to soak it up while Amable and Urbain hastily spread canvas across the cargo, tucking it around the bales.

Emile leaned back and André moved forward, centering their weight to lighten the pressure on the bow and stern. *Perhaps we can seesaw over the waves until we get closer to shore—or the wind drops.*

They met each wave at an angle, swiveling enough to support both the belly and the ends of the canoe. It was a long wet ride before they found a bay to wait out the rough weather.

To make up for lost time, they again paddled later, once the moon rose.

"Tonight is the last supper of pea soup," Hercule announced. "We finish it off at breakfast."

No more food until Sault Ste. Marie, a whole day or more. The mood was decidedly down.

"Then let's eat it all tonight," Louis suggested, hungrily eyeing what little was in the kettle. "Hardly enough for two meals."

"I'm for it. Emile, what do you say?" Amable said.

Emile looked around at the group, all nodding their heads. "Tonight, we eat it all, Hercule."

Pierre said, "The moon is almost full so we can see to find roots. Anyone want to join us?"

Most shook their heads, but Prisque, Hercule and André came along to forage in the bright moonlight that illuminated the darkness. Hercule took a small kettle.

First Pierre and Toussaint set snares. Then the group ventured farther inland.

"Along this stream we might see greens. Look for the one that smells like pepper," Toussaint suggested.

That gave them confidence—cress was a familiar piquant green.

"See there, that one with arrow-shaped leaves in the marsh? We can eat the root. Like a potato."

Prisque and André waded out and cut many of the bulbous roots. "Ah. For soup?" Hercule said.

Toussaint nodded. Nearby, he dug cattail roots with his knife, adding them to the kettle.

"Is this cattail?" Prisque asked, pointing to sword-shaped leaves. "This purplish flower, it looks like the flower on the old flag."

"No, not cattail and not to eat," Toussaint said, alarmed. "Both grow in marshes, but the one you can eat is much taller. Be careful."

Hercule fingered it thoughtfully—he would not like to mistake it.

"Smell—wild onions near. Here." Pierre lifted three small whitish bulbs. "But the ones with wide leaves will make you sick."

Along the root at the base of a dead tree Toussaint dropped to his hands and knees and spotted a dozen brown mushrooms, which he cut off and dropped in the kettle.

"We can eat that? It looks like a sponge."

"But you will like its taste."

"I smell mint—but where is it?"

"Ouch!" yelled André, thrashing some yards away from them. "I'm in a nettle patch!"

"Good. Nettle also is one we can eat," answered Pierre. "Cooking takes the sting away. But I know you found it the hard way. Cut some if you can."

When they returned, following a game trail to the shore, a few were asleep, but not all.

"What did you find?"

"Enough for stew tomorrow for all of us," Hercule said.

With this food, we won't be hungry tomorrow, although it is strange. Maybe being able to tell stories to our families in Lachine will make up for it. Who knows—maybe we will find that grubs and worms and snakes taste good.

CHAPTER 15

They woke to a sunrise streaked with rose—a clear day. Eagerly, the men speedily loaded the canoe. With good winds and good luck, they would arrive at Sault Ste. Marie before nightfall.

Following their usual schedule, they ate breakfast in the canoe after several hours of paddling. It was root stew to which they had added several frogs caught in the snares. No one spit it out. No one said a word. Except "*Merci*" and a nod to the cousins. It did not fill their hollow stomachs, but it was better than nothing.

We cannot paddle faster on less and less food. And because of the fog-bound mornings, it is taking us longer to get to the Sault.

"I wonder how much *pemmican* and dried corn Antoine will have for us," Jean said between songs, practically drooling.

After the Sault, we will eat well again, and my clothes will not feel so loose. André smiled, looking forward to *rubbaboo* for their last leg of the journey, where they would continue to follow the northern shores of the big lakes.

All day they paddled, singing loud to cover the rumbling of their empty bellies.

Late that afternoon, Emile shouted, "The Sault—I hear it. Tonight we sleep at the Sault."

The men cheered, trying to make out smoke rising where he pointed his paddle. The fort and trading post were too far away.

"And we eat again," said Amable. "Ahh."

"A little high wine?" Urbain suggested, but Prisque shook his head.

They paddled determinedly to the North West Company post on one side of the rapids. On the other side was a settlement with homes of Scotsmen, Canadians and Americans, and at the edge, the willow framework of a dozen native lodges.

Pierre gazed at the settlement. "They have all moved to their summer camps," he said in a low voice. "I hoped some would be here yet."

Because it was suppertime, only a scattering of people welcomed their arrival. The community had feted the earliest brigades with music and dancing to celebrate receiving the first news from the eastern cities.

Prisque and Alfred volunteered to stay with their cargo while Emile visited the post master. André and Hercule would come with him to carry back the food Antoine had arranged. The rest of the men could do as they liked.

James, the Scottish proprietor and post master, greeted them warmly. He was as eager to hear about their journey as they were to hear his news.

"Sit doon, Emile," James said. "I ha'e been waiting for ya. Ya are late. Already it is the longest day o' the year. Three o' Antoine's canoes are in Lake Superior some days now. Wha' happened to ya?"

Emile told of the loss of Gerard, and immediately André's eyes teared, hearing it as a story. He looked away while Emile continued with the search for a new *gouvernail*—at which time he introduced André—and the complications of paddling with one fewer man. Though James had heard the information from earlier members of the brigade, he listened carefully, smiling at André, studying his face.

"A heavy yoke for such a young laddie."

André, embarrassed, deferred the comment. "Emile makes it easy for me, for all of us. He's like Antoine."

"Aye, so he is."

The talk turned to other news while André eyed the goods this trading post carried and Hercule took out his pipe.

"But it was eearly this spring, it was, and we was afeered o' this strange weather," James said. "Little rain in the west, the Indians told us. The forests are dry and the prairies, they are beyond dry, with fires here and there. They say the rivers are low. All day we waited for rain but the clouds ha'e lifted."

André was surprised—plenty of rain on their first leg of the trip. He glanced out the window to see clear sky.

"Now aboot the buffalo hunts," James continued. "The tribes who trade here ha'e gone farther out. 'Tis usual they bring in *pemmican* eearly to feed the brigades. Not this year. They dinna return yet."

That surprised Hercule. "What did Antoine arrange for us?" They hoped for a half-dozen bags, ninety pounds each, of the dried corn and the pulverized buffalo meat with fat and berries.

"Antoine, a fine mon, but he was na' happy. Nay—the other company, you know the XY Company? They made shrewd trades, they did. Last autumn, they made deals with every band to trade with them. Kept it in a locked storehouse, they did. 'Twas only for XY canoe-men. Your Antoine, he paddled around to Michilimackinac and more, to find Indians who hadna' promised their *pemmican* or corn."

"Ah, he had success." Emile grinned. "I knew he would."

"He dinna get much. Each canoe took a share. This last, 'tis for you."

He motioned for them to follow around the back where he unlocked a door. One wall was stacked with pelts pressed into bales. In a far corner were two half-bags, one of *pemmican*, one of corn.

"But we need more!" Hercule said, his eyes measuring the bags. "It's hardly enough for two days. Paddling to the New Fort will take us eight or nine days, more because we are one short in the canoe. And more days because we lack food."

"Aye, I am sorry 'twill not be enough." James' eyes showed sympathy, regret and frustration. "But XY men offered much high wine to the tribes before trading and got them to make promises. The Indians wouldna' go back on their word. Though they would rather trade with all groups."

Hercule shook his head. "The liquor, that is not good."

André hefted the corn and Hercule the *pemmican* and they headed out the door. On the way to their canoe, Hercule stopped. "You carry these bags back to the canoe, and I will visit a house or two."

Hercule removed a small bag from his sash with a few silver crosses, colorful ribbons, a tiny scissors, a metal mirror, small fishhooks and a small case with a handful of needles. "Perhaps one of the families has some food to trade. Though it is a hard time of year—their gardens grow little as yet." He walked toward the houses, a hopeful bounce in his step.

At the shore, the *milieux*, watched as André returned.

"Only two bags? And partly full at that?"

André told them about the XY Company encroaching on their territory. Then he looked around. "Where are Pierre and Toussaint?"

Louis shrugged, shook his head.

"They spoke to a man standing by a small canoe," Alfred said, gesturing to a now-vacant place on the shore. "Then they paddled across St. Mary's River to the Indian village on the other side."

Hercule returned an hour later. "First, let us have *pemmican*." He sliced off chunks for each man. "Later I start the *rubbaboo*. And good news! I traded for some fresh peas, new onions and hard biscuit."

He produced a few canvas bags and one very small packet—his greatest prize. "Sage and garlic. What delicious *rubbaboo* we will have!"

Later Emile returned, grinning and full of gossip and carrying a small cask of rum. He and James had already shared a cup of it. Others crowded around, eager to partake.

André stood back, repelled. He vividly remembered his canoe-mates' struggle the day after the last night of drinking. Gerard's death was linked to their impaired skills. The memory of his friend being sucked away by the current was raw and painful—he did not want to feel that ever again.

Most nights since becoming a steersman, André had been so tired he fell asleep as soon as he rolled up in his blanket. Tonight he sat on a rock and looked at the starry patterns in the sky, searching for familiar constellations.

Almost never do I look up. In the canoe I look ahead. On a portage I look down at my feet. At night we are exhausted and trees hide the view. I've hardly thought of stars since we left home. But they cover this whole bowl of the sky, so many more than we see at home. I wish I knew more star stories.

His mind turned to the voyage ahead. So far they worked well as a crew. He hoped that wouldn't change in this last stretch of miles. What would they do for food during the days of hard paddling?

He glanced around, worried that he did not see Pierre and Toussaint. *Would they abandon us to live in the woods?*

At midnight, when most of the men were snoring, the cousins still had not returned.

"Should we search for them?" André whispered to Emile.

"Maybe they are distant kin to the Saulters, the band that lives here. Wait until morning. They will return."

Before dawn, when André awoke, the cousins were there, with birch bark baskets of dried fish and a pile of fine netting.

The new foods raised the spirits of the canoe-men. They stowed their cargo and supplies and readied to leave.

Fortunately this *sault*—a thunderous rapids—did not require them to portage into Lake Superior. A few years before, a canal had been dug and a lock built to take loaded canoes up the rapids. They pressed on toward the *rendezvous*, more than four hundred miles away.

Fifty tiring miles later, keeping the shore on their right, they stopped to camp at a rocky beach.

On Lake Superior as on Lake Huron, they arose before sunrise and paddled with short stops for *pemmican* or pipes until nearly dark. Paddling with less food reduced the number of miles they could manage, and each day it was fewer miles than the day before, though the daylight lasted longer. They stretched the fourteen hours into fifteen, and sometimes sixteen. But they did not catch up with the rest of the brigade.

Evenings, Pierre and Toussaint slipped into the forest, returning when others were asleep. *Will they reunite with their family?* But the cousins did not speak to André about their nighttime forays.

Most days the canoe faced a hard west wind that slowed them.

"Years ago, an east wind rose in the morning on our push to Grand Portage," Urbain recalled during a pipe break. "We make a mast of the poles and we sail, maybe eighty miles in one day."

"One of the few times Gerard let us ride," Amable said.

"Gerard kept us to the paddle most days," Urbain said. "He'd say, 'You'll get soft.'" They smiled at the memory of Gerard.

André turned his head away, his eyes misting. He felt suddenly haunted by the memory of Gerard's being swallowed up by the river and pained not to be able to save his friend.

It reminded him of Basile floundering in the river. *But he is dead. I can forget about him.*

Against the wind, André now steered automatically. He scarcely thought about the physics and geometry. He simply reacted. *No wonder it was hard for Gerard to explain his movements to me—this paddle is like my hand or arm. I am one with the water—I understand now.* But his mistakes made them slower, and he worried the *milieux* tallied up his errors with frustration and disdain.

Instead of cooking *rubbaboo*, Hercule sometimes shaved off slices of *pemmican* for them to eat. It saved time. He rationed their *pemmican*, but it ran out after the third day, and corn on the fourth. Pierre and Toussaint offered their dried fish, and with the last of the onions, peas and hard biscuit, seasoned with Hercule's precious sage, it gave them one more supper. Finally the provisions were gone. Nothing more. They tightened their sashes and gritted their teeth and ignored the aches and noises of their empty stomachs.

They paddled on. And on. Seven days. Eight days. And many miles to the new fort. With good winds, at least four more days, the older *milieux* reckoned.

They woke to a layer of thick clouds covering the sky, and no wind.

"It rains today," Amable said, sensitive to nuances of the weather.

Toussaint nodded, having noted wind and pressure changes during the night.

"Cover the trade goods. Let's go," Emile ordered.

Rain drizzled on them as they left, and it annoyed them all day. Pipe breaks were short.

Supper was porcupine stew. The cousins had spied a porcupine gnawing a branch in a tall pine tree. Toussaint climbed the tree, captured the porcupine and skinned it for the stew.

"Our Porcupine, he has found us a porcupine," Prisque said. "I hope it was not a brother to you."

Toussaint smiled. The teasing nickname would last a little longer.

No one refused the unfamiliar bounty, but it did not fill their bellies the way *rubbaboo* or pea porridge did.

The men now spoke with more interest of eating what bears ate, and looked for birds and frogs and even snails. Grubs and earthworms, snakes and beetles—not yet.

It sprinkled all night. They rigged the oiled canvas to cover themselves as well as cargo but found it hard to relax wrapped in wet blankets.

CHAPTER 16

By the next morning, the rain had stopped. The day quickly turned sticky and warm, the air sultry. Throughout the day thunder rumbled in the distance, but they saw no lightning. The men felt aggressive and edgy.

"Look at the clouds," Amable said. "Those wispy ones on the bottom, they amble to the north. But there are heavy clouds above them. They speed southwest. And those clouds ahead, they are almost green. Me, I don't like it."

High clouds amassed and twisted into strange shapes that were dark underneath and lumpy, as if someone had punched them. A moment later they swelled into other strange shapes.

"That one, it has a flat top, like the blacksmith's anvil," Louis said. "A sign, I think."

Jean grouchily refused to agree. "We are voyageurs. Clouds are nothing to us."

Though the day felt odd—hot and suffocating—they forged ahead.

"Ship oars," called Emile, starting a mid-afternoon break.

While the *milieux* stowed their paddles and lit their pipes, Amable pointed out a large whirling cloud formation. André studied the blackish churning clouds rushing across the sky.

"Look—the winds, they circle, do you see? " Amable said. "A bad storm—it comes soon."

"Head for land," Emile decided, trusting Amable.

When he scanned the shore, André was stunned to see waves running in almost opposite directions—the wind pushed sideways against the normal crests. *We are a half-mile out. About ten minutes to paddle most days. But today?*

The men glanced at the sheer cliffs lining the shore where they were headed. A wave smashed against the cliffs and shot upwards with an immense sheet of white mist higher than the trees. Their eyes widened and their mouths gaped. To come ashore there was as dangerous as being in the water.

André looked for any place to land the canoe and wait out the storm. None. They would have to paddle until they could locate a safe haven.

Their paddles flew, but they made little headway—the wind felt like a solid wall. The current had its own mind about where they should go and pulled them crosswise.

The sky quickly became dark as night. Then lightning flashed high overhead. Thunder boomed seconds later, and the heavy clouds broke open, pouring rain straight down on them.

Dark swells, topped with wild foamy crests that looked like teeth, lifted their canoe. A second later it plunged into a glassy trough. Then they were lifted high as the wave surged. Plunged, lifted, plunged, lifted, plunged.

Each wave posed a different problem for André. He worried about one swamping them. Or one that left part of the canoe unsupported out of the water—the weight of the cargo could crack the canoe.

If we ride the waves, we are at the mercy of the wind and current. Plowing through the waves might get us to shore faster, if we could find a safe bay. But a big wave could fill the canoe to its gunwales in a second. Angling toward the land takes extra time—do we have enough energy? Gerard, what should I do?

"Triple-time." No songs. Every man's shoulder and arm muscles burned.

Water inched up in the belly of the canoe. But no one could be spared to bail.

The wind increased, almost screaming, circling them.

"Amable, what is this storm?" André yelled.

"Like this, I have not seen," he shouted back.

A deafening roar rose, like nothing they had ever heard. Hail clattered against the canoe and vibrated their paddles. Icy stones bounced off their shoulders, stinging the backs of their hands, necks, heads. The world was a curtain of water.

Their arms were exhausted, but they kept at it.

"Forward, men! Forward!"

Suddenly a monstrous thick black serpent dropped from the clouds a league or two away. Its end swirled. The snake's tail grew longer, thicker, dangling and grasping for the lake. When it hit, they watched, horrified, as it sucked up water, spewing fish around and up and down, fish appearing and disappearing. The terrible tail shot sideways, then away.

"Harder! Paddle harder!"

"But which way? How can we escape that?"

The writhing serpent moved toward land and seized everything in range—trees and rocks were lifted up into the tail. Abruptly, the dark waterspout snake drew back into the greenish-black clouds. It dropped again and zigzagged crazily, then lurched in a direct line toward them.

It paused and dipped again into the water. Fish and hail and rain and rocks pelted them.

"*Mon Dieu*, it is coming for us," cried Alfred. "Forgive me, Father."

"*M'aidez!* Help!"

"Are we going to die?"

"Ste. Anne, pull your cloak around us."

"Paddle, men! We have to reach shore!"

Gerard, what should we do?

The spout again veered over the land, and dropped its tail. Tree roots, branches and rocks were flung around and dirt flew into their faces, but they could not duck down—they had to keep paddling. The winds pushed them backwards as the storm roared overhead.

To their amazement, a small window of clear sky appeared, and immediately closed.

"Is it a sign?"

"The eye of God?"

The deluge of hail and rain continued. Waves threatened to swamp them.

"André, I think I see something! That island?" Emile pointed, but when they neared, they found it was too small, rocky and inhospitable.

Fighting the churning crosscurrents, André tried to hold the canoe in a parallel course to the land while they looked for a cleft in the rocks. Emile chose a spot—but seconds later, the surging waves revealed a great shoulder of rock hidden beneath, one that would have ripped open their canoe. He searched again, studying the waters as well as the shore.

Everyone's life in peril, each man's eyes scoured the shoreline for a haven.

"That point?" Prisque shouted.

Too rough. The waves seemed to hide something underneath.

"Is that a sandbar?" Urbain yelled.

"Let's try for it," Emile answered.

Yes! And a small gravel beach where a stream fed into the great lake.

They powered close to shore, the wild waves rocking them. *It felt like this when I almost drowned. But I can't let that happen to us.*

Emile leapt out. A half-second later André and the *milieux* followed, wading ashore, pulling the canoe through the turbulent waters. They guided it carefully towards the narrow pebbly beach. Every step was slippery. In the sirening wind and driving rain, they hefted the bales in a big pile on massive black-red boulders next to the forest. On top of the bales, they overturned their canoe and spread canvas on it, weighting it with rocks, hoping to protect it from a tree branch smashing over them.

Finally, soaked and exhausted, they crawled beneath, breathless, as hail and fish, sticks and pebbles clattered over their birch bark shell. They huddled together, their ears cocked and their eyes wide, listening for a change in the roar of the storm, and their thumping hearts slowed.

Gradually the deluge of debris and hail ended, leaving gray ice balls and rubble on the shore. Silence reigned for parts of seconds when thunder wasn't rumbling. They breathed huge sighs of relief—and waited for lightning to stop piercing the sky, for the black clouds to empty and move on.

Though unnerved, they were exhausted, and fell asleep waiting.

Finally the storm's power was spent.

The men crowded out from the safety of their canoe to stare at the land around them. The forest was unrecognizable—massive tree trunks splintered and spun all around, their giant root balls exposed. They smelled earthiness, pine needles and wet bark and something they could not name. Waves still splashed high on boulders covered with lichens—purple, black and gray-green.

They gazed around, and then at each other.

"The storm, I remember one like this when we lived with our tribe," Toussaint said, his eyes distant with the memory. "It broke the biggest trees and they fell every direction. It plucked people, lodges, animals and whirled them about. We did not find where they dropped. Our band, we lost many."

That sobered André. *We were lucky to survive.* "Thanks to Ste. Anne. She looks after us."

"Well done, Emile and André. You found us a place to pull up before the tempest got us."

They peeled off their sopping clothes and draped them over wet bushes. Then they opened the bales to begin to dry the contents.

For hours, the men wandered aimlessly, staring at the destruction wreaked on the trees, then finding a rock to sit on, then standing to peer at the still-violent waves. Their eyes were again drawn to the forest. They seemed relieved but miserable and fearful. And hungry—there was nothing to eat.

We are strangely unfocused, drained from the exertion but too stimulated from the storm to rest. How long will we have to wait before we can leave?

No one noticed when Pierre and Toussaint left. It was nearing dark when Pierre yelled, "Help! Come to the stream. Bring the kettle. And Hercule, build up a fire."

André was immediately curious. "Where are you? Call out again." He sprang up, joined by others. They waited for Pierre's voice to lead them—uprooted trees and broken branches made it hard to locate him.

"All the wood, it is soaked," Hercule said as he handed André his largest kettle.

They found Pierre and Toussaint up to their waists in a stream, grappling with their net. Hundreds, maybe thousands, of small silvery fish darted around the sandbar.

"Little fish! They are running now!" Pierre said. "Every spring they swim from the big lake into the rivers. Most years it is earlier."

"Help Pierre lift the net! Scoop them into the kettle," Toussaint directed. "We looked before, but did not see the fish. Until today. Maybe it was the storm."

André and Urbain waded in, supporting the bulging net to prevent it from tearing. Louis and Alfred snatched fistfuls of the leaping fish and tossed them into the kettle. It filled rapidly.

They took turns dragging the kettle full of squirming fish back to the shore with the makings of a meal. In spite of the tempest they'd barely survived, they were gleeful, grateful, and their feet were light.

"Ste. Anne, she has turned our luck." André heard several of his men thank her.

Hercule cooked the whole kettle full of fish and they stuffed their stomachs, sated for the first time in a few weeks. The storm and danger were forgotten.

After they had licked their fingers, sat back and relaxed, Jean asked, "How can we bring a kettle of them in the canoe?"

"Your bellyful has to be enough. Little fish, they go bad fast."

While others whittled after supper, the cousins set out again on their nightly forage for food.

"May I come with you?" André asked. "I want to learn what you know."

Toussaint beckoned him to join them. "The fallen trees, they make it hard." He pointed—the game trails from the shore were crisscrossed by branches in every direction.

Stunned by the ravaged forest, André could not speak. Instead, he watched them closely. When they returned to camp to clean their findings, he said, "Tell me about your people."

Pierre was quiet for several seconds. "I am Red Rock, from the Lynx clan."

"Our people call me Spotted Feather," Toussaint added. They told André about their lives.

CHAPTER 17

Because it took two full days to dry their cargo, and for the waves to drop, they feasted again on the silvery fish.

After they had set off, André asked, "Prisque, how long before we see the new fort?"

"About three days," he answered. "But long ones."

"Me, I will be glad to arrive at all," Urbain said, to nods and murmurs. He was not the only one to toss more pinches of tobacco to appease *la Vieille*, the old woman-spirit of the lake and pray to Ste. Anne.

Supper was root stew. The men nodded their thanks, wishing for one more meal of the delicious fish.

Nothing for breakfast, though they tried to catch frogs and fish. Root stew for supper.

Nothing for breakfast again. On they paddled wearily, following the shoreline, looking forward to the feast at the *rendezvous*.

"Tell us again how to get the food bears eat," Amable said.

"To find honey, look for claw marks of a bear," Toussaint said.

"For grubs, look in rotten logs," Pierre said. "But bears may have taken them all."

"Perhaps grubs would not be so different from snails," Alfred mused. "My mother, she cooked the big snails."

"Beetles you can find under leaves, or where the soil is moist," Toussaint said. "Sometimes I like foods that crunch."

During a mid-afternoon pipe break, Toussaint tilted his head, listening intently. He gestured his head opposite from the shore. "Many birds. Emile, go that way."

Emile didn't see or hear birds but, buoyed by the cousins' knack for finding food, he agreed. André angled their canoe where Toussaint pointed.

Because they stood in the canoe, André and Emile were the first to notice black specks, like pepper, swirling in the air, over a small rocky outcrop a mile into the lake.

"Birds!" Amazed, André had never seen so many in one place. *Why are they circling an island? Nesting?* "Gulls?" he asked Toussaint, who nodded. His brain moved from gulls and nests to chickens and eggs. *Perhaps eggs!* His mouth watered, remembering his foster mother Berthe's omelets.

"Eggs?" He said it aloud.

"Eggs enough to feed us all?" Hercule asked.

"On that outcrop," Toussaint said.

A cheer rose and instantly the canoe surged toward the tiny island.

When they neared it, Emile and André slowed to scrutinize their approach. It would be disastrous to scrape or spring a leak here—the island had no trees to shelter them and sleeping on the rocks would be uncomfortable.

But—if they were careful—a few men could steal eggs from the hundreds of nesting gulls. The rest stayed in the canoe, making noise to scare off the gulls.

Toussaint ran ahead, tossing tobacco and shouting in Ojibwe to the birds.

Urbain and Alfred splashed loudly over the canoe gunwales, grabbing kettles and jumping from rock to rock to snatch eggs from the nests.

Pierre followed, calling directions. "Leave an egg or two at each nest, or the mothers, they will not return."

As the men stole eggs, dozens of angry birds struck back in earnest, flapping their wings in the men's eyes and pecking and jabbing with their sharp claws. Toting the kettles heavy with dozens of eggs, the canoe-men dashed back.

"Look how small the eggs are!" said Alfred, holding one up.

Urbain stuffed a raw egg, shell and all, into his mouth, roaring in laughter when the runny yolk dripped down his beard.

As the kettles were stowed, the famished men lost all sense of control. Like Urbain, they crammed raw eggs in their mouths. At home, that would have disgusted André, but he was hungry and wanted food—he tried it also.

"Don't eat them all," Hercule shouted. "Oh, for some of that hard biscuit from Sault Ste. Marie, or a garlic. I could make a feast."

The canoe slid along more easily now, the men grinning through yellow-streaked beards and mustaches and eager to eat more. They sang full of zeal. While setting up camp, they smelled the enticing aromas of Hercule's meal. Their eyes were riveted on the kettle, and they wept with pleasure at his scrambled eggs mixed with roots, ferns and mushrooms. Thinking only of their unbridled hunger, they ate and ate until all the eggs were gone.

As the day closed, several men drifted over to the cousins and, in soft voices, thanked them for finding the eggs.

"Maybe for some of the roots, too." They all smiled.

"Ste. Anne, she takes care of voyageurs."

Before noon the next day, Amable pointed to a long ridge of high hills along the distant horizon.

"Soon we come to the Sleeping Giant," he said.

"I thought we woke that giant some days back," André answered, remembering the awful storm they had survived.

The men laughed—they had cheated death once in the storm. More, if they counted starvation.

"True, but this giant, he will be sleeping."

André recalled from his first trip how fearful he had been of imaginary monsters. And of the *windigo* that Basile Roche had claimed to be, when André first learned of the Ojibwe evil spirit. This year they had faced real dangers. *I can forget about Roche—he is dead and gone.*

Their canoe slipped past the familiar cliffs in the clear sky of late afternoon. It would be a magnificent sunset.

"Do we continue to the fort or stay here overnight to get cleaned up?" Emile put the question to the whole canoe.

"On! We go on!"

"What need have I to scrub up? With that tempest, my shirt it is almost clean."

"They will have *rubbaboo*."

"And—maybe some is left in tonight's kettle."

Invigorated, they swept toward the New Fort, their voices rising in "*C'est l'Aviron Qui Nous Mène*" with great gusto, for truly "It is the Paddle That Drives the Canoe." They had survived near-impossible challenges. With joy in their hearts—and tears in their eyes which none would acknowledge—they would arrive at the *rendezvous*.

CHAPTER 18

A mile from the New Fort, Emile directed the canoe up on a sandy shore so the men could spruce up and don their cleanest, brightest clothing. Though they had not arrived with the early canoes, they wanted to appear full of vitality.

Hercule somehow managed to look nearly as smart as the day they left Lachine, but the rest tried their best to wipe clean their clumsily-patched shirts and stained trousers.

Emile, disgusted with his tangled beard, decided not to shave. "Takes too long."

Finding no comb, Alfred tamed his wild mane by running his fingers through it, while Toussaint simply tied his long hair back.

Prisque and Urbain found their ostrich feathers, bent and faded, and tucked them into their knitted caps with pride.

André wished he could sport a red plume in his *tuque*—announcing that he was a winterer—but it had been lost in the rapids. Now others would not know he was a person of substance. They would simply address him as a pork-eater. He shrugged.

Oh I'm being foolish! Why is it important that others know I survived a winter inland? What they think shouldn't make any difference. Shouldn't. But it did.

Then he realized that all the men except for Pierre and Toussaint had wintered in distant fur posts. And the cousins had lived in their band's lodges. Everyone deserved that badge of honor.

He sighed while unsnarling the fringes of his sash. *At least we are here. Gerard is not with us. But in a way, he is here—and has been with me while steering.* It made André smile, to think of Gerard celebrating at the *rendezvous*.

When they all were adorned as finely as could be, Amable unfurled their flag and set it in their stern. They paddled with vigor and precision, singing jubilantly on this beautiful evening. Their hard work, the lack of food, the difficult times—were now behind them. André was happier than he could imagine—they had survived. They would arrive!

At the *rendezvous*, they would work, as their contracts stated. But tonight they would celebrate!

It was nearly twilight when Pretty Mouse, sitting alone at the shore, heard their voices and picked up their tune, singing along. He and Antoine and the whole brigade met them at the wharf— cheering, whistling and shouting greetings. While they unloaded the cargo bales and hauled them to the warehouse, André and the men from canoe No. 2 were peppered with questions.

"Finally you are here. What kept you?"

"Did you have trouble?"

"Where were you when the tempest hit?"

"What did you find to eat? You don't look as thin as we thought."

"Antoine, he has asked every canoe if they saw you."

"Oohhoo, was he mad at us for leaving you alone."

"André, you did it," said Old Louis, shaking his hand.

André gazed appreciatively at the large fort—or so it would be when fully-built. He inhaled the scent of fresh-cut wood from the logs of the newly-completed palisade around the fort.

Pretty Mouse pointed out their place to camp outside the fort's stockade, and others eagerly carried their canoe to a grassy area where they would sleep and eat.

"Aha, you chose a sleeping place with no rocks," Prisque noted with pleasure. "My back, it thanks you."

"Do I smell *rubbaboo*?" They spied kettles simmering over the embers.

"What work detail were we given?" At the Grand Portage *rendezvous,* their contracts had required pork-eaters to work six days, carrying the Nor'westers' bales over the nine-mile Grand Portage, because Nor'westers had withstood much harsher conditions and had traveled a thousand miles and more. Their assigned tasks here could not be so arduous as traversing the Grand Portage.

"We are woodcutters," answered Matthieu.

Urbain was sour. "That's not work for voyageurs."

"Ah, this fort, it needs us to build it," Pretty Mouse said. "But we can do anything. We are voyageurs—*Nous sommes voyageurs.*"

"On the way here, we carry cargo. Now it is trees—we are the beasts of burden, like always." Amable was discouraged.

"What does it matter? A voyageur's life—it is still the best life."

After they had groused or guffawed or regaled their friends with the drama of the trip across the great lakes, André and Emile examined the canoe one last time to make it seaworthy for the crew who would return it to Lachine. While painting pitch on its seams, André's memory drifted back to his first *rendezvous*. He'd felt too shy to dance or bargain with Indians for their fancy beadwork and moccasins.

He recalled his "baptism" as a winterer after Basile Roche had bullied Pretty Mouse. Using a diamond-willow tree branch as a sword, André had confronted Roche and stopped him. Infuriated, Roche had left angrily, but not before spitting out a menacing threat: "I will remember your faces, and when you least expect it, I will come for you. Remember that when it is late and dark at night. I will come for you."

Months later Roche lived up to his threat. He had leapt from a tree to attack his brother Denis and try to drown him. The memory flooded André's brain, like clouds darkening the sky before a storm. The air felt chilly and he shivered.

But it is a memory. Basile drowned in the waterfall, not Denis. I am wasting my time. André shrugged off the ugly thoughts. *Since we left home, I've done hard things. Now I'm going to have fun. After being steersman, I've earned it.*

During the next days, they toiled long hours felling trees and removing and stacking tree limbs. More buildings were planned for the fort, so trees had to be cut and hauled and sawed into planks. Crews of voyageurs were assigned to the heaviest of these tasks, which they accepted with stoic pride.

"We are voyageurs. We can do this—and more."

"But I hate these mosquitoes and black flies!" To fight swarms of biting insects, the men tried various potions, attempting to stop the sting.

They were not the last to arrive. More brigades came—canoes of pork-eaters from Lachine and the rugged northmen and from fur posts that dotted the great interior. Up to a thousand men would swell the fort. Cries of joy rang out when men saw former canoe-mates.

When Charles Chaboillez arrived, the wintering partner to whom Antoine and his brigade were contracted as *engagés*, André greeted him warmly. He owed him a debt—not only had Mr. Chaboillez accepted him as a clerk, but later he had helped him in the search for Denis.

André hoped to connect with Joseph Charette, Marie-Thérèse's father and interpreter for the Dakota at a western fur post, to hear his news to pass on to the couple.

One day an express canoe arrived carrying a *bourgeois*, an important North West Company owner from Montreal, in a tall black beaver hat. This partner wore a dark green waistcoat with many shiny buttons, a yellow patterned vest and tan knee breeches. On his feet were shiny black shoes, buckled with silver. His stockings were pure white.

How does he keep the stockings so clean?

Then André saw the *bourgeois* being carried ashore on the backs of three strong voyageurs. After that, the voyageurs carried the man's personal gear—a dozen locked wooden cases.

The Montreal partner said, "Careful with those. The red case contains my finest wardrobe, the brown has my china and glassware."

"Glassware, sir?" One of the lesser clerks seemed surprised.

"We must keep high standards and wear our finest clothing. That is how we keep distinct from those who serve us, so they know who is important."

André glanced at his own shabby clothing—his shirt gray with dirt, his faded sash, his stained trousers, his frayed black neckerchief—and wished he could appear better.

Do the Ojibwe also use clothing to show their importance? Maybe. Makwa's eagle feathers show his bravery. Runs When He Walks wears buckskins embroidered with colored beads when he comes to trade.

So I will buy myself a new sash while I am here—I have enough coins for that. Perhaps next summer when we come back here on our way home, Antoine will advance me some of my wages and I can get new trousers and a shirt. When they pay me in Lachine, I won't have spent much so I'll be able to give most of it to Joseph and Berthe.

CHAPTER 19

Every day at the *rendezvous*, every hour, brought exciting things to André's eyes and ears.

After supper, he ambled along the water's edge to inspect the "Invincible," a sailing ship moored next to the pier. Others had unloaded its huge wooden crates and told how sails propelled it swiftly over Lake Superior during the tempest.

André was puzzled by the vessel's complicated ropes and sails. During the next days, he found countless reasons to wander past and examine its rigging, which fascinated him.

The ship looks invincible, like it would withstand much more than our birch bark canoes! It would make our life so much easier. But, if the ship carries all the trade goods, will that end work for voyageurs? I do not want that.

Once, while André was studying the steering wheel intently, a young sailor sitting high on the bow, carving something, spied André and called out in English, "Hey, boyo. I could use a hand here."

André stopped, surprised to hear the language he had studied, though it sounded different than it did coming from Father Goiffon. He looked up as the sailor slid down. *Does he mean me?*

"I been trying to make this round again. Kin ya pull this here, hard-like? When I say, pull fer all yer worth." He handed André a flat wooden plate with a hole through its center. A rope circled its outer edge held by a groove. André had never seen such a device before.

"I can. What is it?"

"A pulley, it is. See that one up there, and yon?" The sailor pointed to the mast and other locations. "They make lifting things easier. This pulley, she lifts the sail. Or is s'posed ta. But lightning hit this'n in the big tornado some days back. See the burn mark?

'Tain't round no more and I'm not sure the groove will hold. If'n I carve off more, she'll be too small."

André waited while the sailor tightened the rope around the groove. When the boy signaled to pull, André tugged hard, grunting. But the rope kept slipping out of its groove and would not operate smoothly.

"It still don't work. But thanks, mate. Cap'n, I s'pose he'll want me to switch this'n and another. Better get to it or he'll blister me."

The sailor started to fling the pulley in the river but André stopped him.

"Could I have that, if you don't want it?"

"Why'd anyone want a busted pulley?" he said as he handed it to André.

"I want to see how it works. Maybe I'll copy it and make a good one of my own." André waved goodbye.

When he returned to the campsite, he showed it to Pretty Mouse who was fascinated. Mouse walked around camp searching for something they could use it on. "Let's move this rock. It's in the way."

Though their ropes slipped out of the pulley groove as often as they stayed, Mouse loved this new toy. But when he suggested lifting their canoe, André knew Antoine would be angry if they damaged it, so they tried a log instead. Mouse continued delighting in using the damaged pulley, and urged others to discover how it might ease their own loads.

Warmed by the sailor's open nature, André stopped by the "Invincible" as often as he could, to ask about the sailing ship and learn more of how it worked.

CHAPTER 20

On days when he hauled Nor'westers' pelts to the smelly fur warehouses, André would eavesdrop on their conversations.

"Many from the tribes were sick over winter. They came late with furs."

"But they were the best pelts—thick and big like you have not seen."

"Our second food cache, it was spoiled. We went nine days without food—not even rock moss."

"The rivers, they were still frozen when we left. Dogsleds carried our pelts to Lake Winipic, but this year we had to camp nearly a week before the lake ice broke up."

"Did you hear—some posts may be closed?"

"Not ours—we brought a record haul this year."

André had thrilled to hear Joseph's exciting stories of the far north. Suddenly he realized how difficult the northmen's lives were—nine days without food compared to his brigade's missing meals for a few days! He noticed he could barely carry two of their bales—they were heavier than the usual ninety pounds—and wondered why. Getting to the *rendezvous* was not an adventure story for them—it was stark survival. *No wonder Nor'westers look gaunt. No wonder they think pork-eaters have it easy.*

Late one afternoon while helping a small brigade of Nor'westers, André heard familiar voices. He looked up and recognized two men.

"François Laurent! Pierre Manet!" He bear-hugged his canoe-mates from his first voyage, then stepped up to hoist their packs.

"Bon-à-rien! You are back!" Pierre laughed, punching his shoulder. "I thought maybe the wolves and lynx, they scare you off!"

André grinned, reddening at their teasing. He had been so very young—and gullible.

François, who was much shorter, looked up at him. "You are beeg! Look at you now! You grow more and you will not fit. Or we build a new size of canoe—an André canoe—for you!"

They laughed, and settled into sharing their tales.

When André told them about Gerard's death, they doffed their caps and crossed themselves. "I think he knew every stone of every river and lake he'd been on," François said.

"You are the steersman? Ho! That's a surprise. And worth a feather in your cap!"

"Perhaps you will winter one year with us."

André helped to carry their canoe and personal goods to the separate campground reserved for Nor'westers. *Back in the village I don't have friends, but here I have many. We suffered together and are forever bound, almost like brothers.* It made him glow inside.

He sauntered back to the stockade, heading toward the company stores and the Indian Shop.

André peeked inside the Outfits storehouse at immense stacks of trade goods being baled for distant posts, each one wrapped in white canvas and marked with "NWC" for North West Company, a number and letters to show its destination. The letters puzzled him so he glanced at a map tacked to the wall showing the districts. He'd heard many of the names—Fond du Lac, Upper Red River, Lake Winipic, Rainy Lake, Peace River, Nipigon, Rat River. Red-painted wooden chests had "Michipicoten" and "Lac des Isles" painted on them—André wondered what was inside.

The pile of bales and boxes for Athabasca was so much larger than any other district's allotment of bales and barrels that he drew nearer, to count them. *That's because they bring the largest and glossiest beaver pelts. And more furs than the other districts.*

On the map, he located Athabasca in the far north, and then other districts. *Where is Antoine's Moose Horn River post?* André's fingers traced the rivers that he thought led there. Then he pored over the route they had traveled from Lachine. *It doesn't have all the streams and bends I remember. The northern shore of Lake Superior has more islands and rivers than this shows. Who made this map—and how would I make my own?*

Finally André meandered to the Indian Shop, looking for a feather for his cap to show others he was a winterer. First he browsed the red ostrich plumes, but other goods caught his attention—knee garters, brass tinder boxes and flint for starting fires, shaving gear, fine soaps, wax candles, silk ribbons in a dozen colors, packets of tea, playing cards, dice, tobacco and pipes and skinning knives. He fingered the coins in the small bag around his neck—*how far would they go?*

In the far end of the store, a half-dozen voyageurs with plumes in their *tuques* milled around, smoking. They conversed with a *bourgeois* wearing a maroon cutaway coat, a black brocaded vest and gray striped trousers, and leaning on a cane. The man pulled uncomfortably at the ruffle topping his white shirt.

"I dinna wear these fancy clothes all year. 'Twill take getting used to again. That and sitting through the meetings."

His accent sounds like James at Sault Ste. Marie, like a Scotsman. André knew that McTavishes, Mackenzies, McGillivrays, McKays, Macdonalds and McLeods had financed canoe brigades before the North West Company had been organized.

They sound like Nor'westers. I'd like to hear their stories. André edged himself into a corner, listening to their tales of survival in the harsh climate, the vast lakes and icy rivers, the caribou, the northern tribes. Some bragged, surely, but others simply chronicled their stories of drama or tragedy. He imagined himself living that life, paddling and trading.

He was startled to hear someone addressing him.

"Wha' be your name, golden-haired lad hidden in the corner? I ha'e heerd that Gerard LeMoine is na' with us. That you became steersman in Antoine Felix's brigade," said the *bourgeois*. "Be this true?"

André, rattled at the sudden attention, nodded. "Yes, sir, it is true. I am André … Didier," he stammered.

"Many years Gerard paddled as *gouvernail*—and once I rode in his canoe. A fine man, he was. The company depended on his knowledge and skill. Pray, tell us of the circumstances."

Most of the Nor'westers stayed as André painted his picture of the trek—seeing Gerard catapulted out, then overturning their canoe and losing provisions and personal packs. He told of Antoine's search for the right steersman, and his own test on the French River and the great waters. His lack of food on Lake Superior did not compare to their days of starvation, so he recast the story to give credit to the native cousins who had found nourishing roots, silvery fish and gull eggs.

When he was done, no one spoke for a few moments—they nodded and continued smoking, their eyes distant. *They attended to my words. Like they were measuring me. Maybe getting us here safely was a feat equal to theirs.*

"Well done, André Didier," the *bourgeois* said. "I reckon you are young to be a steersman. Your skills of observation commend you. As do your studies." He paused and looked around for his cane. "Before you leave the fort for the next leg of your journey, I may ha'e something of interest to you. If that is so, I will send for you."

André nodded, barely able to speak after the praise from such a man.

With that, the *bourgeois* picked up his cane and limped toward the Great Hall. The Athabascan voyageurs, now thirsty for high wines, left as well.

"Now I be closing." The storekeeper held the key in his hand, and gestured at the door.

Walking back to their campsite, André knew that Antoine would have reported Gerard's death—the company needed to know. But to be publicly acknowledged for his role was something new. *I must tell Joseph about this encounter, and Denis. About Gerard. About becoming steersman, and the food we ate. I wish I had bought paper and ink at the Indian Shop.*

While their campsite usually bubbled with activity—men boxing, others playing games of chance or skill, still others whittling—tonight no one was around. André was startled to find it deserted.

Then he heard music and laughing. Yes! Tonight there was a dance. André hurried to the fort's main square. Two men with violins sat facing each other, their bows moving rapidly. Music cascaded with each movement.

Another man, wearing a dark plaid kilt with a matching wide sash thrown over his shoulder, stood with a bag that had several pipes arising from it. When he blew into it, the sound was strange and piercing, but André found it pleasing.

And there were native women—which stunned him! He tried not to stare.

Pretty Mouse, though a little tipsy, was light on his feet and danced to nearly every song, choosing many different partners. *Look at all the friends he has here. I thought Mouse would be single all his days but maybe that is not so.*

With Mouse's prodding, André shyly invited a young Ojibwe girl to dance, but neither knew what to do. They giggled nervously, and after clumsy attempts at the steps, they both looked relieved when the musicians stopped for refreshments.

André saw Toussaint and Pierre at the edge of the crowd and went to stand by them. "I've hardly seen you. Have you found family here?" Their success might help him feel more connected with his own brother.

But Toussaint shook his head. "Perhaps some are here, but we do not know them," he said. "For too many years we have lived away from our people, so we are not close to our tribe."

André was stunned. "Please tell me more."

Toussaint began, telling of their fathers who ended their voyageur years with enough money in their pockets to buy farms, and send their sons to school. "One day an ox, it stepped on Papa's foot. Many bones were broken. His foot, it puffed up and got very red and hot. It hurt him to walk. Then his foot, it turned dark and he became very quiet. He did not want to talk or to eat."

"His Papa was the brother of my Papa. That winter my Papa, he took ill with the lung fever," Pierre added. "He coughed and could not breathe. By spring both had gone to the Great Spirit."

"Our mothers kept us in the school as long as money lasted. They talked of returning to their tribes, but lung fever took them and they died last winter. We have no other kin that far east. We do not fit in the towns. And we will not return to Lachine."

"Antoine, he knew our Papas, and told us about his canoe brigade. So we signed on. We are headed to Lake Winipic, a fur post on the Red River."

Their wistfulness told André how hard it was to be ostracized, looked down on for their mixed heritage. *In the village I felt as isolated as Pierre and Toussaint. We were outsiders, but for different reasons. At least they had each other, which made it easier for them. They are the kind of friends I want.*

"The roots you found, the tiny fish and other foods, they kept the men in our canoe alive. Can you show me how to find them?"

"Our grandmother, she taught us," Toussaint said. "Maybe tomorrow night, if the moon is bright."

Not long after, all three slipped away to their campsite. For others, though, the dance, laced with high wines, lasted late into the night.

CHAPTER 21

At the end of the next day's toil, André wiped his sweaty face with his neckerchief. The summer days were sweltering, and the voyageurs roasted while cutting and sawing trees. He had looked forward to being in the cool quiet forest with Pierre and Toussaint, but they had not returned.

Hearing boisterous shouting and laughter from the waterfront, he meandered in that direction. He looked out at the big lake. *It might refresh me—but what if I get sucked under? No, water is not my friend.*

At the shore, a crowd heckled two burly voyageurs, each standing in the bow of a small canoe, balancing and rocking. Aha—"cat and mouse," the voyageurs' tug of war.

"I bet on Michel. He won last year."

"*Pas*, Michel, he can't hold a candle to Albert."

"Two *sous* on Albert."

"*Non*, the feet of Albert have not the speed. I say Michel."

"*Oui*, bet on me. I am Michel. Every year I win this bet for you," said the shorter one. "Make it worth my while. Me, I am the one who is giving you fun." He placed his bare feet carefully on the gunwales, straddling the canoe, and tossed a rope to the other, grinning.

The second man, Albert, eyed his competition and threw his head back with a loud chortle. "That old man, he is nothing but talk. I will show you who is quick on his feet. And smart."

Those standing on the shore pitched coins on the ground. A man from Antoine's brigade, Jacques Comeau, placed the coins on top of Michel's *tuque* or Albert's, keeping the bets separate.

How can men swagger while balancing on a tippy canoe? Hearing them boast, André decided to watch, but keep his coins—he could enjoy their skill and the camaraderie without losing his money.

Un, deux, trois … the game began.

When their canoes were a few yards apart in the water, Michel and Albert pulled the rope taut between them, keeping up the banter. In their separate canoes, each rocked confidently while eyeing the other. Albert yanked the rope, hoping to catch Michel off his guard.

"Oho, that old trick! I know you," called Michel. He played out a little slack, flexing his knees.

Back and forth, the cat and mouse played each other to much hooting of the crowd. More coins were bet.

Suddenly, Albert bent his knees, twisted—and loosened the rope. Michel, not expecting it, lost his footing and toppled backwards into the water.

The splat doused half the spectators. Their laughter increased to a roar, and Jacques paid out the bets as a sopping Michel stepped to shore.

"You are young," Jacques said, beckoning to André. "You could beat Albert. What do you say?"

André shook his head. He did not choose to play at cat and mouse. Besides, the waters were dangerous, so he turned away and wandered toward the Indian encampment. *Maybe the cousins will be there.*

Many trees along the shore had been cut to build the fort, but a large grove remained, with ten or twenty summer lodges nestled among the trees. *If I can remember enough Ojibwe words, I might trade for a pair of buffalo hide moccasins for Joseph, or a beaded bracelet for Berthe. It will be good to practice my Ojibwe.*

As he neared the native village, he noticed its quiet in contrast to the boisterous voyageurs. He heard birds chittering, hidden in the trees, and a flute player who mimicked them. Ojibwe women stirred aromatic meaty stews over smoky campfires or scraped wet deerskins to soften them. Several infants were snuggled into cradleboards that hung from shady branches while young giggling girls rocked them, and whispered secrets to each other.

A circle of men, natives and French-Canadians, sat under a leafy tree playing a game of chance. They tossed marked pebbles, and when two pebbles with the same design landed face upward, the men yelped good-naturedly and slid pebbles to a man who was amassing a large pile. A few throws later, his pile was halved, won back by other men.

From one lodge, he heard a long low chant, followed by rattles and the beat of a small drum. *It smells like cedar and sage and sounds like the medicine man who helped Denis. Perhaps it's a healing.*

When he got closer, he heard angry voices coming from another lodge.

In the shallows of a rocky beach, a dozen children bobbed and splashed, swimming as easily as the otters he'd seen along the French River. *They're having fun.*

The day's heat lulled him and André sat in a shaded spot on the shore, watching the children who played in the water, tossing rocks and diving for them. *They're like loons—they go down in the water here, but come up over there! I wonder how long they can stay underwater.* He began counting to see which ones held their breaths the longest, how far they swam. *Un, deux, trois ...* and got to eleven, then fifteen.

Splash! His head was drenched with a spray of water. A second later another splash soaked his shirt.

Surprised, André looked up. It was the young Ojibwe girl he had danced with. She smiled, waded closer and beckoned for him to join her.

Then she ducked underwater and was gone. *What?* He looked around. *Where did she go so fast?* She popped up again, this time holding a fist-sized rock with multicolored bands. She called to a group of her friends to wait for her.

"I, Black Duck," she said, pointing to herself. "You?"

"My name is André," he answered, feeling awkward.

"André, come."

"I don't swim," he said, suddenly immobilized. *The current might pull me under. I might drown! Rivers are treacherous.*

He looked across the water—wide, shallow and slow, the opposite of the rivers he'd paddled. The water was clear enough to see fish darting at the bottom. It seemed harmless. He took a deep breath. *Their parents aren't worried about them. Maybe ... I could try.*

Black Duck motioned again to him. "Come." To her friends, she seemed to add, "He will come, I'm sure of it."

Though his heart thumped rapidly, he choked down a breath, and shook his head to clear his thinking. *Albert and Michel weren't afraid of the water playing cat and mouse. These Ojibwe children aren't afraid. I will try this.* André pulled off his sash and shirt and untied his moccasins. He waded toward her, his body rigid.

"Down. Like this," she said and sank to her shoulders in the water.

Uncertainly he mimicked her movements. No current swept him away.

The next time she dunked her whole head under water.

He stiffened, his eyes wide. *Is it safe?*

She rose, seeing he had not followed. "Try." She pressed her fingers lightly on his shoulder. "You can."

I can. He ducked down to his shoulders. She nodded, then took a deep breath and held it. André imitated her.

Then she ducked her body fully under water. *Is that how to do it?* André sank to his knees, water covering his neck, his chin, his whole head. He jumped up, water flying off him. *I did it! It wasn't so bad.*

She placed her fingers to hold her eyes wide. "Open eye. See in water. Yes? And hold breath." She plunked herself underwater again.

He dropped down. This time he kept his eyes open. Amazed, he looked around. He could see his feet, her feet, the rocky bottom. The water was crystal clear, with rippling light patterns.

André rose, grinning, nodding, breathing again. He was thrilled with his new discovery. *I saw underwater!*

"*Oui. Merci*, Black Duck."

She tossed the rock a few feet away from him, and he stepped near, keeping his head out of the water, and reached to retrieve it.

"No. Like this. See under water." She took the stone from him, tossed it in the water and swam underwater to it, shimmying her feet. She retrieved it and tossed it once more toward him.

André dropped into the water. This time he propelled himself with his feet, the way she had. When he saw bubbles rising from the pretty banded rock where it had landed, he reached down and grasped it. Standing again, he looked to see where Black Duck stood, and flipped the stone a few feet away for her to retrieve.

The game began. Ready to play again, her friends scrambled to get it first. Each toss increased the distance, the depth. *They often play this game. Friends playing. We don't play like this in the village, and never in the river. When was the last time I had so much fun? And I am not afraid. What could happen to me, in these shallow waters anyway!*

They added more rocks, more players. Splashing and laughing needed no language. The game went on and on as the sun dipped low into the sky.

Suddenly André felt a sharp blow between his shoulders, driving him deep in the water. Dizzy and disoriented, he tried to rise but stumbled and choked. *What happened? Did someone miss their toss?* His back stinging, he stretched his fingers to find the sore spot—and discovered blood on his hands. At his feet was a large black rock. Confused, he turned towards the shore.

Another rock hit him in the belly and he fell backwards.

The game stopped.

Black Duck yelled to a friend nearby. The two of them huddled around to help him stand.

Stunned and in pain, he looked toward the village. A man stood at the water's edge, holding a large stone in one hand.

CHAPTER 22

André stared at—an apparition. *Basile Roche? No, it could not be! Not possible! How could it be? Roche was dead!* His breath caught. It shook him to see Basile, alive. André reeled, his knees buckling. Impossible. He had seen Roche careening over the falls.

Now that dead man was sneering, his body oddly cramped, his face twisted. Roche leaned on a stick to steady himself, his arm holding another rock.

"I said I would get you," he spat. "Here I am. Yellow hair makes you easy to find."

André's mind tried to focus.

Furs were heaped over Roche's voyageur shirt, though it was a hot day. An expensive beaver hat topped his rough mane of unkempt, stringy hair.

"Quevillon? Didier? Bon-à-rien? What you call yourself matters not," Roche rasped. "Like cat and mouse, but I am the cat. I toy with you. You will live only as long as I say."

Basile's face looked pale, his body looked broken, a misshapen leg and arm. His voice was hollow and reedy, but oozed bitter venom. Two men stood behind him, one on each side.

"I will come when you least expect it. Or, one of them will surprise you." He indicated the two men. "You will never be safe!"

Roche let fly his last rock at André, though it fell short of him. Roche turned and hobbled away, the two men following.

André tried to make sense of it. *I thought Basile drowned in the fast waters of the river, arms writhing. He bounced from rock to rock. I thought he perished. Nobody could have survived. Nobody!*

I wanted to believe his lifeless body was sucked under the ice. But I saw no proof. Basile is back. And now he will kill me.

Roche, like a *windigo*, had returned.

He looked from Black Duck to the others. They were as confused as he was. Bleeding, he left the water, dressed and returned to his own campsite to be alone, to think this through. But alone, unprotected would be worse—Roche could easily track him.

His stomach was a knot. Fear flooded his mind. His body felt taut, alien. He dreaded going to the dance, in terror of being seen by Roche, but more afraid of being caught alone.

Once his friends, Silent Wolf and Ghost Wind, had helped. This was different. Basile knew him by name, had scouted him. He would know which post André was bound for, and would wait to attack, cat and mouse. André had to be ready—for anything, any time.

A new nightmare had begun.

CHAPTER 23

Basile did not come to the dance or festivities at the New Fort that night. But André, waking repeatedly from a mishmash of terrifying dreams, encountered him dozens of times. When the day dawned bright and inviting, he felt foolish at allowing fear to control his actions.

Of course he will not pounce on me when others are around. But what might happen on our way to Antoine's post in the wilderness? He will wait until I don't have the protection of others. And then ...

He shook his head and tried to put the matter out of his thoughts. While toiling at the woodcutting, he found he could forget. But at other odd times of the day, an intimidating fear found him, and he felt his bones turn to water.

When he saw someone who reminded him of Basile, he would jolt and freeze, then glance around when he realized Roche was not there. André berated himself for this weakness.

Early one morning another express canoe arrived with a *bourgeois*—again carried ashore by voyageurs.

Grabbing many parcels of oiled cloth, the gentleman partner hurried to where they held their annual meetings. "Company news. I have instructions," he bellowed. "I bring letters."

That drew other gentlemen, the wintering partners, out of their rooms.

"Hurry with my desk. We shall need my calculations." He pointed to where his harried assistant had placed the gentleman's portable desk used on their voyage. "Put my baggage there but don't unpack. I shall do that myself."

113

The *bourgeois* pulled out a dozen sheets of paper covered with minute handwriting. "Distribute these to the wintering partners, quickly, before the next meeting. Don't forget the letters."

After his other tasks, the assistant delivered a large pile of document bags to a young clerk who began to sort several dozen letters, slipping them in separate slots, one for each partner, along a wall. He came upon two letters, stopped and scratched his head.

"André Didier? Who is he?" he muttered. "Must be a mistake, but where am I to put them?" He set them aside until he could ask.

Several hours later, the word was passed to André—from Mr. Chaboillez to Antoine to Prisque, who happened to walk past the campsite—that he must speak with a clerk at the main office. It aroused the curiosity of his canoe-mates, and their teasing.

"Is our André being called to task—a bad boy?"

"*Non.* I think they give him more money—he was steersman for half the trip."

"So perhaps he will sign a new contract."

When he arrived at the headquarters, the clerk smirked at the shabbily-dressed canoe-man. "A voyageur who can read? Why are you receiving letters? Will someone have to tell you what they say?"

André rose to his full height. "I read and write in French, Latin and English."

Surprised at his direct answer, the clerk grudgingly handed over two flat packets.

André felt many sets of disbelieving eyes on him as he took the packets outside and sat on the grass to open them. One letter was from Father Goiffon, one letter from Denis!

He broke open the wax seal on the letter from Father Goiffon, who wrote: "Joseph asked me to open the letter from Denis, in case there was news they should hear. For Joseph, I have answered Denis and sent the letter on the next ship to France. We thought you may not receive this for some time."

That was wise of him. André continued reading.

"My latest booklet is about a Swede named Linnaeus. He devised a way to classify plants and animals. How I wish we had known this before you left. You could describe God's unusual creatures of the New World. It would help me see them better."

It made him smile. There were other messages from his mentor. When he was finished, he savored Father Goiffon's words for a while.

He examined his brother's letter, its wax seal broken but resealed. Marks on it showed this letter came from France and he had written in March! So they had survived the voyage and arrived at the estates of Ansereau.

Denis had written on crisp paper embossed with a gold crest that he had seen once before.

"My dear brother André, I hope this reaches you before you leave on a brigade—then you can cancel your contract and sail for France. Grandfather and Uncle Georges send greetings. They desire to meet you soon. And the Didiers would like word of Joseph and Berthe. The sea voyage was wet and cold, hard on Marie-Thérèse— she was often ill."

André tried to imagine the voyage. *Would I be seasick?*

"When we arrived at Ansereau, the family ordered a feast to celebrate. You would like it here—it is a plum of an estate, far away from cities. That way we live our own lives and do not worry about the problems of the government and army. Our house and lands are small compared to nearby estates, but our farms are rich. There is enough work for the two of us—make plans to return immediately."

Father Goiffon will have told him I signed on.

"Uncle Georges said Basile Roche is distant relative, because his mother was kin to our Grandfather Quevillon." Andre almost dropped the letter. *Related to Basile Roche?* He felt ill. After a few moments, he continued reading.

"Basile had a sister—a nun—and a brother who died but left children. Roche's family lived at court for years, where their father collected taxes. The court was full of spies then—perhaps he learned to use them. He amassed a fortune, but lost his position in the Reign of Terror. People think Roche or his brother responsible for some ugly deeds but cannot prove them. Like the carriage accident Mama and I had when I was little, or Father's favorite hunting dog who was injured. Georges thinks Basile returned to France once or twice. But it matters not—he is dead."

At that André gritted his teeth. *It's not true! And how could our good family be related to him?*

"Marie-Thérèse has not made friends here—she does not speak this kind of French and feels others look down on her. But that will change. She misses her family. I beg you to send news of the Charettes."

It was signed simply, "Your loving brother, Denis."

Though André's gut was churning since his encounter with Roche, the newsy letters brightened his mood. *But I must tell Denis about Roche. He may be in danger.*

He returned to the Indian Shop to purchase paper, ink and a goose quill. In the twilight, while others danced to the music of bagpipe and violins, flutes and jaw harps, he wrote to Denis—telling him of his second brigade, becoming a steersman, the tempest, of eating roots and of the New Fort.

But when he started about Roche, André faltered. The bruises on his shoulders and ribs throbbed as he searched for the right words to describe the attack. Putting it on paper made his hand shake. Finally he wrote simply that he had spoken with Roche who was alive, and seeking vengeance.

André began to doubt the safety of a letter and his agitation spread. *Could Roche ambush the person who carried letters? Where was he now? Who was helping him? Did Roche have friends among North West Company men? How had he survived the winter? Who were the two who surrounded him?* André shuddered at how quickly he was filled with rampant fear.

He looked at his letter and signed it. He walked over to ask the post clerk to seal it with drops of hot wax when he remembered he had no news of the Charettes to comfort Denis' wife. He needed to ask if Joseph Charette was at the *rendezvous*. Perhaps Mr. Chaboillez might know. But his door was closed.

CHAPTER 24

Early the next morning, he went again to see Chaboillez, who was asleep. He walked to the office to ask about sending a message, knowing he had to speak to the snooty clerk, not looking forward to it. He phrased his questions in English instead of French.

The clerk had acted superior before, but now answered quietly. "Yes, letters can be taken to Montreal."

André, puzzled at the change in his attitude, smiled. *Was it speaking a different language?* "Is it too hard to speak in French?"

The young clerk's eyes misted and he spilled his problems. "I'm not good at it. And my *bourgeois* is unpleasant. When I make mistakes, he berates me. After my parents died, my uncle contracted me to the fur trade. But I do not want to be here."

Holding out his hand, he said, "I am André. What is your name?"

"I am Hugh," the clerk said, accepting André's outstretched hand. "Did your parents die too?"

"Yes, long ago," André said. "Where are you bound?"

"Pembina, or Rainy Lake, both places now need a clerk. My contract is for five years. About this life I know naught." He looked forlorn at the dim prospect.

"They are north of where we winter." They chatted for some time. Then André remembered his errand. "Do you know Mr. Chaboillez? I must ask him about Joseph Charette, one of his interpreters."

Hugh offered to pass the message.

André returned, thinking about Hugh, only a few years older. *Where would I be without Antoine, Pretty Mouse and Emile, and my other canoe-mates, all who are my friends? And my native friends? But Hugh has no peers—the voyageurs won't befriend clerks, nor will the trader he works for. The class differences are too great.*

At the campsite, Antoine stopped him, a light dancing in his eyes that André had not seen since Gerard's death. "I want to leave for our post the day after the feast. Starting today, find a way to work with the head man at Outfits. Help him. And see how long our provisioning will take. Convince him to get our trade goods ready first, if you can."

André grinned. That work sounded more interesting than tree-cutting.

He hurried to the great Outfits warehouse. Ahead of him was a *bourgeois*, resplendent in fine city clothing, whose demands took a long time.

While André waited, he wandered away to study the wall map of rivers, lakes and North West Company districts. It also showed the rival posts of Hudson's Bay Company and XY Company. He searched for Pembina and Rainy Lake—and then Lake Winipic—to see how far they were from Antoine's post.

Before he could take his turn, a man wearing rough clothing, much like André's, entered the storehouse. André was surprised to hear him addressed as a *bourgeois*.

"Oh, sir, you are here finally," the head clerk said. "It must have been a difficult trip, sir."

"'Twere the last miles be the hardest. I hope the company builds a portage road around Kakabeka Falls." He sat on a bale of pelts.

"For my return, I shall need extra provisioning. Here's my list— please put things aside for me. And, oh—can you get me a compass? Mine was lost in a gale. 'Twas from an uncle. It ga'e me such good service, I hated to lose it. Well, I canna stay. I shall be back."

Finally the head clerk turned his attention to André, first giving him a hard look up and down as André asked, "Antoine Felix wants to know how soon his provisioning can be ready. This week—can that be done?"

"No. Priority is for special crews heading to Rainy Lake. If they don't leave in two days, the trade goods for Athabasca will not arrive before freeze-up." The head clerk brandished a dozen sheets with long lists. "And you heard the two *bourgeois* before you—their orders will be done next. Your Antoine Felix, he must wait."

"I helped with Antoine's provisioning once before," he pressed.

The clerk frowned. "They trusted you with an inventory of trade goods?"

André nodded. "Simon showed me how. But I don't see him. Is he here this year?"

"Simon was my oldest brother! God bless his soul, he returned to Montreal."

André was disappointed, for Simon had been a kind taskmaster. "I can help you with the urgent orders. Tell me where things are, I'll make the pile and you can check it."

Overloaded by the number and complexity of his tasks, the head clerk agreed. Many hours later he was well-pleased to see André's work correctly done.

"I could use your help with these orders before the Rainy Lake brigades leave." The head clerk pointed to his lists. "How soon does your Antoine want to leave?"

"The morning after the feast."

The clerk shook his hand. "That's plenty of time. Come first thing tomorrow."

André was glad to help—working his brain helped keep it off Basile Roche. He did not know how to tell Antoine—or Mouse or Emile. Or if he should.

After supper his ruminations on Roche were cut short. Toussaint and Pierre offered to teach him woods lore. While gazing at the sky, the cousins told him Ojibwe stories of the stars.

Helping the clerk during the day and spending time in the forest kept him active, but in the back of his mind, he could not forget Roche's threat: "I will be there when you do not expect me."

How can I prepare for that? There was no answer but to be constantly alert.

CHAPTER 25

That evening André was waiting for the cousins when a young man with shiny straight black hair stopped to see him. He said, "Please to come with me, I bid you."

That request was intriguing. *Am I being led into the clutches of Basile?* He decided to take the chance—he would watch where they were going, and veer off if he had suspicions. Besides, the young man was clean, polite and not intimidating, all the opposite of Basile. So he followed.

They went to the gentlemen partners' rooms and stopped by one. The young man knocked.

"'Tis open. Enter," said a deep voice.

When the young man opened the door, André saw the wintering partner who had asked about Gerard. Deeply engrossed in reading a book, he sat in a chair next to a desk with many drawers. A candle with a shiny reflector lit the pages.

"André Didier has come, sir."

André bowed while the man slid in a paper to mark his place in the book and set it aside.

"Well, 'tis a trial to spend the winter with nae to keep me mind active. Last season I read 'Robinson Crusoe.' In it a sailor is shipwrecked on an island and spends years alone."

He reached into a desk drawer and pulled out a book, bound in dark green leather. André's heart quickened. "I brou' it for another man who likes to read. But since he dinna come to the meeting this year, you shall borrow it, if you'd like. Though it is not physics, your book that was lost, you will ha'e something to read this long winter."

"Oh yes, thank you, sir." André was humbled by his astonishing kindness.

"This cloth, 'twill protect it from the weather." He wrapped the book in oiled canvas, tied it and handed it to André.

"Next year you shall return it at the *rendezvous*. That is all."

André's eyes shone as he grasped the book to his heart—to be trusted with such a gift was an honor. "*Merci*, thank you, sir. Thank you."

The *bourgeois* turned back to his own book, and the young man ushered André out.

"Please thank your master again for me."

"He is my father—and my master, for this year I have entered the fur trade."

André was speechless.

"My father read the book to us last winter. Perhaps you will read it aloud to others? It is an adventure many enjoyed." The young man slipped away quietly.

I like that idea. I hope Antoine will too.

He walked slowly back to the campsite, feeling the package between his fingers and the weight of the book, like gold in his hand. In the light of the campfire, he examined his treasure.

Pretty Mouse, pleased from having won a handful of coins in a leg-wrestling contest, sat down and peered at the book. "A book, André? Where did you get a book?"

"A *bourgeois* lent it to me, because I lost the other one from Father Goiffon. It's a story about a sailor who was shipwrecked. Do you think you would like it?"

Mouse sniffed, a bit sorrowful. "Me, I do not read."

"I mean that I could read it out loud, after supper at the post. When we have enough light."

"Now that I like. You make sense of all those little letters—the Mouse will whittle." He leaned against a tree and took out his knife, looking for a nubbin of wood to shape into something. "You could start now. I have nothing to do."

André grinned. That was like the Mouse. Though it was too dark to read, the pleasure of having a book was so immense that he forgot his dread about Basile Roche. *Bad things happen, but good things too.*

CHAPTER 26

With André helping to organize the trade goods being sent to fur posts, his last days of the *rendezvous* swirled by. The wintering partners made their final decisions about the year to come—who was retiring from the fur trade after a lifetime in the wilderness, who would rotate back to Montreal after their five-year term. André paid little attention to some announcements. But he smiled to hear they would not close any posts, though that question lingered for the future. To celebrate their successful year, the *bourgeois* presided at a final night of feasting and dancing.

Antoine, his bales of trade goods ready, chafed to be on the move to his wintering post. At their campsite, many canoe-men were organizing to go to their wintering posts. From canoe No. 2, only Amable and Urbain were returning to Lachine, and the others were bound for distant posts. André said his goodbyes to the rest of the brigade and gathered up his gear.

On his last day, André returned to the Indian Shop to select a new sash. *But no red plume. I will wait until the next rendezvous, so it won't get broken or bent.*

Among the goods, he saw a compass, and fingered its shiny brass and glass, marveling at the way its needle always pointed north, no matter which direction he stood. *The clerk will have chosen the best one for the bougeois, so I will buy this one.*

After paying for his purchases, André made a final stop to say *Au revoir* to his new friend Hugh, who would clerk at a post on Rainy Lake.

André heard news of the Charettes, and finished his letter to be carried back to Lachine and sent on to France.

André would be safe once they arrived at Antoine's fur post. Would Basile attack on the way?

Chapter 27

Antoine's canoe was loaded shortly after sunrise, ready to slip along the western shore of Lake Superior. André glanced at Pretty Mouse, who was quiet as he dragged himself to the waterfront. André reached out his hand to steady the Mouse as they prepared to paddle.

"Today Emile and André will steer," Antoine said, raising his eyebrows at Pretty Mouse. "Tomorrow they are our *milieux* and we shall work the bow and stern."

"Not for me. I want to be the *bourgeois* and ride in the middle," Pretty Mouse said. "You can carry me to shore. Where is my fancy hat?"

They all laughed. The camaraderie brought André joy.

From Lachine to the New Fort, his canoe-mates had worked well together but, with the heavy responsibility of steering, André had not relaxed. Now that work was shared. *This is the voyageur life I want, like old times. Together, we can do anything. That's what Joseph said.*

The friendly atmosphere helped lift the dark cloud of Basile Roche, the cloud that had begun poisoning his mood and silencing him. André had not felt ready to tell them Roche was alive. *They won't believe me.* And sometimes he, too, wondered if it hadn't all been a terrible dream.

Paddling past the old Grand Portage, they slowed their pace, gazing silently at the few buildings that remained of the *rendezvous* site. It held memories for each of them.

Antoine examined the place carefully—the XY Company, their competition, used warehouses at the Grand Portage. He eyed the canoes nearly ready to leave for wintering posts.

André waved to a young man about his age standing on the hillside watching them. *Last time I was the youngest one. This year*

I saw others like Hugh at the New Fort, and here is an XY Company person my age. I wonder where he will go.

At a pipe-break, Pretty Mouse became agitated. "André, this new book you have—can I see it again?" When André dug it out, Mouse handled it reverently, but upside-down. "When do you start?"

"In the winter we need a good story," Emile suggested.

"Winter? Too many weeks away," whined Mouse. "He should read now. André said it was about a man lost at sea."

"We won't get lost—we follow rivers." Emile liked to tease. "But does this Robinson Crusoe trade for pelts? That might help us."

"A story, you say? I like it." Antoine tapped the ashes from his pipe. "Our post is already built—we don't have to hurry to get there. If we paddle a little less each day, we can hear some of the story along the way."

André grinned. "Tonight?"

"Tonight," Antoine nodded. "We stop—before the sun sets."

"The moon, it is almost full," Pretty Mouse said. "We could read longer then?"

The rest of that day they paddled vigorously, with a new look of anticipation in their eyes and slight upturns of their lips.

After a quick supper, they sat around the small fire. In hushed respect, they watched as André removed the book from its bag and opened it. They leaned forward as he turned to the first page and began reading.

Pretty Mouse interrupted at nearly every sentence. "He was born in 1632? So old he is now. Or dead. How did he write this?"

"His brother killed, so sad."

"A free school? We did not have that."

"Humph. You should never go against your father."

"Me, I was not sick on the ship, not me! Maybe I will not like this story."

Finally Antoine intervened. "Patience, Mouse, patience."

From that night on, they unloaded quickly, ate fast and sat like school children waiting for André to begin. Each night he read. Each night they listened, and were disappointed when darkness crept over them and he closed the book.

Someone would inevitably cry, "But André it is not yet too dark. Look, I can see." But he stopped. They had many miles to travel each day, and needed to rise early.

They discovered that Crusoe's sea journeys often mirrored theirs, when dangers, like contrary winds, meant all hands needed to work together, to help each other.

The paddlers made good time and entered the St. Louis River a few days later. Antoine described their new route with fewer portages, though they had to cross the six-mile Savanna portage.

"I heard they had little snow in the winter," André said. "And that the ice left early on the rivers and streams—a dry spring. It's why the river seems low—look at all the rocks."

"Less mud on the portages," said Pretty Mouse gleefully.

"And maybe not so many mosquitoes," Antoine said, swatting at flying insects. "But nothing keeps the black flies away."

Even with irritations like black flies and mosquitoes, I like being here. Paddling upstream on these smaller rivers is almost a holiday compared to the boulder-choked rapids on the Ottawa and the Mattawa. The rivers were narrower and shallower, but the hidden rocks as deadly.

With others sharing the responsibilities of steering, André's shoulders eased. On portages, he grabbed handfuls of blueberries and raspberries. Along the shores, he noticed fragrant purple and pink flowers. *Father Goiffon would want to know what they are. How do I describe them? How could I bring him samples of the plants I see?* Sometimes he spotted grasslands between the trees, birds twittering, moose wading in marshes. *This is rich country. What would it be like to stay a whole year, or maybe more?*

For several days they smelled smoke in the air.

"Where are they? I do not see camp places," said Pretty Mouse. "No footprints in mud. But every day me, I smell the smoke, that little bit. How do they hide from the Mouse, who has such good eyes?"

It was a puzzle, especially for Mouse who noticed things that others did not.

Paddling through a fire-blackened area, they saw massive trees reduced to crumbling skeletons, the ground burnt black, small brush surrounded by ash piles. Here no birds sang, no frogs croaked, no insects buzzed. Though the fire was long gone, the air was harsh and acrid.

"It smells different than camp fires," Pretty Mouse said. "Now I see why."

"Ah," said Antoine, knocking his forehead with his knuckle. "My old friend Cruzette, he told me—no rain. Then lightning hits, a little wind, and *voila!* The forests and the plains, they all burn. A big fire, it races, eating everything. The grass—it is nothing for the hungry fire. The fire wants more, more, more. The tree—it is so dry it makes a great fire, so hot that the fire eats the next tree and the next. Only a river can stop this kind of fire."

In awe and silence they paddled. Few shoots of green poked up out of the scorched earth. When André flipped a stone into it, wisps of smoke arose and the smell wafted in the breeze. They had never seen such devastation, except for the tempest.

"How long will it take to grow back?" he asked.

"The brush, maybe three or five years," said Pretty Mouse with sorrow, "but the great trees, never in our lifetime."

Evening rain often sprinkled them. André, knowing that rain would damage his borrowed book, shook his head—he would not read that night. His canoe-mates protested in disappointment.

"But I must know," said Pretty Mouse. "You know the story, do you not? Tell us what happens next."

André had not looked ahead and could not tell Mouse what he wanted to know. He shrugged and carefully kept the book inside its oiled canvas cover.

A few days later a bountiful crop of mosquitoes appeared, swarming and humming in their ears and around their backs, usually out of range of being swatted. During the days, the men were easy targets—their hands were occupied with paddles or packs. But each night they slapped, scratched—and swore, as red welts grew unbearably itchy. They fanned smoke from the fire onto themselves, hoping to deter insects. Pretty Mouse tried sleeping in the shallow water, but the mosquitoes buzzed and bit his ears.

"At the *rendezvous*, a Nor'wester, he told me—skunk urine keeps them away," Mouse said. "But how do you suppose we could get some?"

Emile and Antoine shook their heads and laughed. No one offered to find skunk urine.

"My hair is getting long now," André said, untying it. "Maybe the bugs will get lost trying to find skin."

"Too bad you don't have a beard," Pretty Mouse said. "Whiskers keep them off my face."

"Toussaint said bear grease was good," Emile said.

"That we have," Antoine said, and dug into the pack.

"Grease—too thick for their skinny stingers," added Mouse. "Me, I hope they will get their little feet stuck."

They rubbed grease on their arms, legs and necks.

"And my ears," Pretty Mouse said. "I hear them singing, circling me. I slap. But they are not there. Then my ear sings the rest of the night, because I hit it too hard."

The mosquitoes continued their sneak attacks, reinforced during the day by black flies, which bit and left bigger welts that itched much longer.

"Tonight we camp on an island," Antoine decided. "Maybe it will be too far for them to fly."

After a few hot dry days, the mosquito hatch disappeared, swooped up by bats, birds and toads, but the black flies remained—the men were resigned.

On a portage, André was the first one over. As he neared a resting place, he spied a barrel and a bale of trade goods on a grassy hill. *How can this be? Who is ahead of us, faster than Antoine?* He peered uncertainly. The insignia painted on them was not the North West Company's. His second thought: *Is this a trap of Basile's?* Since leaving the New Fort, André felt safe with his friends. He had pushed aside fears of Roche and his whereabouts.

André reasoned he was safe. *Roche needs a cane and cannot carry packs. But he has henchmen—two of them, maybe more. So who is ahead? He will have to return for his last load.* André waited, and steeled himself.

Soon a voyageur with square shoulders appeared, whistling. *I know him, but who?*

The voyageur wiped his sweating forehead on his sleeve and looked up, startled to see André.

It's Jean Ducharme—he was in Antoine's brigade the other time.

André stood, holding out his hand. Oddly, Jean did not seem pleased to see André. "Jean, I thought you were Antoine's man."

"Ah, André. I am with the XY Company now—they give me the winter post of my own," he sighed. "Our brigade, we did not have so good a guide as Antoine. It was, how should I say, a difficult voyage from Lachine. But with this company, I can make money because now I am the trader, like Antoine. All these seventeen years I have been a voyageur, but never could I do more than paddle and carry. If I am a winterer for the North West, and I buy their tobacco or extra blanket or rum, then I get behind. I owe them my wages, which are little. I never come out ahead. But with XY, I have a chance."

Being his own man—that André understood, and helped Jean shoulder his load. "Where will you build your post?"

Ducharme was haughty. "My *bourgeois*, he oversees many posts—a busy man. Others built the post already, and traded for food. We do not have that work."

"Where is it?"

He named rivers and portages that weren't familiar to André.

"Do you know what to do? To keep the accounts, how the trade works?"

"In Lachine they talked many hours with me. I know how to be the trader—that will be easy. Keeping the records—I am not so good."

It sounded like Antoine's first years as a trader.

"I go now. Me, I do not want to see Antoine. He will think I am traitor to him."

André didn't answer. The word "traitor" reminded him of Basile Roche.

"*Au revoir.*" After they shook hands, a little more at ease with each other, Ducharme continued on and André returned for his second load to portage.

I wonder if that rival company will affect us. When Antoine came into view, André told him what he'd learned.

"Oho, Jean Ducharme has been hooked by sweet promises. Maybe like I was," Antoine said. "When I was filling up my brigade, he did not come, *non*, he did not. He is strong, with many years left to work. How close will he be, I wonder?"

André repeated what Ducharme had said about the rivers and portages.

"Some days' journey north of our post. Maybe he will try to lure 'our hunters' away by offering more goods. We must keep our Indians loyal to us, or Chaboillez will close our post."

With that sobering thought, they portaged on. There was no further sign of Ducharme and his canoes.

We won't be near so we won't see him. But our hunters—will they choose to trade with the XY men instead? What could they offer that Antoine wouldn't?

He had an unsettling vision of Basile pouring Jean Ducharme a large drink of rum, the same as the day he had bullied Mouse at André's first *rendezvous*. Recalling Roche rattled him—he felt chilled, though it was warm.

CHAPTER 28

The next day they arrived at a portage with a few skinny trees. "You remember this place, André?" Pretty Mouse asked. "The earth, she sinks into a great mire. Each step, it is like torture."

"Ah, the moccasin-eater," André remembered, laughing. "So much muck—though you tied on your moccasins tight, the swamp sucked one off your foot."

"Not only a moccasin-eater, but almost a man-eater," said Pretty Mouse. "The foot goes down, down, down. A monster, it waits on the bottom."

"The Savanna," Emile groaned. "I hate this portage the most. There is hardly a step of solid footing the length of it. And the stink—how can I hold my nose?"

"But to reach our post we have to cross it," said Antoine as he reached to hoist the canoe. "Enjoy this clump of birch where we stand—there are not many bits of dry ground until we are on the other side."

Emile pointed to shreds of birch bark off the path, the remains of a canoe. "How could they go on, without their canoe?" He looked perplexed.

Antoine shrugged. "One winter a group of us cut tamarack trees and laid them in a row, to make a kind of road to help when we carry the canoes," he said. "But that spring, we sank to our waists—and deeper. We couldn't find our road."

"Me, I tie my moccasins tighter," Mouse said, "or I will end up barefoot until we reach the next trading post." He bent to bind his leggings and moccasins with long leather cords.

As soon as André stepped into its oozy mush, he smelled the rotting swamp. Though it was a dry year, he found himself knee-deep, and sometimes hip-deep in slimy dark mud, never sure how far down his foot would drop before finding solid ground for the next step. It made him nervous.

Would Roche lay in wait on this portage? No, but if I fell, the muck might swallow me up. Who would ever know where I was? At the realization, André stayed close to his canoe-mates and was grateful for their companionship.

He and Emile slogged on, loaded with double packs, grateful that Antoine and Pretty Mouse carried the canoe. He wondered how they would find enough dry places to camp each night, but they did. It took the better part of five days to reach the Mississippi River.

Each night they stopped early to hear more of Robinson Crusoe. André read with enthusiasm, slowing his words to pace the story. He used different voices, whether hushed or shouting, to dramatize the action, so the others could create vivid pictures in their minds.

Aspects of Crusoe's adventure spoke differently to each one. Emile liked the thrilling story, Antoine liked that a man could find his way through complicated problems. Pretty Mouse, who had never heard a book read aloud, loved it all. For André, reading to them covered up his growing anxiety of Roche's threat. Each night kept the threat at bay.

Listening to the story made the hard work of their journey easier and inspired conversations.

"What would you save from the canoe, if we were to shipwreck?" Emile asked.

"Me," Pretty Mouse said, "a bale or two of trade goods. There are many things I could use." Then with a twinkle in his eye he added, "and a keg."

"Tools and food," Antoine answered, his eyes closed and imagining such a situation.

One night after reading of Robinson Crusoe's struggles, André asked, "What is the worst time you ever had?"

Antoine took a deep breath, looked at them all and set his pipe on the ground.

"I was young, and we were far in the north. My *bourgeois*, he gave liquor to the natives often, not only in the fall when the trade was made or when the hunters brought the furs in. He told them drink would give them visions like the medicine man had, so the chiefs and hunters desired that power."

Antoine picked up his pipe and frowned at it, then set it down again.

"After a while all they wanted was to drink and they did not go out to hunt—no beaver, no elk, no food, no pelts to trade. They fought with each other and then with us. Joseph, your father, he was in the wrong place and was attacked by a warrior—who was his friend. With no hunting, the people in the villages began to starve. We voyageurs, we too had less food—everything we ate came from them."

Emile and André looked at each other with concern, remembering their hungry days on the big lakes.

"The *bourgeois*, he often gave us high wine, and with so much liquor, we got lazy and did stupid things. Me, I thought I could do everything—paddle, carry, find my way in deep woods. But I could not master drink. Nor could any of us."

Pretty Mouse closed his eyes. He too was remembering such a moment.

"One day I was coming back from trading and too addled with rum to notice a moose," Antoine went on. "Big horns, how could I miss it? But I did. That moose, he didn't want me around and he charged toward me. I couldn't outrun him, but I was lucky and climbed a tree. He rammed my tree and it swayed. I thought he would knock it down, with me in it. He stomped my pack to shreds. For a few hours, I stayed on that hard branch, cold and hungry and getting sober. It was dark before I was brave enough to get down."

They all relaxed. The worst had not happened.

"That taught me, but not Louis. André, you remember Louis— the one with the scars? Louis, he was not afraid of anything after he had been drinking. One day, he dared a bear, big and black and with teeth like sharp knives. This bear, she was a fearsome bear, because beyond us was her cub. She watched and maybe she would have left Louis alone. But Louis threw rocks and taunted her. And the bear, I think maybe she did not want Louis to speak so in front of her cub. In two steps, she was upon him and reared up. He yelled once more, this time in fright. She cuffed him on the neck and head. Her claws raked deep gouges, long bloody scrapes. Louis, he did not lose his life—but many scars pucker up his face."

André shuddered, recalling Louis with terrible scars.

"But did we stop our party? *Non*. My good friend Pierre hit his head when our dogsled swung wildly and crashed into a tree—we were not paying attention. A big barrel of rum was also smashed— people cared more about the lost liquor than Pierre's injury. After that he was never the same. He could not remember everyday things. It was his last year in the fur trade—the *bourgeois*, he did not hire Pierre again. Now Pierre, he lives with his family and never comes out."

Antoine picked up his pipe again and lit it, and was silent for a few moments.

"Finally we ran out of high wines. There was no other trader to give out liquor, so after a while the men hunted again, the children ate once more and the women laughed and sang while they worked. That was when I decided too much trade in alcohol is wrong. The next year, I signed on with a different *bourgeois*."

They sat in silence. Emile had not heard the details before. Nor had Joseph told André. *It's why Gerard's death affected Antoine so much, because it came after our celebrating.*

After a long quiet, Pretty Mouse said, "But for me, the rum helps me forget a very bad time."

That seemed out of character for the joyous Mouse.

"You know that narrow chute on the Ottawa, with high cliffs on both sides?" Pretty Mouse said. "It was my third spring on a brigade. We sang and paddled. But we did not see the band of warriors hiding at the top. Suddenly their bows rained arrows on us. We could not defend ourselves—except to paddle as fast as we could. They shot and shot and shot at us. It felt like hours passing through. We did not stop paddling until we were far away. All of us, we were hit. I took three arrows—here, and here, and here."

Mouse peeled back his shirt and pointed to long scars from his ear to his collarbone, across his shoulder blades and slanting over his stomach toward his thigh.

"My blood, it did not stop leaking out. Many days afterwards I was dizzy. I could not eat or drink. I could not carry much. I didn't get my strength back until after the *rendezvous*. Every year at those same cliffs, I remember those warriors. A wee dram, it helps me forget."

They did not speak again that night as they contemplated the stories of Antoine and Pretty Mouse and listened to the haunting calls of loons.

CHAPTER 29

When they finally reached Antoine's post on the Moose Horn River, André heaved a sigh of relief as they hauled the packs inside. *No bales to tote until next spring. No portages with black flies. No sleeping with mosquitoes, no shortages of food. Once we move our new goods into the trade room and cache our provisions, we can start trading. The Ojibwe will bring lots of pelts—Antoine will trade here as long as he wants. And I'll be his clerk as long as he wants me. I'm safe here.*

As the autumn leaves changed their colors and fell to the ground, the weeks at the post were filled with chores—amassing wood piles and stacking them high, fixing the small dock and the stockade surrounding the post. Antoine repaired the shed and fur press. Pretty Mouse and Emile enlarged the space to store high wine, because this year they had brought more barrels. Antoine added water to the smallest casks that would be given out at the first trades of the autumn, while André marked it in their inventory. Mouse built caches to hold the wild rice they'd traded for, while Emile and André foraged for the last hazelnuts and edible wild foods. André and Antoine reviewed their trading records, and Emile and Mouse chose sled dogs to begin training.

At the post, Pretty Mouse often suggested uses for the pulley, like lifting bark slabs to reinforce their rooftop or straightening their stockade poles. Finding different purposes was a game with him. Mostly they were successful, though sometimes the rope slipped from the damaged pulley.

For a month they were so busy that there was barely time for Robinson Crusoe. But as those tasks were completed, André again took out the book and read, sometimes by the flickering light of a reed-candle that burned smoky bear tallow. They learned how

Crusoe had raised corn, dried raisins, made baskets and clay pots, tamed goats and built a boat.

"He did well," Emile said, inspired by Crusoe's resourcefulness. "But so many years alone—I cannot fathom it."

All were yawning, ready for sleep. André's eyes glanced to the next chapter title—and he jolted.

"Oho. The next page says 'The Footprint.'"

"Only one?" As usual, Pretty Mouse was eager to hear more.

Even Antoine agreed. "Keep reading."

Despite the heavy eyelids, including André's, he began the chapter. In the middle of a sentence, their reed-candle sputtered out.

"No!" yelled Pretty Mouse. "What happens next?"

"Tomorrow," Antoine said.

Though they could not see each other in the darkness, discussion continued.

"But only one foot?" Pretty Mouse demanded. "How can someone make only one print, not two?"

They were mystified.

"Me, I think it will be a friend," Antoine said. "He needs one, *oui?*"

"Could it have been a she, do you think?" Emile mused. "Maybe that I would not mind."

Only André felt the fear and danger that Crusoe foresaw. *Another person threatened everything Crusoe had built. Someone had arrived in quiet, and left without making his presence known. Why? For evil? Should he hide from it?*

It echoed his own questions about Basile Roche. When André left the safety of the post for his tasks, his eyes again darted about, suspicious of shadows. The danger posed by Crusoe's mystery footprint became personal, connected to Basile.

Bit by bit, Roche's threat took on a life of its own and grew. Noises while working outdoors made André's head jerk around for its source. A snapped twig, a hare or raccoon scurrying past, a flock of geese lifting up—each sound or movement caused him alarm. *Is it a spy, an enemy, a trap?*

He began to arm himself—"Is this not the season for hungry wolves?"—with a hatchet or knife when he left the palisade enclosing the fort. *I must be ready at all times. But ready for what?*

Wolves were about—all had heard baying. André felt jumpy and frazzled, though no one mentioned the change in him.

Sometimes he could use logic to dismiss Roche from his mind and release the fear. *Dry leaves are noisy. So lurking, or sneaking up on me in the fall will be harder for another person.* It didn't always work. Often he pretended a lightness he did not feel.

The novelty of this life as a winterer was no longer an adventure. Survival was uncertain, difficult. The adventure stories Joseph told had skipped over that aspect.

In André's first winter, Ojibwe hunters had come often to take new goods on credit and to visit. Now when they came, he understood more of the language, and greeted the hunters and chiefs, though his use of Ojibwe words occasionally caused laughter. He alternated between being expansive and friendly while visiting with hunters, but somber and thoughtful when alone.

It was a brisk afternoon when an old friend, Runs When He Walks, and two other hunters arrived. "Open Face, we come to trade," Runs When He Walks said. They sat by the fire, sharing news with Antoine, whom they called Open Face, over a cup of high wines he had warmed for them.

While André tended to the post's chores and stirred Pretty Mouse's soup pot, he caught snatches of their conversation.

"Dry this year. Wild fires on the grasslands. It drove animals away from our hunting area. Hard to find good furs this year—maybe we go into the big forest."

"One fire started without lightning. Spoiled good camping areas."

"Big trees burned near the river—and Makwa's winter camp."

"Some families cannot move to winter grounds. Instead they go to spring sugar camp."

And they brought news of a new trader, who had built a fur post early in the summer, elbow-to-elbow with a trader they knew. Three sleeps away.

"New man gives rum each time. Some hunters camp there, stay there to drink."

"Sounds like trouble," Antoine said, his face darkening and wondering about Jean Ducharme. "Will you trade with him?"

"We trust you, Open Face." Then Runs When He Walks paused. "But we trade with all white men, if they are fair." After taking goods on credit and sharing a supper, they left.

"Having an extra trader, that complicates our business," Antoine said. "Some of 'our hunters' owe us from last season because they couldn't find enough furs. I hope they don't hunt in contested areas or Dakota hunting grounds." He ran his fingers through his long hair. "No, it is not good."

Emile said, "Runs When He Walks told me that since the fires, animals are smaller, harder to hunt. There is less to eat." He blinked several times. "We know what that's like."

"The post gate is open," Antoine said. "André, step outside and close it. You can finish writing up their credits afterwards."

André did, though he felt vulnerable in the dark and cold. The night's normal sounds—an owl hooting, the wind, a branch rubbing repeatedly against the wall—bothered him. Each one seemed like Roche, spying, sending messages, taunting him.

A few mornings later Antoine counted the groups who had not yet come to trade—it took both hands.

"I thought we weren't as busy this year, but it was because we didn't have to build the post," André said.

"I will wait for Makwa and Lame Hawk," Antoine answered. "But for others, you must go to the bands and start to get their furs. I cannot wait for all of them to visit." He began to plan for Emile and André to visit the winter lodges.

"Tomorrow, you head to Badger Creek. Be ready to leave early. Before their furs go to another trader. We take no chances."

André was torn. Encouraging trade had been exciting. Before the *rendezvous*, he had especially looked forward to seeing Makes Thunder, the grandson of Makwa. Makes Thunder had uncovered the clue which led to finding Denis. Though grateful, now he dreaded the trip to Makwa's band, a long distance away. He feared leaving the safety of the post.

Tomorrow's jaunt was only as far as Badger Creek, a half-day away. He and Emile would be in the forest. *Will we be vulnerable to Basile Roche?* He fretted while they piled up an array of tools—fire steels for sparking a fire, awls, fish hooks and metal chisels. They added blankets and cloth, tobacco, silver jewelry, ribbons and beads. Each item they added made him feel anxious. Until Antoine placed a gun, and shot and powder on the pile.

Stop, he finally commanded his brain. *Roche cannot know when we're going. Or where. Because I will be with Emile, Roche will not attack me. And with the gun, we are more evenly matched.* After that he could make preparations again.

That night a great weight pressed on André's chest. He tried to cough but powerful fingers squeezed off his air, stifling his breath. He smelled the foul, filthy breath and powerful body odor of his enemy. A guttural voice from his past whispered in his ear. "Now I have you!"

Basile Roche!

André couldn't breathe. He scrabbled at the fingers squeezing his neck. He scratched. The light behind his eyes began to dim.

Then he jerked free. Took a deep breath. Opened his eyes.

Woke up. His blanket was wrapped tightly around his neck. He pulled it off quickly and rubbed his skin.

A dream! But so real.

He could not fall back to sleep. The uneasy feeling about Basile Roche would not leave him.

André listened for the snores and sleep-breathing of his friends. They had not wakened at his nightmare. Which meant they would not look at him with questioning eyes during the day.

When they arose, he discovered snow swirling and a rising wind—the first blizzard of the season was in full force. André was safe at the post for a few more days. They contented themselves with the adventures of Robinson Crusoe and games on the checkerboard.

Now in the snow André could see occasional animal tracks—rabbits and a fox. No human prints. He sighed with relief—safe again.

When the storm cleared, André and Emile packed a sled and left for Badger Creek to cement friendships, present gifts and gather what Antoine hoped was a hefty pack of pelts. Over supper, they listened for news. Antoine had asked them to focus on when and where different bands might be hunting and what luck they had.

André also pricked his ears for whispers of Basile and wondered about visitors to the tribes. Outwardly he showed pleasure in being with hunters in their village; inwardly he felt edgy and sharp.

Back at the post, Antoine asked, "What did you learn, my boys?"

They relayed what they had heard, and showed the pelts—more than Antoine had expected. He was pleased with their success. "Good work. Tomorrow, no, the next day, you go again."

André had felt relieved to be again under Antoine's protection. *I can't keep hiding here or I won't be able to do what Antoine needs me to do. Joseph said my friends would help me, but I don't know how they could. I feel foolish burdening them.* He didn't say a word.

Instead of releasing the burden, he stayed closer to the post and used reason to combat his anxiety. Basile would not visit the post, he was sure. Roche himself could not easily move about easily. If he came, he would need help from his henchmen—and word would travel.

Gradually the memory of Basile's threats eased during the days, and nightmares no longer dogged his sleep. Trees and thickets were no longer hiding places from which Roche might leap.

Daily the snow piled up and soft drifts became too deep for them to move easily. Only a few native hunters visited, bringing news, or a rabbit to share.

Soon, however, the cold would harden the snow and they could travel with more ease. Then it would be time again to set out to visit the bands in their winter lodges.

CHAPTER 30

While they waited, Antoine set them to plugging leaks in the log walls and other minor tasks, but there was little urgent work to do.

One darkening afternoon, they all seemed to wait for something. André wrote in the post's diary before the day's light left them. Snowflakes swirled through a crack they had missed in the log chinking, landing on his neck.

"Tomorrow is Christmas," he said suddenly. "*Le Noël.*"

They all looked up.

"Marguerite will be hurrying off to the midnight Mass," Emile said, a faraway look in his eyes. *He's thinking about that pretty black-eyed girl who said goodbye so sadly at Lachine.*

"Me, I would be at the tavern by the river," Mouse mused. "The maid, she brings us an extra pitcher of ale and we sing all the songs of Christmas."

"After my father butchered a pig," Antoine said, "we would make blood sausage, *boudin.*"

"'Black pudding,' we called it," Mouse said, a sparkle in his eye. "And my mother, she baked us a special cake we only ate once a year."

André was quiet. Joseph and Berthe would give him little presents—something whittled, something knitted. She would make André's favorite supper, a meaty *tourtière* in a crisp crust and a dish of baked apples with cream. Denis—what would he be doing?

He longed to be with them, and sighed. It would be ten months, maybe more.

"Christmas, eh?" Antoine gazed at his men. "Then we celebrate. Mouse, what is in our larder? Something special?"

Mouse cocked his head, grabbed his *capote* and headed outdoors. A moment later, Emile got a funny look on his face, and he also left.

André muttered. *What is Christmas without gifts to share, but what can I do?* Then it came to him—he would entertain them with magic tricks that Joseph had taught him. He began tidying their living space, though it was hardly big enough to become untidy.

When Mouse returned, he went to the food corner, humming a French carol André remembered. Absorbed in their tasks, no one said another word that evening. They skipped reading Crusoe.

Though the morning seemed as cold, snowy and windy as every other, André awoke with a sense of surprise in the air.

"André, look at the hearth. *Père Noël*, he visited us."

Stockings! Not one but three homely gray woolen stockings lay on the hearthstone. Lumpy and not especially clean, they looked suspiciously like Antoine's.

The men rose from their bunks, dressing with speed. Feeling each stocking, Antoine handed them out, one at a time.

"This one, it is for you, André."

André poked his fingers in and pulled out a small silver cone. "An earring?"

Puzzled, he glanced at Antoine. "A pen point for your quills. For writing in the diary and log book. Look, there is a small slit to hold the ink."

André fitted it onto his goose quill which had been sharpened many times, dipped it into ink and scrawled "*Merci*" in the margin of the day book. "Thank you, Antoine." His wide smile showed how useful a metal point would be.

Emile received the second stocking, which he upended. Out tumbled two tiny silver bells.

"So Emile, will something special happen after we return home? What do you say?"

Emile reddened and grinned. Then he held the bells and rang them, like church bells.

When Mouse dug into the bottom of the third stocking, he found a jaw harp.

"Oho, now I can play the tunes. My songs, they will be so sweet."

They were pleased, contented with their gifts.

After they had eaten breakfast, Emile stood to open the door, letting in a snowy cold draft. He pointed to a corner of the palisade wall. "Look. I have made us a *crèche*."

They went outside to inspect the figures of Mary, Joseph and the Baby Jesus he had shaped with dried grasses, nestled under a peaked roof made of thin sticks of wood.

"Ah, and *L'Enfant Jesu* is wrapped in a bit of rabbit fur to keep him warm," André said. "He needs it this winter."

When they came back inside, Mouse handed them each a tin cup with a warm fragrant mixture. "Do you like it?"

André guessed it was tea with rose hips, but Mouse refused to divulge his secret.

"For our supper I could not make the blood sausage—we have no pig," Mouse said. "No, this year we only have stew. But later I have a surprise." He added a few things to the stewpot, and presently the aromas of garlic and onion and mushrooms filled the room.

While they waited, they told the Christmas story, as well as they could remember.

They sang the carols of Christmas: *Noel nouvelet, Patapan, Un flambeau Jeanette Isabelle* and the sweeter voyageur tunes. They read more adventures of Robinson Crusoe. They feasted on the stew.

"It's my turn," André said when they had finished supper. "Emile, choose one of these playing cards, but don't let me see. Show Mouse and Antoine. Now, put it back in this pile. *Abracadabra!* I will magically tell you which one you chose."

He shuffled the paper cards and waved them importantly. Counting as he dealt them out onto the table, he said with drama, "This is the one, the … jack of diamonds. *Oui?*" It was.

André repeated the trick, twice for each man. They frowned and their jaws fell open. "How you do this?"

Then he reached into Antoine's pocket and—*voila!* A pine cone. He peeked under Mouse's pillow—Emile's silver bells!

"Not me, I did not take them," Mouse exclaimed. He laughed, knowing it was a trick, but not fast enough to catch André's deft sleight of hand.

To their delight, André continued to pull pipes, spoons and small trade goods from the most unlikely places.

Darkness had fallen when Mouse brought them something wrapped in a cloth—a steamed cake he had made by grinding hazelnuts and wild rice as finely as he could, adding maple sugar and dried berries and some of Antoine's cocoa and currants. It was not much like any sweet they had eaten before, but that made no difference—they were impressed. A Christmas cake like no other.

They were talking by the fire when Emile said, "Antoine, did you miss a stocking earlier? It is on your bunk."

Sure enough, a stocking with a red stripe lay on his blanket, a roundness in its red toe. André was mystified—he had not seen a stocking like that.

Taking his time, Antoine held the stocking and admired the knitting. He stretched it, rubbed it, hefted it, sniffed it as if he were trying to guess the object and the giver.

"What is it?" Mouse yelled.

Finally Antoine dumped its contents onto his lap—a brier pipe. He looked with great pleasure at all three, though he guessed it was a gift from Emile.

"'Twould not be *Noël* without a wee dram?" Pretty Mouse said hopefully. With a nod, Antoine poured some of his special brandy into each cup, André's included.

After they toasted each other as friends, and André handed his cup to Mouse, they sang more carols. It had been a most memorable Christmas, shared with friends.

What a gift my friends are. Joseph was right. He had not thought of Roche all day.

Chapter 31

A few days later Makes Thunder thrust open the ice-crusted door to the post. A flurry of snowflakes descended on them all.

"*Boozhoo*, André. *Aniish na?*"

"*Boozhoo*, my friend. I am well. And you?"

"The best. But it was a long way here." Makes Thunder grinned.

Beaming with great pleasure, André jumped up and placed his hands on Makes Thunder's shoulders. In response, Makes Thunder stepped back and offered his hand in a handshake. He looked much older, though it was only two years since they had first met.

"Much has happened. Now I am almost a man." Then he added, smiling and looking up at André, "But not tall, like you. I was hoping."

It made André laugh.

"You are alone?" Antoine asked. He had wondered if Makwa would visit.

"No, others are coming. Makwa hurt his knee yesterday, it slows him," he said, removing a heavy pack from his back, moving close to the fireplace. "They be here soon."

"Emile and I were going to visit you," André said. "Runs When He Walks told us about the wildfire burning your winter campgrounds, so you are now farther away."

Over tea, they caught up on news—of Makwa's band, of Denis, of the fires which altered the landscape and reduced the animals for food and furs, of the new trader.

Makes Thunder suddenly stood, squared his shoulders and looked intently at André. "I go on my vision quest soon," he said quietly.

Holding himself with pride, he stepped over to the trading counter.

"This day I take debt," Makes Thunder said. "For a gun, this many beavers. Yes?" He held up all ten fingers spread apart. "I have half now, in the pack. I bring half when days get longer."

André knew that Antoine hesitated in giving credit to young hunters for the most valuable item the post carried, but Makwa and Crow Man were important leaders. He glanced at Antoine, who nodded.

"André, you take this trade," Antoine said.

"You have half the pelts already. Good work, Makes Thunder," André said. *This is a big moment in my friend's life. He is now adult enough to trade his skills and time for goods. I've watched Antoine do this, so I know what to do—treat him with the dignity of an esteemed hunter.*

"First I write your name in the book," he said, pointing to a page. He picked up the ink bottle from the shelf, warming it in his hands to thaw it. He wrote easily using the new metal point on the goose quill, and showed Makes Thunder. "This mark says we have given you a rifle."

With that André helped him select the best flintlock rifle they had. Together they examined its fine metal handiwork and satiny-smooth wood stock.

Makes Thunder hefted the gun, pointed it at the ceiling and made soft shooting sounds. André thought the transaction was complete.

But Makes Thunder did not move. He looked to Emile and Antoine.

"A gift, André. Make him a gift," Emile reminded him quietly. "Shot and powder he needs, but also a gift that befits his new status."

Of course he needs shot and powder or his rifle is worthless. And he should have been offered a gift before we started. This didn't start like our usual trades so I forgot. That could offend some people, but not my friend, I hope.

He placed small bags of powder and shot on the table, and then reached for colorful items.

"A hunter should have bright ribbons for his shirt," André said. "Or vermilion paint?"

"He brings meat for his family—maybe a fire steel or fish hooks," suggested Antoine. "The large barbs, perhaps," he added, looking at Makes Thunder for confirmation.

André felt befuddled. He had watched Antoine and Emile trade dozens of times, but he had stumbled over the basic steps in his first trade. He had misjudged Makes Thunder—and had offered style over substance. *Again I forgot something I should know. The process of trading is harder than I realized.* He reached for the tools.

"Perhaps Little Berry would like beads?" he said, displaying hanks of yellow, red and black seed beads.

Makes Thunder was gracious in accepting.

More than an hour later, Makwa, Crow Man and two other hunters arrived. Makes Thunder looked concerned—it was much later than he had expected. Makwa's knee must be seriously hurt.

"Tonight it is too late to see the targets. Tomorrow morning let's practice with your new gun," André offered. Being outdoors at night eroded his confidence.

Makes Thunder nodded. Over a hearty supper the talk turned to news of the tribes.

"Winter always brings the starving time," Crow Man said. "Already this year is a hard winter for us. Beavers small, when we find them."

"New trader, this Ducharme gave much firewater to hunters in fall," Makwa added. "Now they owe him many pelts. When the firewater is gone, they have no tools or blankets to show for their work!" He was disgusted with their choices.

André looked up at the mention of Ducharme, but said nothing. Makwa's band was much nearer to the new trader. André wondered if they had taken debt at the new post.

He caught Antoine's eyes—Antoine had been wondering the same thing.

"Ducharme, you say," Antoine said. "He paddled with me until this year. For some years we wintered on the Lake of the Woods."

"I have met him," Makwa said, nodding. "Open Face, I save my best furs for you, but to have more traders, that is better for the tribes. Others will trade with Ducharme too."

The next morning, André and Makes Thunder left the post to practice with the new rifle. His friend had already learned from other hunters how to use the weapon—Makes Thunder smoothly poured the correct amount of powder, stuffed wadding, loaded a pellet and shot accurately.

André had less experience with firearms. While aiming at a target, suddenly an image of Basile Roche whirled through his brain, saying, "What do you know of guns? You would miss if I stood next to you. But I will get you, when I'm ready."

He shook his head to get rid of the ugly scene. His shot missed. And the rest of his shots were no closer to the targets.

Before departing that morning, Makes Thunder gave directions for their new camp. André and Emile would visit them later in the winter—it would take them across open areas and forests. André's stomach tightened—he would have to prepare himself carefully.

CHAPTER 32

André distractedly moved his checkers piece and Pretty Mouse grinned, jumping several.

"Your king, it is mine," Mouse exulted, leaping to his feet. "Today it is three games for the Mouse and only one for André. Perhaps you are thinking about something else?"

André growled back. It was true. Basile Roche's threat was like a seed. It had taken root and grown in his brain. Though he had meant to hide his worry, it was unusual for Pretty Mouse to best André in checkers.

After a while, André said, "No one will come in to trade today—it is too cold, too late. I could read while it is light."

Pretty Mouse's eyes lit up, and he got comfortable, sitting forward in anticipation. Emile and Antoine stopped their tasks to listen. André opened the book at its marker, a scrap of ribbon. He took a deep breath and read about cannibals coming, and Crusoe's paralyzing fear.

"On my first trip, I was afraid of imaginary creatures—mitten biters and werewolves," André admitted sheepishly.

"Cannibals, they sound like the *windigo*," Pretty Mouse said.

"Don't feel too bad," Emile said. "Lots of people were threatened by the *windigo*. Until we learned that the Ojibwe evil spirit was Roche."

Maybe everyone has their windigo. Basile Roche is mine. But he didn't say anything. Reading about someone else's problems felt safe.

André read about Crusoe finding a ship wrecked on the shores of his island, then trying to build his own boat to leave.

"A cruel thing, that all were dead."

"Twenty-three years on the island? Without talking to anyone?"

The others could not imagine the isolation. *But it happens in different ways. Like Denis' years in the forests and plains of the vast interior,*

Joseph and Berthe leaving their families after the French Revolution to keep me and Denis hidden from the enemies of our grandfather.

He read about five canoes of natives returning to Crusoe's beaches with a captive that Crusoe helped to escape.

"Who would name someone Friday?"

"Dark skin, straight black hair—that sounds like our hunters."

"Oh, I forgot. The story reminded me," Mouse broke in. "At the *rendezvous*, did you see the man with very dark skin and black hair like wool?"

"He is a Bonga," Antoine said. "Very smart traders, that family."

André read about the savages returning, this time with a Spaniard and the father of Friday.

"His father is a captive?"

"Why didn't Crusoe learn Friday's language? Like we do with the tribes here?"

Daytime activities, like chopping wood, helped André forget about Roche. But when the light dimmed, he felt nervous and questions arose. In the dark, he couldn't see if someone was watching him. A crack of ice or a swoosh of wind made him anxious. *What made that sound? Why did that bird call? Is it a real bird—or a signal? Dakota braves spying on us? Or Roche?*

After doing heavy tasks, if he was tired enough, sleep would come. If not, fear might bring nightmares.

With fewer Ojibwe visitors on the cold days, Antoine called again for trips to their winter lodges, these more distant.

André agreed to Antoine's plans, though it unsettled him. Then he remembered how Robinson Crusoe had worked to conquer his own fear. *He hid and he worried, but he also planned. He was able to act, though he was afraid. I can plan a way to be safe.*

"This time visit the bands of Lame Hawk, since he has not come here, and Bobtail Bear." Antoine listed two Ojibwe hunters he most wanted to encourage. "André, what goods did they want before?"

As best as he remembered, André named the items those chiefs and hunters had traded for and what goods they had eyed. He and Emile packed the best of their trade goods—heavy blankets, cotton and wool cloth, four sizes of copper kettles in a nest, rasps and chisels—in addition to the usual tobacco, twine, thread, pins, beads, ribbons and lace. A small keg of high wines was added at the last minute. In the morning, they set out, their sled heavy.

Antoine knew that other traders freely shared high wines and quickly made bargains. It was becoming the standard way to trade. He instructed Emile to dole out liquor in small amounts. When those hunters brought their furs to the post, Antoine would be more generous.

Emile was not bothered by this, but it unsettled André.

Besides the high wines, this year the voyageurs also brought *pemmican* to share. When visiting to trade, the tribes usually fed them as guests—but the bands were low in food. Wild rice had not been as plentiful in the summer, and the tribes had harvested less game. Most felt a pinch in their stomachs.

They arrived at Lame Hawk's band late in the afternoon. It was quiet, with little activity, though Emile noted thin trails of smoke rising from each dwelling. Occasionally they heard uproarious laughter from one bark lodge or another.

"Halloo, we are here," André called, giving them time to make ready for the traders, though he was sure a scout had already signaled their arrival with a bird call.

"Maybe they are telling stories," Emile said. "Some stories are secret, not for our ears."

They were greeted by Lame Hawk himself. "*Boozhoo,*" he said. "Come into my lodge. Sit. Eat, then we talk."

He gave them a bowl of meaty stew and a tart lemony beverage.

"What is this?" André asked, holding up his cup.

"That red seed cone on the sumac. In the fall we gather. We mash it and soak it in water, so we can drink it," Lame Hawk said. Then he invited others in to tell stories. He introduced his band—this man a skilled hunter, that one a clever trapper. One hunter spoke at length about watching a fox hunting rabbits. Another told of being challenged by a hungry wolf while bringing home a good-sized beaver—and hacking off the head to leave for the wolf.

Much later Lame Hawk began the ceremonial process of trading, talking about the cold year, not a good season for pelts or food. The starving time had come.

André didn't talk—that was Emile's job as leader, and his own skills were not up to the task—but it felt like they were speaking in circles. *I know enough of the language to follow what is being said. But I wish this would move faster.*

Emile sensed it. "Remember how hard they have to work for each blanket and kettle," he said quietly. "They wade in icy water to snare beavers, haul them back, scrape the fat, stretch the pelt. Let them take as much time as they want."

Chastised, André sat back. *Emile is right. They are good friends, and I want them to know we value them. I don't have to be in such a rush to return to our post. Here we are safe.*

"I trade with Open Face," Lame Hawk finally announced to the group of hunters. "We are friends. New trader, he gives much spirit water. Is not good for me. I do not like, but each hunter ..." and here he paused to look at his men one at a time, "choose for yourself."

The younger men around him nodded agreement, that they would respect their elder but would choose for themselves.

Though Lame Hawk's hunters did not commit to exclusive trading, Emile viewed their visit a success—they collected many pelts. André carefully noted their credits in the account book. They had not been ambushed by Roche or his helpers.

They headed next to the winter lodges of Bobtail Bear's band, a full day away.

"Look at these strange footprints," said Emile, laughing as he pointed to marks in the snow. "But more than one, not like Crusoe, eh?"

At first, André grew tense when he saw the wide, odd-shaped tracks. *Roche?* Then he realized a trapper had probably wrapped his feet in a pelt. André relaxed and blew out his breath. With Emile he felt safe—and they were in open area.

They arrived at nightfall, exhausted and hungry, having given most of their *pemmican* to nourish the dogs. There was no longer enough to share with Bobtail Bear's band. He hoped they had more success in hunting. Smelling campfire smoke and hearing raucous laughter, André was glad to be among friends.

Bobtail Bear was not as friendly as the previous year. In his lodge, several men were focused on a gambling game, with piles of stones shoved from one player to another. Two appeared to be winning most of the rounds.

After they shared a meal. Bobtail Bear's son invited other hunters to join them to trade. When they came, one wore the red uniform coat of a British soldier. The next man held his head high in a fancy top hat, adorned with shells and feathers, and a fox tail. Each hunter wore some insignia of worth—a brass medallion, a colorful flannel shirt, even ruffles.

Emile paled.

Someone has honored many men as "made chiefs." Could all of them be distinguished hunters? This trade will be much harder.

They listened carefully to what Bobtail Bear had to say about his band. The XY Company had offered these excellent gifts, and firewater each time, he told them. "I watched how white men drink—they like a lot of rum. We will do it like you do it. First we drink your firewater, then show us the trade goods."

Emile gestured for André to bring in the keg. They offered it to Bobtail Bear. He took a long pull and passed it to the person on one side, and around the circle the keg went. Then to Emile, who took a drink. Emile handed it to André, who glanced at him, trying to send a message, *This is not good. Must I?* But Emile nodded grimly. André uncertainly took a short drink.

The keg made another round, and another. Each time he took as small a sip as possible, holding the keg as if he were taking a longer drink. Finally it was empty, and one man tossed it outside against a tree trunk, where it bounced. The hunters laughed loudly.

"Now show us what you bring," Bobtail Bear demanded.

While Emile spoke, André displayed their goods to their best advantage—thick fabrics, durable and shiny kettles, useful metal tools—but the hunters remained impassive. He showed beads, needles, wires, twine and thread, soap and playing cards—which seemed only slightly more attractive to them.

The hunters handled razors and laughed. They had no beards, but the sharp cutting edge could be useful in other ways. One man twisted a snare out of the wire—that held possibilities. By now they had lost their reserve and argued noisily. Emile gestured emphatically in response to their comments.

André felt nauseated and unsteady. The cold night air might clear his head. He stood, which made him dizzy. Suddenly it seemed there were two fires—his eyes could not tell which was real. Not sure where the doorflap was, he stepped hesitantly.

He teetered and reeled—his foot slipped and he pitched forward toward the fires. Seeing him falter, a man leaned heavily against him, steering him away, but he now bumbled into the group of men.

André grabbed for something to balance himself—his hand clutched a support branch holding up the lodge roof. It broke under his weight and the bark roof caved in.

Snow cascaded through the opening, dumping its chilly load on each of them. They yelled in surprise and discomfort.

He lurched back, falling almost on top of Bobtail Bear, cracking birch bark containers decorated with colored porcupine quills.

Disaster!

The noisy disturbance alerted Bobtail Bear's wife, who rushed in. She looked at the birch bark containers and all the work she had done now destroyed. She dug under André to get her food stores—and came up with a now-dented copper pot. Her eyes shut, she hugged the kettle and moaned, a valued item.

She glared stonily as Emile handed her a kettle from their pack, with his apology. She ignored him, gathered her blankets and left.

"We brought a dozen lengths of the heavy canvas," Emile said quietly to André. "That could cover the hole in the lodge tonight, until we can fix it. At least we can help them."

They spent the morning repairing the damaged roof. None of the hunters offered pelts to pay down debts, though several asked for more credit. As early as they could manage, they left Bobtail Bear's lodge—with no furs to show for their effort.

It was a long hike back, André's stomach heaving and head splitting.

Antoine looked glum when they explained themselves.

Pretty Mouse said, "The rum, I see it is not for you, André."

"*Non.*" He felt foolish, his shoulders slumped.

"I should have foreseen. You are too young for this," Antoine said. "That is my mistake."

154

Chapter 33

Late one night, well after they'd gone to bed, they heard beating on the outside gate, then yelling, "Antoine, open up for us. We bring a message."

Pretty Mouse hurriedly unbarred the gate, admitting a pair of snow-covered voyageurs and a panting team of dogs.

While Emile and André watered the dogs, Pretty Mouse heated supper. Antoine hung up their *capote*s and greeted them—fellow-voyageurs who also worked in the district overseen by their *bourgeois*, Mr. Chaboillez. Their trading post at Otter Creek was several days northwest.

The message had been written hastily on a single sheet of paper, folded and wrapped in oiled canvas. André read the words aloud.

"To Antoine Felix: My main clerk at the post on Bear Tooth Rapids, Jean-Baptiste Bousquet, hurt his head in an accident. This was nearly a fortnight ago, and he has not yet recovered his senses. When the Indians come in with the rest of their winter furs, I must have someone who can sort out our business—send your André to help. They need him immediately. There is no other to ask. Have him bring two large kegs of high wines."

The note was signed "Chaboillez" with several flourishes.

André was stupefied. *A different post? Away from my friends?*

While eating, the two men told the details of what had happened, first one, then the other, as fast as they could tumble the words out.

"He is Louis and me, I am Pierre. We work at the Otter Creek post."

"But the post on Bear Tooth Rapids, the one on the river with the big rocks, they send us the runner to tell us of this accident. Jean-Baptiste, they said he fell on the ice."

"You remember Bousquet, the quiet one?"

Antoine nodded. Emile, Pretty Mouse and Andre leaned forward, not wanting to miss a word.

"It was late at night, and he went outside the post. They did not find him until early the next morning. Me, I think they had too much high wine."

Pierre, the younger one, winked. "They carry him with blankets to warm him by the fire indoors. Almost like ice, he was."

"Me, I am cold too. Ah, but a dram would warm me up." Louis looked hopefully at Antoine, who unlocked the chest with the keg and filled their cups.

"Oho, I said bears, they come out of hibernation—it was not so cold some days back. But *non*, a bear did not attack him."

"Scare him, maybe. They saw tracks."

"No blood, nothing broken, he has one big bump on the head—but he doesn't wake up."

"For days and days he is asleep in his bunk—how do you say?—not there." Louis shook his head, his eyes wide, showing the strangeness of this predicament.

"They wait. And wait more. Even they ask the tribe's medicine man to bring him back. But he say Jean-Baptiste's spirit, it is out wandering and the medicine man, he cannot call it back."

"Finally, after more than a week they send a runner to ask the *bourgeois* for help. And the *bourgeois*, he sent us to ask for André who, he said, can write and do sums—with ease. This is so?" Louis raised his eyebrows in surprise. "An *engagé* can do that?"

They both sized him up as André nodded.

"But I thought, we thought you would be … older."

"This year, it is not your first winter here?"

André shook his head, numb with shock. He looked at Antoine.

"*Oui*," Antoine finally said. "Since André helps me, my accounts they are right. The *bourgeois* asks this, so, *oui*, he could go."

André was stricken—he could not speak. He did not want to leave.

It was plain that Antoine did not want to release him, but saw no way to refuse the *bourgeois*. Antoine—or Emile—would have to make sure the credits in the book matched the goods given out.

"Tell us more of the post on Bear Tooth Rapids," Emile said. "Who else works there?"

They spoke at length of the three *engagés* who worked under Bousquet—Vincent and François and Luc.

"And we have heard now a rival post is nearby. What do you know about it?"

"*Oui,* so it is. The XY Company, they have built their trading house barely a stone's throw away. Built this summer while we were at the *rendezvous.*" Pierre and Louis eagerly added what they knew. Their information soon fell to gossip.

Antoine was irritated and needed his own time to think. Gruffly he interrupted. "You must be tired—it was a hard trip for you. Tomorrow we talk more, about the best route, the provisions."

Soon André heard snores from the others, but he did not sleep. *I hope the post at Bear Tooth Rapids will be like here, the same tasks, the same way to keep records, some of the same hunters.*

He scoured his mind to recall the wall map he'd seen at the New Fort. *Where exactly was Bear Tooth Rapids? What had Makes Thunder—or anyone—said about Ducharme? Louis and Pierre will return to their post going a different route. So I have to make a three-day journey, by myself.*

His head whirled with questions. *Will anyone—the voyageurs or the Ojibwe hunters—listen to me? How long will it be before Jean-Baptiste Bousquet recovers and I can return to Antoine's post?*

And suddenly—*Is Basile's hand in this? He threatened me, but he has not followed through. Nor has he been seen. Will he have done this terrible thing to draw me out, alone?*

The thoughts paralyzed him. With the uncertainty of the journey and his new assignment, he did not sleep, until exhaustion overtook him.

CHAPTER 34

Early the next morning, the two voyageurs rose, poking their fingers in the ashes of the fire and drawing maps on the floor to show André how far he could follow their trail, where to turn off to the north, and the different routes he might travel. One way had long stretches of open plains and flatlands—not hard, but expanses where he could lose his bearings. Or he could follow winding rivers which would keep him on the right path, but that would take longer. If he traveled in forests, game trails would lead him through. His dogs would sniff out the way, even if he couldn't see it. Then the voyageurs pointed out good places to camp.

After breakfasting, they cheerily bundled in their *capotes*, attached their snowshoes, harnessed their dogs and returned to their own post with the answer for their *bourgeois*—*oui*, André would leave immediately. He would arrive in three days. "Follow our tracks for an hour or so. Then, at the old stump, turn north and you're on your own."

Emile and Pretty Mouse discussed the provisions for the journey: Boiled wild rice—yes, it would only need heating. Tea—yes. *Pemmican*—yes. Dried moose or fish—maybe, if the scent wouldn't draw animals. A leather bag for water, so he wouldn't need to stop during the day to melt snow. And why did the *bourgeois* ask for high wines?

Antoine was silent for some time. Suddenly he stood, and stomped towards the door.

"André, which dogs do you want? Come."

Mechanically, André followed him. He was afraid he would cry, so he tightened his face. He could not trust his voice.

"Me, I do not like this. Not one bit," Antoine said as soon as they were outside. "That you must travel alone—I do not like it. You at a strange post—I do not like it. Who will be your friend? Who will help you?"

He pulled his pipe from his sash. "Too many things I do not know. But I saw no way to refuse." He put his pipe between his lips and lit it.

André knelt by the dogs, looking at each one while Antoine continued.

"Every day there will be problems. For the important problems, listen and do not hurry. Sometimes you must be the big man, stand up, assert authority. You will have to choose what is good for all, not simply for yourself. Maybe no one else will agree with you, but if you take enough time, it will be the best answer. Do not hurry to decide. Remember that."

Hearing Antoine's advice, André relaxed a little. It reminded him of Joseph's words.

"About Jean Ducharme. He has a good heart, but the XY men, they will push hard this first year to make sure their new post is a success."

He spoke of the Ojibwe hunters who would trade. "The tribes, they will test you—they need to know who you are. Learn all you can about them. Some Indians may come who have not traded there before—pay them special attention. Maybe they are your friends, maybe not."

André nodded as Antoine continued to talk about the intricacies of trading, how he might dispense high wines and ways to put his own stamp on a trade.

Finally Antoine looked at the sky to check the time. "There is so much to tell you, I do not know how to begin."

"*Merci.* This post seems to almost run by itself," André said shakily. "Maybe theirs will not be so hard."

Antoine grinned, and paused. "Now what about the dogs?"

"Yellow Eyes and Arrow are young," André said. "They can pull better over the three days."

"Both strong dogs, as you say. I will harness them."

Pretty Mouse joined them outside.

"With the big kegs, we can use the pulley to lift them onto the sled," he said brightly.

The rope stayed in its groove and moved the load easily. Mouse had finally found a real-life use for the pulley. Mouse and Antoine lashed the heavy casks securely while André went inside to wrap canvas around his belongings—clothing, the quill tip, the borrowed book, his letters, blankets—tying the bundle with a long length of basswood cord.

Emile handed him another bundle. "Tools—a fire steel to spark a good flame, kettle, ax—other things you need for the journey." Then he said, "I wish you did not have to go. I will miss you, friend."

"Pierre and Louis gave clear directions. Antoine had useful advice. From you, good training," André said. "Besides, I'll be back in a month to get our furs ready for the *rendezvous*."

They carried the packs outside.

"Looks like a blizzard coming," Emile said, studying the cloud cover as he packed the sled. "Tonight, I think. Leaving now—you only have half the day to travel before dark. Maybe you should start out tomorrow morning."

André looked into the low gray sky, wind buffeting his hair.

"Probably a normal snowfall, like when we were visiting the bands to trade." André wanted to say, *Please don't make me go.* Instead, fighting for control of his feelings, he added, "It's been more than two weeks since Jean-Baptiste's accident. They need someone."

I can't speak my true feelings. Neither can they. To show that they regret my going, they invent reasons to keep me longer.

Antoine looked mournful as he patted the harnessed dogs. He re-balanced the packs Emile had added to the dog sled, shifting the tools, the water and food, but not the two kegs of high wines.

"Your pulley, I'll put it in here," Mouse said, showing him. "Tomorrow I'll carve one for me."

"I tied your compass on the handle of your sled," Antoine said. "So you can check it while trotting alongside."

"You remember how to build a shelter?" Emile asked. "You remember the Ojibwe words?"

"Here is something for later," Pretty Mouse said, tucking a packet into André's *capote* and snugging up his hood. "Maple sugar."

André grinned his appreciation. "*Merci*, my friends." He pulled out the stake holding Yellow Eyes and Arrow, and yelled "*Marchons!*" for them to start. "*Au revoir.* I will see you soon."

"Or at the *rendezvous*," they called back.

Then Pretty Mouse yelled, "Wait. We never heard the end of Robinson Crusoe. Does he get rescued?"

André did not answer—the story would have to wait. And he didn't want them to see his tears.

161

CHAPTER 35

After he came to the big stump, he turned off the trail of Louis and Pierre and took out his compass and aligned it with a tall tree in the distance. He planned to take the most direct route over open land. Using the compass, he could stay on course in the snowy conditions he expected. *If Basile Roche is behind this, an ambush in open country will be difficult for him to carry out.* He felt confident.

The first leg of the journey crossed open hilly country. In the distance he could see trees lining a river that made it easy to stay on course, if he kept them to his right.

The wind gusted flakes into his face. Loping alongside the dogs, André kept a pace slow enough so he would not break a sweat. Wet clothes would freeze quickly, and chill him dangerously.

He remembered that Robinson Crusoe was nervous in venturing across his island. *This is open friendly territory. Exploring the hills and forests of this land—I can do this.*

André regularly stopped to water his dogs and rest them. He was grateful not to have to melt snow or cut a hole in the ice, and use up valuable day hours. Tonight he would replenish his water bag.

He studied his compass and carefully chose his next landmarks. Yellow Eyes and Arrow, rested and eager to get back on the trail, took off again.

When they circled a large reedy patch, André was glad the hillocks were frozen hard—the sled slipped easily over the crusted tops. Once in a while he let the dogs stretch out their legs and run.

They continued across prairie, occasional tall grasses spearing up through the snow. He chose features to guide him—a single tree, a massive boulder or a cleft in the hills—each time checking his compass heading while his dogs rested. The blowing snow did not hinder his distance vision.

André kept a lookout for animal tracks, but snowflakes quickly drifted over the prints of the occasional deer or rabbit and the tiny holes of burrowing mice that he spotted.

To keep his mind sharp, he reviewed the upcoming turning points of the trail. Then he reflected on Antoine's advice and how he might need to apply it. He recalled the Ojibwe greetings he knew. Then, he counted in Ojibwe by ones, twos and threes, and then backwards—André liked using Ojibwe words.

During one break, he watched in surprise as a marten left its burrow and, a minute later, a badger left the same hole. *They share a home. And the Ojibwe are sharing this land with us. What is the Ojibwe word for "marten"?* He scrunched his eyes trying to remember: *wabizhashi.* It was miles before the word for "badger" came to him: *misakakojiish.*

After that, each time he encountered an animal, he tried to recall its Ojibwe name—and its Latin name, if he knew it. *I should start my own word list at Bear Tooth Rapids, when I have time.*

The wind picked up and loose snow whipped across the open hills. As he tightened the hood of his *capote* with its long tails, he found his ears were cold—and wondered if the temperature was dropping.

André gazed on drifts of prairie sculpted by the wind, forming sharp edges. In the white landscape, he found it increasingly hard to distinguish the hills. Once the sled dropped down in a hollow of dry fluffy snow that could not hold their weight. André laughed in surprise but Yellow Eyes and Arrow kept pulling, and he had to struggle to untangle their harnesses before they could go on.

Finally, they came to a snow-covered cairn of stones that marked a turn. *Another inch of snow and I might have missed this. Now I need to look for the little stream.* While they rested, André mentally chanted the directions: *Next the rocky hill, then watch for a game trail into the forest. A ways in, follow a stream to the big lake. On the south shore, Makwa's sugar camp, where we can spend the night.*

His cheeks smarted from the cold—the temperature was falling. A howl followed by several yips told him a wolf had scented him. He looked at the sky, calculating the time until dark. *The clouds seem lower—I can't see as far ahead. And I'm getting tired. Time to move on.*

At the rocky hill, crowned with a few spiky bushes, he veered toward the forest, glad for the shelter from the snowy gusts. But these woods looked dense, dark and unfriendly.

There would be no trees blazed with a tomahawk to mark a trail—Makes Thunder had explained that his tribe did not leave signs that enemies could easily read. Instead they marked their path in subtle ways, moving rocks or aligning branches. *I won't find their trail markers under the snow. But at least the wind's power will be blunted by the woods.*

As he entered the forest, André scanned for bear markings, in case the *makwa* might have wakened early from hibernation, feeling hungry and grouchy. But this late on a cold day, a bear would have returned to its den, he hoped.

The trail through the forest was difficult for him to detect but Yellow Eyes and Arrow found the animal scent with ease, sniffing where to go. They confidently zigzagged their way on an invisible route. He felt vulnerable, not being able to see as far ahead, but relieved they could find the trail.

A large barred owl flew across the path, barely inches from his head, and dipped toward the ground. André stopped. Seconds later, he saw it flap upwards, a mouse in its talons. He shivered. For the owl to live, another creature had to die. *Owl and mouse—cat and mouse.*

The forest closed in on him, and he peered anxiously around the larger trees. *Could someone hide behind them? Are there human tracks? How long ago was someone here?*

Night was coming. With snow falling, soon there would be no light. Though he had not traveled as many miles as he had hoped, he reached the stream that would lead to the lake. André decided to stop and camp before the last bit of daylight dwindled.

He felt weary, but first he kindled a fire and scooped a pot of snow. While it melted and heated, he eyed nearby tree boughs to cushion and cover themselves. The low branches of spruce trees would have made the most comfortable bed, but he saw none.

Instead he cut piles of brush. Hazelnut shrubs, he decided, pulling a few empty seedpods from the branches. *I wish the squirrels had left a few nuts.* Though stiff and lumpy, the brush under him would at least lift them off the snow and insulate them from its bone-chilling cold.

"For you," he said to his dogs, slicing off a chunk of *pemmican* and handing it to them. His voice startled him, after nearly a whole day without conversation.

They shared the water and he put the rest in his water bag—it would be comforting to sleep next to its warmth. Then he tended the dog's feet. To bed down, André wrapped himself in blankets and covered them all with a length of canvas to protect them from the snow and wind.

The dogs fell asleep quickly, but André's brain was still active, with one unsettling thought after another. The baying of a distant wolf, the cold, the fear of stepping into an established post—almost as soon as André cleared one thought away, another took its place.

What kind of men work at the Bear Tooth Rapids post? Will they like me? Will they respect me? If I get lost, how will they know where to look for me?

He recited his multiplication tables, and then Berthe's medicinal uses of plants. He would not allow his deeper fears of Basile to surface. As night deepened, the wind rose, a hollow whistling through the forest that reminded him of how alone he was. Finally he slept.

CHAPTER 36

When black night gave way to gray morning, the dogs woke him. He built a fire and warmed a hearty stew for himself and the dogs, and kept half to eat during the day. Today would be his longest travel day—he should arrive by mid-afternoon on the third day. He brushed the snow from his canvas, folded it up and tucked his things into the pack, the cold seeping into him.

The morning air was hard and biting as he harnessed the dogs and started out, following the stream. *I like open country better than the forest, though there is more wind.*

At noon he came upon the lake and the frames for the lodges of Makwa's maple sugar camp. Here he saw well-used trails. It felt welcoming. He realized that he'd not relaxed since waking.

Far across the ice-bound lake, winds blasting in his face, André glimpsed a burned area. *That's where their winter camp used to be, before the fire. Emile and I visited there once, and hunted with them. Now those big trees are gone.*

Then he turned the dogs westward into open hills again, met by a nearly horizontal wind whipping their faces, snow stinging their eyes. It was difficult to make out land features very far ahead, and he felt less certain about his compass readings. Inside his furry mittens, his fingers tingled with cold and his chapped hands burned. He clapped them together to regain circulation.

Where the snow was deep, he walked ahead to break a trail for Arrow and Yellow Eyes. To keep his mind occupied he reviewed his Ojibwe vocabulary, the thirty-six portages and the thirty-six *décharges* between the Ottawa River and Lake Huron, the names of all the voyageurs he could think of and where they paddled in the canoe.

In late afternoon, when he spotted an eagle's nest atop a lone tree skeleton—Makes Thunder had once spoken of it—he exhaled in relief. They rested, and finished the stew and drank water, and then turned northward away from open prairie toward deep woods.

His shoulders felt tight, but he kept going. André was confident—mostly. While there were few hiding places in the prairies, unspoken fears of Basile slid into his consciousness. Again and again he pushed out the thoughts with his lists or facts, but often something would remind him of moments that tightened his gut.

Passing a willow tree, he recalled his first *rendezvous* at Grand Portage, where he shaped a willow walking stick for Joseph—and used it to prevent Roche from taking advantage of Pretty Mouse. *But now Roche means to do me harm. How will I stop him? I have no weapons, except for the knife Joseph made or the ax. Maybe tonight I will look for a stout stick.*

On they slogged in the lonely cold and blowing snow.

A sharp high bank topped by birches reminded him of Basile's leaping attack on Denis by a waterfall. Ghost Wind and Silent Wolf had knocked Roche into the frigid river. *Where I thought he died. If he comes, when he comes, I will have to face him by myself.* His scalp felt cold, his mouth dry.

Fighting the wind and gusting flurries, they trudged on. He realized he was getting tired. Time for a rest. But he could not see the next landmarks. *Where is the jutting stone ledge and the small round lake? I should have come to them by now.*

He had missed the point where he had to change his heading. André felt confused trying to repeat the landmarks. He looked at the sky, but there was no sun to help him determine the direction and his compass seemed to point him the wrong way.

Now what? He looked for a sentinel tree to use as a guide. But there was none, only the dark woods ahead, so instead he chose a place where there seemed to be a break in the trees.

Maybe we need water. He reached for the water skin, and they all drank, savoring the last drops on their tongues. Never enough.

He looked in each direction for a stream. *A stream will wander and following it will take longer, but it'll be easier. And I won't get to Bear Tooth Rapids until at least supper tomorrow night.*

No stream. Only the forest. *Arrow and Yellow Eyes will have to sniff out the way through the deep woods. Because I don't see the trail.*

In the fading light they entered the forest. The trail through the woods had disappeared, covered by snow, but his dogs sensed one. André heard the call of a raucous blue jay, but he did not see movement and he listened for it to repeat the call. Was it a *deedeens*—or a *deen de se*?

Deeper in, he was startled to see huge trees, tipped over, uprooted and broken. He saw exposed root balls higher than his head. Trees were twisted, torn apart and spun in many directions, as though a giant had crushed the forest in his hands. *I wonder if they were destroyed by the same kind of tempest as on Lake Superior.* The young sailor had called it a "tornado" and Toussaint, a *geezheebasun*. It amazed him that he had seen no trace of the storm damage until he entered the forest.

When he paused, he heard a CRAAACKK and turned to see a pine that had exploded in the bitter cold. He stood for some minutes, gazing in awe at its clear heartwood, exposed like an open wound.

His breath made great white billows which evaporated instantly. The dogs looked at him, eager to move. It was eerily quiet. Only their breathing broke the silence.

The dogs wanted to follow an animal trail, but trees had fallen in every direction. Veering around them slowed them, and they tried to shortcut under a deadfall where the branches were high enough for them to slither under. But though André moved slowly, he accidentally brushed against it—and it creaked. He froze momentarily, then hurried the dogs and they dashed out from under the branch.

A few seconds afterwards, it crashed to the ground, throwing up a cloud of loose snow into the air. A dozen small birds flew to safe branches, chirping. Then it was hushed once more.

André gulped. Too close! *I won't make that mistake again. I've been worrying about Basile, but it's my mistake that nearly brought us to our end.*

New questions filled his anxious mind: *Why did the pine explode right then? Did my brushing against the deadfall make it drop?*

Unsure, André watched for signs of people—smoke, sounds, prints, a trap, an item dropped. He saw none—a thick layer of snow covered everything.

Trudging around the dead trees confused his sense of direction. André hoped the dogs knew their way, for he was lost. It was nearly night and they were all hungry and tired. He felt defeated.

Time to camp. Again they would not get as far as he had hoped. But he didn't want to camp among the trees with broken-off tree trunks pointing every which way, some balanced crazily on slim

169

branches holding them up. Seeing them and the bare roots of trees thrust into the sky bothered him.

That cottonwood, and a dozen others like it here, grew for maybe a hundred years. But in a moment of terrible wind, it no longer lives.

Detouring slowly around the downed trees, they plowed through thick bushes that scratched his face. Finally he spied a clearing to camp in. *Are there spruce boughs to cushion the snow? Yes!* André relaxed.

Suddenly a pair of rabbits darted ahead. The dogs lunged after them.

"Stop, Yellow Eyes, Arrow." André tried calling them back, but they chased at top speed. He could not keep up.

They ducked under the top of a fallen tree.

"*Non*, don't go there! Stop!"

The dogs veered and plunged down a small ravine. A large spruce tree had partly fallen across the trail—they should go around.

"NOOO!"

Suddenly the deadfall pitched toward him.

André tumbled, off balance. He reached up to fend it off, his small arms inadequate against it. The huge tree smashed over him. A branch dragged him into the ravine, pinning his body.

Spiky branches slashed his face, splintered over his head and shoulders. All he knew was stunning pain. The scream died in his throat.

CHAPTER 37

André gradually came to his senses. It was dark. He was buried among the branches of a spruce tree that pressed against every part of his body. His head throbbed. Flakes of snow drifted over his cheeks and chilled his head. The pungent smell of high wines intermingled with the piney boughs.

What happened? His brain could not focus and he closed his eyes.

In the bitter night, his breath made frost crystals on the black-green needles around him.

When he became conscious again, he was shivering. Cold from above and below seeped into his body. He was numb. As he moved, loose snow trickled around his neck. His face stung and the side of his chest ached, deep and searing. He remembered feeling a snap inside when the tree struck him.

A howl. Then, a whimper, closer, something in agony. *My dogs? Hurt?* With a weak voice, he called their names. Only more whimpering. And a distant answer from a wolf.

A wolf?

He wiggled his toes and fingers. They tingled. His right arm was wedged beneath his back and his hand prickled. He squirmed, his chest exploding in pain. He couldn't move. Trapped! Except his left arm which was free—he slid it in a wide arc. He moved his head side to side until sharp spruce needles poked him. With each movement, a fierce pain emanated from his chest.

A branch lay heavily on his right side, pinning him down, jabbing into his ribs and shoulders and legs. Another branch pressed against his head.

He couldn't turn over. Or slide out. He squirmed to the side, drawing in a breath at the sudden stabbing in his ribs. Nothing he did worked. *But I have to get free!*

The effort exhausted him. He lay, waiting for his brain to clear. Beads of sweat collected on his spine. He felt snowflakes drift down onto his ears. His eyelids fluttered—and shut.

The louder baying of a wolf in the darkness jolted him awake. *Wolves? I have to get out. How long have I been here?*

Death was certain—by wolves or by freezing, if he did not get out from under the branches. He needed to move. Free his arm from beneath his body. Free himself. *Moving will hurt. But I have to do this. Fight, André!*

He took a deep breath and wrenched himself upward as hard as he could, twisting his right arm out from under. Pain mushroomed in his side. His shoulder ached but both arms were free, and gradually feeling returned to his fingers. He rested. *What next?*

He edged his hips left. More pain. But with his arm out from under himself, the pressure from the branch above him lessened. He moved his arm. Felt something catch. *Still stuck.*

My capote! It's hooked on a branch. Have to take it off.

Removing his fur-lined mittens, his cold fingers worked the knot on the sash until he could untie it. He snaked his sore arms out of the sleeves. *It will be cold but I can get warm later.* Feeling the cold on his back, he shivered.

André dug his foot and knee in the snow and levered his body left. Slight movement. More pain. He breathed and rested. Edged himself an inch away from the tree. More pain. He rested. Again he pushed. More pain. Inch by inch he dragged his body out from the imprisoning tree branches—and away from his warm *capote*—resting between spikes of pain.

Finally he freed himself. *I'm out from under!* His teeth chattered. He forced himself to sit. With a trembling hand, he reached for his *capote*. When it didn't move, he tugged hard until he heard it tear as he wrenched it from the branches. Panting with exertion, he rolled the woolen *capote* around himself and curled up. And waited for the pain to subside.

When he felt stronger, he probed the side of his chest. Pain blossomed when he touched certain spots—and made him queasy and light-headed. *A broken rib? Or two? But no blood.* In the dark, his numb fingers couldn't find his mittens. So he slipped his hands under his arms inside his *capote* to warm them.

Exhausted, he wondered how badly he was hurt. He slumped down, and fell asleep.

Hours later—or was it minutes?—he woke to the growling of wolves. Very close. He could smell them, and hear them patter back and forth nearby. He could see vague shapes moving against the dim white of the snow. He sat up quickly, sucking in breaths as the pain hit him. *Everything I do will hurt. No matter—I have to start somewhere. And keep on until I'm done. But what first?* He waited a few moments until the pain lessened. *Take care of the dogs.*

He felt violent jerking of the dogs, yet in their harnesses. Then growling, the snap of teeth and a cry of pain he didn't recognize. He broke off a branch and yelled, flinging it in the direction of the wolves. One yelped and another snarled, and then the sounds began to dwindle.

Yellow Eyes—did she snap at a wolf, injure it?

"Yellow Eyes, is that you?" André reached into the mess of spruce branches for his trembling dog, trying to pet her. She must have protected them from the wolf. But Arrow was silent.

André winced as he slid his arms back inside his torn *capote,* tied it around himself and found his mittens and put them on. Brushing snow away, he saw the sled jammed under the fallen tree. *I hope it's not too mangled, but I won't know until daytime.* He rested, his eyes closed.

Yellow Eyes barked again. *She's half under the tree and still harnessed to the sled. Doesn't sound hurt. Maybe between branches or in a hollow?* Arrow, hidden by branches, made a weak sound. Yellow Eyes barked softly. *Is she comforting him? Encouraging him?*

"I'm coming. I'll get you out," André said, hoping to soothe them, wishing for something to soothe the jabbing pain in his ribs. Yellow Eyes' tail wagged and she barked a response.

He tried to stand, but his left snowshoe was buried, and he fell, wrenching his ankle. Frustrated, he sat to remove the snowshoe and rub his ankle. *The other snowshoe must be under the tree.*

"Almost there, Yellow Eyes."

On his hands and knees, sinking into the snow, he dragged himself closer to them, despite the pain. The effort sapped his energy. He broke small branches above Yellow Eyes so he could see her. When he unfastened her tangled harness, Yellow Eyes sprang out and danced around, yipping with joy and licking his face. It made the scrapes on his cheeks sting.

It took time before he could muster enough energy to reach through the branches and unfasten Arrow's harness. Arrow whimpered in pain. André could hear him flick his tail, but slowly.

Maybe the branch injured him. Getting him out will be difficult. I need the ax.

He reached toward the pack of tools lashed to the sled and now buried beneath a mound of snow and sharp branches. He untied the basswood cords that secured it. His numb fingers delved inside and found canvas, fire steel, cup and kettle. Finally his ax.

In the faint light he studied the branches that surrounded Arrow. With the ax, he chopped away at them, lightly, carefully, so as not to spike his own pain. But it made no difference—his chest throbbed with each movement. Arrow, pinned by a large branch, made no attempt to move—he moaned. *He must be in agony. Worse than me. But I need to rest now.*

"I'm sorry, Arrow," he whispered, panting, tears in his eyes. "I can't figure out how to help you. Yet."

André reached to pet Arrow's head. The dog groaned piteously and snapped in pain when André's hand neared the dog's spine, his teeth clicking. He covered Arrow with a layer of small branches to keep out falling snow.

Breathless and sweating at the exertion, he plopped down. *It hurts but I can't think about it. What next?*

"Water. We need water. And warm food."

Yellow Eyes woofed.

"Are you as hungry as I am?"

Yellow Eyes answered, Arrow did not.

He scooped snow into the kettle and, using pieces of dead branches, made a small fire a few feet away. From his food pack, he dug out *pemmican* and shaved off slabs for Yellow Eyes, who ate greedily. Arrow sniffed but turned his head away. When the water was warmed, Arrow only lapped up a little bit, Yellow Eyes drank thirstily.

André finished the rest of the water, then slowly chewed a slice of *pemmican*.

I want to sleep. But I can't yet. What should I do next?

In the light from the fire, he saw the wolf tracks in the snow. *We were lucky. Merci, mon Dieu.*

Then he gazed up and down the length of the spruce. When it fell, it had sheared off branches on one side of a standing tree, an oak with its leaves rattling in the wind.

The snow reflected enough light to see shadows of the dark trees on both sides of a ravine, many of them fallen. *The tree fell across the path at the same time as we went into the ravine. Its full weight didn't crush us—we were partly protected. Why did it fall—did the bitter cold freeze the sap and split the tree? Or was it because of the tempest, like so many around here?*

He stood, wrapped his arms around the trunk and tried to lift the tree, gritting his teeth against the searing pain in his chest. It was monstrously heavy. He tried a second time, grunting. Nothing. *Far too heavy. How will I ever free Arrow?* He wanted to cry, from pain and from wasted effort.

Puffing, he sat down to recover his own waning strength. *I'm too tired. I have to rest. Curl around the dogs and share what warmth we have.*

André piled other branches into a large mound. With blankets, he fashioned a bed for himself around the dogs, sheltering them all with the canvas.

Please God, help us survive.

His arms across his dogs, André dropped off quickly into a troubled sleep. Waves of nightmares flitted through his brain. At first he couldn't tell if the wolves that howled and crept near, baring their fangs, were a dream. When they dashed away at his wild rantings and the fierce growls of Yellow Eyes, standing spread-legged near her master, he knew they were real.

Exhausted, he fell asleep again.

CHAPTER 38

The sky was light gray when André awoke. Wind whooshed in the forest, blowing loose snow around everywhere he looked. His breath, and that of the dogs, made balloons of white—and immediately disappeared. Colder than yesterday. But some of his energy had returned.

Yellow Eyes licked him, her wet warm tongue chafing the raw scratches on his face.

"It's day already," he scolded. "You didn't wake me." She woofed.

"How is Arrow?" He flicked snow off the canvas, lifted it up to see them and rubbed both dogs' ears. "What good dogs," he said, relieved for their company.

Yellow Eyes nuzzled him, then turned and began licking Arrow, who barely responded. André looked carefully at Arrow for blood from a gash or for a broken bone. Nothing. He touched Arrow as gently as he could, but with each brush, the dog groaned. *Not good.*

Though the snow had stopped, several inches had piled up around them.

What day is today? How long have we been gone? Only their third day, he decided. *We would have arrived at Bear Tooth Rapids tonight. Will people at the fort worry about us?* His shoulders sagged when he looked at the tree that had smashed over them in the ravine, now covered with snow. *It's impossible.*

Then he stopped. *Don't think about such things. We will take care of ourselves. Like Robinson Crusoe did. It's not impossible—but it will take longer. Eat first.*

When he stretched and slid out from under the canvas, every part of his body ached. His face was stiff and crusted, his chest on fire with every breath. He examined the tear on the right sleeve of his *capote* and across his back. *No wonder I felt cold.*

Moving slowly, he built a fire in the same spot and melted snow, water for now and later. While he prepared stew, he sniffed the strong smell of high wines. A heavy branch had struck one keg, and a slushy brown puddle formed beneath it. *Leaking. How much is lost? Would there be enough to save?*

Again Arrow turned away from the warmed food, but André and Yellow Eyes gulped it hungrily. Then he gently placed canvas over Arrow to maintain his heat while he and Yellow Eyes were working. *Next I should figure out about the sled. Getting it out will be a slow job.*

André began to free the sled, moving deliberately so as not to hurt more. First he emptied the packs and slid them away and removed the lashing that tied down the nearly-empty keg. He leaned his shoulder against the full one, but it did not budge. *I will leave it for now. Maybe it will not be a problem.* Then he methodically began to remove branches, enough to allow the sled leeway. Last, he reattached Yellow Eyes' harness so she could pull. With each exertion his chest hurt but, if he moved carefully, he could work.

When everything was ready, he shouted to Yellow Eyes to pull, and he leaned against the sled, trying to push it out. Nothing—it remained wedged under the branches. The pain and effort drained his energy. He doubled over, holding his ribs. Even breathing hurt.

He unharnessed the dog and sank to his knees, and then sat. Yellow Eyes jumped onto his lap and they rested, André's head against hers.

Eyeing the gigantic spruce tree, his heart sank. *How can I possibly move it? I'm not strong enough to lift it—even if I weren't injured.*

He put his hand on the rough bark and felt depressed. The tree was a monster. *If I walk to Bear Tooth Rapids to get help, how long would that take? Two days? Four to get back? By that time, my poor Arrow will ...*

Exhausted, he curled up next to Arrow and saw pain in the dog's eyes. He put his arms around both dogs and cried. *What if we can't leave?*

Finally he sat again. *I have to get us out.* He glanced at the pack items he had strewn around the tree. *The pulley! I forgot I have a pulley! And I need a plan. It's not impossible, but I need to think to make it work. Just lifting or having Yellow Eyes pull—that wasn't a real plan.*

"I need more time, Arrow. We'll help you." His words were to encourage himself as much as his injured dog.

He reached the pulley and, seeing a length of rope, smiled. *Emile gave me a good rope. I hope it's long enough. And the packs were tied with braided basswood cords—maybe that will be strong enough.*

André trudged slowly to the end of the deadfall, the snow crunching under his feet, and sticking to his *capote*. *Where could I attach the pulley to lift this?*

Looking at the trees one after another, the answer became obvious. All the upright trees around the spruce deadfall were either too far away, too small, or had branches too high or too weak. That left a stout oak tree growing near the end of the deadfall. The oak, its dry brown leaves attached, was on his side of the ravine. *The angle is awkward and the best branch is high, but it's solid enough to work.*

He pulled off his mittens to hold the basswood cord in his hand, and tossed it up. It missed. The effort cost him. *Try again—get it higher.* After four throws, each increasing the pangs in his chest, the cord flew over the strong branch where he wanted it to go.

Now to test it—will the branch be strong enough? He matched the tail ends so they were equal in length, and wound an end of the cord around each hand. He pulled his body up, lifting to test the branch. *It holds me, but doing it hurts. And it will hurt more when I try to lift this tree.*

André rested against the trunk, sagging, panting for some time, waiting for the pain to release—and made a surprising discovery: *When I don't think about the pain, I don't feel it. So it's best to stay busy.*

He slipped the cord through the center of the pulley and made a large loop, tying the ends tight. Now it hung on the strong branch above. It would have to lift a heavy load. He wrapped the good rope around the thick deadfall near its top, where it would provide more leverage, and knotted it securely. Finally he threaded the rope over the groove, noting where it was damaged, and turned the pulley so that area would have the least effect. Would the rope stay in the pulley? He shrugged. He could only try.

André tested it. Smiled—the pulley held. The rope held. And his body cooperated.

As best he could, he slipped a canvas under Arrow and knelt beside Yellow Eyes to harness her. "When I raise the tree, run fast to slide Arrow out. I will count—*un, deux, trois*. Then pull. Ready?" She woofed.

André said a silent prayer.

"*Un, deux, trois—allez!*" André grabbed at the rope and pulled. "Go!"

"HEE-YAH!" he grunted. He pulled until his arms trembled, but the tree didn't move an inch. He increased the pressure as he yelled hoarsely, "HEE-YAH!" His bare palms stung with rope burns. The tree didn't budge.

His chest was on fire. His arms weakened, then gave way. His knees collapsed and he fell, raising a billow of loose snow. Sweat dripped down his back as he loosened Yellow Eyes from her harness. He put his hand on Arrow's head. "I can't do it, Arrow. I'm sorry. I tried."

Is this the end? For him? For all of us? He sighed, and rested.

Somehow he would have to lift the tree. Or remove it somehow. André felt weak at the thought. Seeing the splintered broken trunk on top of Arrow and the sled made his stomach tighten.

It's much heavier than I realized, hundreds of pounds—it wasn't a plan. How could I have moved something like that? How can I muster enough strength to lift a tree that size?

He slid on his mittens, his fingers like icicles. *I have no more strength. I'm tired now. I'll close my eyes for a moment or two, and rest. I'll think of something.*

CHAPTER 39

André woke to Yellow Eyes nudging him. He looked up into the sky—still gray, but a shade darker. *Maybe an hour or two before night.*

He kindled a fire and heated the remains of the stew frozen in the pot, adding wild rice. Pretty Mouse had generously supplied him for four days, but after tomorrow they would get hungry. *I'm starving all too often.*

After he and Yellow Eyes ate, André studied Arrow's body. His leg stuck out at an odd angle. Something must be broken. A lump had risen on his backbone where the branch pressed against him. Arrow yelped if he probed near it.

"Arrow, hang on."

When he examined the sled closely for the first time, hope seeped out of him. Part of it was crushed beneath the sheer defeating size of the trunk. It would need repair before they could leave. If they could get it free. Impossible.

But I must—our survival depends on it. Joseph said I could do the impossible, if I thought long enough about the ways to attack the problem.

André wished he remembered what the young sailor had said about making pulleys more efficient—adjusting part would ease the lift. Two pulleys would be better, but that was a dream.

"Help," he cried to the world, though there was no one around. Only himself. He would have to be his own hero, like Robinson Crusoe.

At the smell of high wines, he looked at the leaking keg. *The other post will be disappointed but I'm glad Yellow Eyes will only have one keg to pull. But that is not the key to the problem.*

André looked again at the sturdy oak tree, and saw what he had missed before—branches on both sides were sheared away. He shuffled through the snow around to the far end of the downed spruce. And yes! Another downed tree, laying almost parallel to the first one, with the oak standing tall between the two. *Could I somehow use the second one with this pulley? As a counterweight?*

In the parallel tree—a red-barked long-needled pine—he saw a possibility for lifting the spruce that trapped them! Hope surged through him. The hair stood on his arms. André felt almost warm.

Merci, mon Dieu. "Thank you, God. I know what I can do."

He clomped up and down the length of the pine. It was thicker than the spruce that trapped the sled. And better, the red-barked pine was three feet above the ground at one end, held up by two big branches spearing down into the snow and dirt. Smaller branches surrounded the larger ones, but didn't support the tree. *I could connect it to the spruce with the rope and pulley. Then, when the pine fell, that would lift the spruce and free Arrow and the sled!* He closed his eyes and pictured how each step would work. *I could ...*

Yellow Eyes yapped about his feet, sensing André's excitement as he grabbed the ax and loops of rope. He wrapped the loose end of the strongest rope around the red-barked pine and tied it tightly, near the end highest above the ground where it would provide the greatest force when it fell. He made sure the rope rode smoothly through the pulley groove and that the other end was tight around the spruce. He smiled—pulling hadn't loosened it. Then he doubled, and tripled the basswood cord that connected the pulley to the branch of the oak. Basswood cord wasn't meant to handle this punishing a load—it would break first.

With his ax he haltingly clipped the small branches holding up the second tree. Thwack, thwack, thwack. Each movement sent a throb of pain.

He was about to start on the thick branches when he realized that night was falling. To finish the work properly, he needed light. Good daylight, not firelight. He blew out his breath, frustrated.

But I am tired. We need water and food—and rest.

He made a fire, and cooked. Yellow Eyes, curled around Arrow, only lifted her head enough to gobble what André spooned for her. Arrow took nothing.

While he ate, he heard wolves baying. *We were lucky they didn't get at us. Tonight I will be ready, in case they come back.* He stockpiled branches he had cut. Then he reached under the fallen tree and carefully dug out his snowshoes, the webbing and foot lacings torn.

Darkness seeped in, until it was complete, except for his small island of flickering firelight. To keep himself awake while he repaired his snowshoe, he talked of his plans to the dogs.

"I think we can leave tomorrow, Arrow."

André thought about his aching chest, and wished he could ride in the sled instead of loping alongside it. But he couldn't. The sled already would carry a heavy load for one dog. He sighed. *I can't think about how much I hurt or I won't be able to get us out.*

"Stay with us, Arrow. What wonderful dogs you both are."

Tears in his eyes, André crawled under the canvas and hugged his dogs. Seconds later he was asleep.

In the middle of the night, he awoke to voices—and barking. *Or is it my imagination? My dogs are right here.*

After listening intently, the woods remained silent. *Another nightmare? Spies from enemy tribes? Cannibals? Basile Roche?* He shivered. Then he remembered to combat his fear, not let it take over. *Maybe the voice came from Joseph—or Denis—or Silent Wolf.*

Robinson Crusoe kept on when he was scared. Joseph was right. Maybe it's easier to do hard things for someone—or something—you love. He was surprised at the warmth he felt for the dogs. They were deeply bonded. The thought comforted him.

He glanced at the night sky above him and saw pale stars winking. Although the snow had been a nuisance, the clouds had formed a blanket and held in a bit of heat. Now, the temperature would drop. He dreaded tomorrow's cold.

When he looked up again, he noticed a greenish cast across the sky, flickering and shifting like Berthe's curtain in a light breeze. A wave of purple rippled through, and then faded. Mesmerized, André watched as colors flared and darkened overhead, the whole dome bathed in mysterious shimmering lights. Finally they disappeared.

Northern lights! Never as colorful as this, nor as long. I would have missed them, but a noise woke me. I wish I could ask Toussaint about them.

André was deeply grateful to have seen the amazing lights. He rolled back under the canvas and fell back asleep, a small smile on his face at the sign of hope.

Chapter 40

Instead of gray clouds, they awoke to a sunrise—after so many snowy days, André was relieved to see streaks of rose and gold in the blue morning sky.

But it was bitter cold. To stay warm, he needed to keep active, though his chest stung at every breath. *I don't know what to do about my ribs, but I won't let that stop me. I have to keep working.*

He started the day by heating water and stew which Yellow Eyes lapped up eagerly. Arrow only took a little water from André's hand, and refused the warm broth. *The trek to Bear Tooth Rapids will be hard on him. Harder on Yellow Eyes who has an extra burden to carry. As slow as we have to go, it will take us two days. Help us, Ste. Anne.*

But first he had to free the sled—and Arrow—by chopping the big branches left that held up the tree. *This will hurt, but I have to do it.*

He checked the pulley and ropes, which were tight. Satisfied, he examined the branches, and was sure only two of them were left supporting the tree three feet off the ground. He grabbed the handle of the ax with both hands. He lifted it into position, took a deep breath—and swung.

He smacked the support branch as hard as his burning chest would allow, swinging the ax, seeing the chips fall away. He chopped slowly but steadily at the closest branch holding up the red pine.

With each swing the pain grew in his ribs, a pinch worsening with each breath. When the burn became too intense, he stopped to hug his ribs for a few moments. Then, pushing himself again, he continued—the branch had to be chopped. Sweating and panting, he struck and struck. Suddenly the branch gave way. The great body of the red pine lurched.

André jumped back, staring at it. Would the second branch hold? If Yellow Eyes wasn't ready to pull at the right time, André feared the spruce would lift for only a second, and then crash down again. *Do I hear creaking? Will the pulley cord hold?*

He took a deep painful breath. Though his chest ached, he went after the second branch in a flurry of cuts. His ax, getting dull, made small chips of bark and wood. It took longer than he had expected— he panted, winded and sore.

After what seemed like hundreds of swings, the remaining core of branch was very slim. Two or three more cuts would weaken the branch so it snapped. Then the red pine would fall and, at the same time, the pulley and ropes would lift the spruce that trapped Arrow and the sled. *Now I will sit, for a minute, and think my plan through one more time.*

He examined his work where he had looped the trees together— tight as a bowstring. If the plan worked right, Yellow Eyes would yank Arrow to safety, along with the sled and the remaining keg. If the ropes held. If the red pine dropped enough and lifted the spruce high enough.

Running the braided strands of basswood through his fingers, he examined every inch. The rope would have to be strong enough. He rotated the pulley so the weakest part was on the bottom. *I have only one chance to get it right.*

Everything was in order. He petted Arrow. "Forgive me. This will hurt, but she will pull you to safety. This is the best way I know." Arrow's head stayed down and André was relieved that he could not see the pain in his eyes. He reattached their harnesses.

"Yellow Eyes, run when this falls." He patted the lighter tree. "The basswood cord won't hold it long." He pointed across the ravine. "Pull to that side." He was asking a great deal of his young dog but she was eager to be in front of the sled.

After checking the loops once more, he grabbed his ax and looked at Yellow Eyes. "Ready?"

She woofed and braced her legs.

Pain shot through his ribs as André swung the ax into the narrow core of the last supporting branch and chopped. Again. Again. Then he stopped to listen. A faint groan from the ropes being stretched. He made one more cut.

"Allez! Go, go, go!!"

The red pine dropped with a resounding crash and cloud of loose snow. The ropes creaked and through the snow haze he saw the spruce shoot up almost three feet. It was going to work! But the sled barely moved.

Yellow Eyes strained in her harness. The sled jerked. The spruce swayed.

A branch of the spruce, but now only one, held the sled. Yellow Eyes barked sharply. André strode over and swung his ax as hard as he could, smashing the branch, freeing the sled.

Yellow Eyes shot forward, dragging Arrow and the sled fifteen feet across the ravine. Free!

Seconds later, the basswood cords on the pulley creaked, and split. The spruce crashed down, spraying snow high in the air.

André shouted, "You did it! We did it!" Yellow Eyes leaped in glee and he clambered to hug her. His tears mingled with her licking. "Good girl, good girl. *Merci*."

Merci, Ste. Anne. Merci, mon Dieu. His knees buckled in relief and tears streamed down his face. *What if we had been under it?*

Arrow whimpered. André, exhausted, shook his head—he could not have freed the sled without hurting his dog. He made Arrow as comfortable as he could. He and Yellow Eyes rested while he considered what was next.

He warmed more water for them, but Arrow refused it. Only Yellow Eyes drank deeply. The rest went in the water bag.

Fewer chores than before: Gather the ropes, tools and pulley. Fix the sled—a big job. Close the tear in his *capote*. Make sure the full keg is securely lashed and balanced on the sled. Fixing the sled was first. Repack the gear. Place the packs and Arrow onto the sled. Rest.

Robinson Crusoe chose a problem and worked at it until he solved it. I did it like he did. It made him satisfied, almost warm, as he mended the wooden structure.

The broken basswood cords won't hold much any more. Should I leave them here? Then he thought of a use—knotted together, he wrapped them around his tender ribs. They would give support while he walked to Bear Tooth Rapids. They circled his chest many times.

His fixed his *capote* by pinning the tear with small slivers of wood. At the post, he could sew it with their needle and thread.

One by one he completed each task. Everything was ready except loading Arrow.

André glanced at the sun's position high in the clear blue sky. While chopping and working, he had barely noticed the day's beautiful brightness—it had been too cold to stop moving. With a few hours left in the day, he could get miles closer to the Bear Tooth Rapids post before bedding down. Then, after this night, maybe only one more night of sleeping in the open.

He tenderly lifted the listless Arrow, who moaned as André settled him on the sled in a nest of blankets and tied him in.

"Let's go, Yellow Eyes."

She tugged, and the sled began to move around broken tree after broken tree. The forest seemed like a tangled web. *How will I get the sled through this mess?*

After winding around downed trees for a mile, André spotted a glint of sunlight off a frozen stream. He recalled the rough map the Otter Creek *engagés* had sketched on the floor. The stream should lead to a lake—and then trails to Bear Tooth Rapids. However long it took, he decided to follow the stream.

The snow was incredibly white, brightened with sparkles of light and blue shadows from trees. But he paid little attention to the day's beauty. Instead André pulled his *tuque* down to block the intensity of the light and prevent snow-blindness. Then he tightened the hood of his *capote* and tied its long tails, leaving only narrow slits over his eyes.

He focused on each step, listening to the dry hollow crunch that broke the quiet. Step after step after step, he navigated through the forest and over the hills.

Late in the day he took a few moments to rest and reorient himself. While he and Yellow Eyes rested, he glanced at the western sky—and saw short rainbows, one on each side of the brilliant sun.

"Sundogs, Yellow Eyes! Look at the sundogs, one for each of you. A good omen. It means you'll get better, Arrow." Watching the sundogs, they trudged until the rainbows disappeared and the sun set in a color-streaked sky.

"Last night I saw the northern lights in the sky and today sundogs. It's got to mean something good. *Merci.* Ste. Anne. Thank you for showing me sundogs."

When Yellow Eyes began tiring, André picked a place to camp that night. He bedded beside the dogs. "Arrow, you are too cold. Get close, Yellow Eyes. We need to warm each other up."

The sheer effort of walking, of helping Yellow Eyes haul, of thinking for the three of them, of blocking his own pain while trudging, all had taken its toll. He fell asleep, missing a second night of northern lights.

CHAPTER 41

In the morning, André heated the last of their food, and extra water to carry with them.

"After this, we have no more," he said to Yellow Eyes as they left. He knew from his hungry days on Lake Superior that he could manage on less than he wanted. Harder on her, though.

Oh, and we have Pretty Mouse's chunk of maple sugar. It'll keep us going for a little longer. He thought of Pretty Mouse as he dropped it into the water skin—that small kindness would make this day a bit better.

The trek would be difficult with his chest so tender. Nothing he could do about that but try not to breathe deeply. With good luck they would not spend another night in the woods.

Joseph was right—although something is hard, you can do it. There is no other choice.

They plodded through the woods keeping the stream in view as it widened. When they came to hills, André helped Yellow Eyes pull the sled through the loose snow.

Each breath coated his red *tuque* with frost. Despite having patched the tears in his *capote*, the icy wind seemed to find every hole.

André's ears and hands and feet grew numb. As the gnawing pain in chest grew, he slowed his pace.

When he felt his energy ebb, he began talking to Yellow Eyes and Arrow. He told them of how he came to be a voyageur to find Denis. He told of his second brigade, learning from Gerard and the haunting moment of seeing Gerard's face right before he was lost in the river. Tears streamed down his face as he told them how that awful death had made a gaping hole in himself that had not been knitted together. Though the other men wouldn't talk about it, he had tried to honor Gerard's memory by steering as well as he could.

And now, somehow, talking with Yellow Eyes and Arrow helped him to feel more at peace with his inability to help his friend.

At sundown, when they emptied the water skin of its last drops, he decided to heat water and refill it, in case the trek took much longer than he expected.

They began seeing signs of habitation—a trap set for fox, the print from a snowshoe, a tie from a voyageur's legging, and then trails, which showed him he was headed correctly. Each one cheered him. *Night or not, we keep going. Finally it's not cloudy—Emile said to watch the North Star, that it would help us find our way.*

CHAPTER 42

Well after dark, André spied a column of smoke rising over the high spires of trees against the background of stars. The Bear Tooth Rapids post!

There it is! Finally! The sight heartened him and brought new energy. Yellow Eyes pulled to her limit—she too wanted to reach shelter. Hoping they might arrive in an hour, they pressed on.

But it took longer. The moon provided light in the star-speckled sky, enough to keep him on the faint path. When they arrived at the post, André leaned against the gate, feeling the rough wood. Tears welled in his eyes.

"We made it," he whispered. "We made it!"

The post's gate was barred for the night. He beat on it. "Halloo. Open up."

He patted the dogs while they waited. "You did it, Yellow Eyes! *Merci, mon Dieu.* Thanks to God, we are here. We wouldn't be here without you. I know you need food. Hold on, Arrow." He knelt and hugged them, relief washing over him.

When there was no answer, he summoned the last reserves of energy and yelled loudly, "Halloo. It is André Didier. Open the gate." He banged and whooped, and Yellow Eyes echoed the demand. He noted that Arrow had barely moved to breathe—*like how I feel.*

As the new leader of this fort, he must appear mature, strong and wise, though he did not feel that way. Despite the deep ache in his chest, he straightened his shoulders, as Antoine had advised.

Long minutes later, the heavy wood gate creaked open and three disheveled men appeared. One held a candle. They looked at him as if he were a ghost. He almost looked like one—only his eyes showed, he was so well wrapped. A thick layer of white frost covered his entire head.

"I am André Didier, from Antoine Felix's post. Mr. Chaboillez sent me a letter about Jean-Baptiste Bousquet. Is Chaboillez here? And how is Jean-Baptiste?"

"Didier? We ... er, thought ... you were dead." The speaker with the candle looked uncertainly at his companions. "How you make it through the blizzard? So cold it was these last days."

"I had to burrow down during the storm with my dogs. Please take them inside. One is injured." He untied his hood which fell back to reveal his face.

"You had an accident!" Another man eyed him in horror. "You are hurt!"

"You are ... so young!"

I forgot about the scrapes on my face and my torn capote. "*Oui,*" André answered simply. "And we ran out of food."

They surrounded him, taking his packs and rolling the keg of high wine—almost picking up André—in a mad swirl and ushering him indoors.

One said, "*Non,* Chaboillez, he does not come here, oh, *non.* It is just us—I am Vincent and this is François and this is Luc." They were all short barrel-chested men with lively eyes and unkempt wiry beards, their faces vaguely familiar.

I probably saw them at the rendezvous. Vincent is the oldest, probably the leader. François is heavy—maybe he is the cook. Luc is the youngest—he has a fancy mustache.

They seated him on a three-legged stool before the fire, unwrapping his *capote* and removing his fur-lined moccasins. They frowned at the basswood cords wrapped around his chest.

"Leave them for now. They help me feel better." André's chilled and exhausted body almost swooned in the delicious heat.

He looked for a stew pot on their hearth, but saw none. "A meal would be welcome."

Luc pointed to the cask of high wines. "This? It warms after such a cold day."

André shook his head. "No, but tea, please, if you have it."

François stirred the embers and settled a pot of water over them.

"The storm, it was so long—we did not think you would come. You must be lost, frozen to death," Vincent started. "We decided— tomorrow we would tell Mr. Chaboillez you do not come. We must send a runner. But who? Then tonight, you come. You are here, and we do not have this predicament. That is good, eh?"

André nodded. They had given him up as dead. "Where is Jean-Baptiste? Is he better?"

Vincent tugged his beard, then looked at the others. "Bousquet, he …" He shook his head. "One night he went off. But he … he … did not come back."

"He is dead?"

They nodded, as a group. They seemed very reticent.

André was confused. These men might be superstitious about unexpected death, like his canoe-mates when Gerard drowned, but he needed to know the details. He pressed further.

While André devoured a plate of rabbit meat, they told him that Jean-Baptiste had never regained consciousness and that a week ago he stopped breathing. Because the ground was frozen, they had wrapped him in a blanket and covered him with a cairn of rocks in the forest by the river, instead of digging a grave. They would show him.

André was silent for some time. *I have become their permanent head clerk, not a helper until the rendezvous. Now I can't go back to Antoine. He did not prepare me for this.* He was crushed. He had not wanted this new responsibility, even for a short while. But how could he refuse? *I have to manage this post and go the rendezvous from here. Should I send Mr. Chaboillez a letter? What else should I tell him?*

He sighed, which hurt his ribs and reminded him that Yellow Eyes and Arrow were not inside.

"Please bring both dogs in. One is hurt and I need to see to him," he said. "They can return outdoors tomorrow, but tonight I want them close."

His request surprised them, but Luc nodded and slid his *capote* from its peg by the door. When he returned, he nervously looked from André to Vincent and back.

"One dog is … frozen," he stuttered. "Not alive."

André nearly dropped his cup of tea. He had talked to Arrow the entire way back. He couldn't be dead. His throat felt full. Finally he stammered, "He … Arrow …"

Luc glanced at Vincent and François.

Do they think their new chief trader is crazy? That I don't know a dead dog from a live one? Would they understand that I got attached to an animal? A sled dog, meant for work?

They stood, taking the measure of each other. "Come, I show you." Luc led André outside.

Kneeling down by Arrow, André touched the stiff body and cold fur and knew Luc was right—Arrow was gone. He had died along the trail and André had not noticed, because the journey had taken all of his energy and thoughts. He felt terrible. He couldn't meet

Luc's eyes, so instead he examined Arrow laying there. He wanted to be alone with his thoughts. *But later.*

"You want the other dog inside?" Luc said incredulously. The request was highly irregular.

André nodded. Yellow Eyes hesitated, not wanting to leave Arrow. Her eyes on André, she finally moved into the living area, nuzzled him and curled up by his feet.

His voice was hoarse. "Yellow Eyes got us here. She hauled Arrow and all the goods, and found the trails in the snow. I want her by me tonight."

Vincent raised his eyebrows, but said nothing.

François asked André about the scrapes on his face, so he told them of the tree falling on his sled and smashing one keg of high wine, of searching for a place to bed down until the storm abated.

"Now I see why you came with only one keg, though we asked for two," Luc said.

François interrupted. "You look tired. The journey, it was hard. Tomorrow we show you the credit book. Vincent, he knows the trades that came in these last two weeks. It was not so very many, because of the cold. Now, sleep."

They offered him their best bunk, closest to the fire, in a show of respect of his position. When they were sure he was asleep, they stepped outside to compare their impressions of their new, and very young, and somewhat unusual, leader.

CHAPTER 43

After breakfast, they showed him the trade goods on hand and the inside storage areas. He complimented them, as Antoine had suggested, but they were honest heartfelt words. "I'll look at the account books this afternoon, but the post looks good. The trading room, it is clean and organized."

"But of course. Better for business," Vincent answered.

When they stepped outside to tour the post, Yellow Eyes followed André closely. He could see Luc was put off by her friendly presence. The rest of the post's dogs kept their distance, growling and yipping. He did not want the Bear Tooth Rapids men around when he spent time with Yellow Eyes, but for the moment he had no choice. These men did not understand that this working animal had become special to him.

On the way to the grave site, which was covered with a massive pile of round stones, they filled in details of Jean-Baptiste's years at the post. *Here I will place stones over Arrow, my friend.*

They unlocked their fur storehouse where André estimated the number of pelts. He examined their small dock, glad to see it was in good repair.

They looked over at the river, where a dozen sharp stones rose from the snow. "So that's why it's named the Bear Tooth Rapids," André said. "Are there bears around here?"

"Not so many. Only the usual ones," Luc grinned. "Not the one that owned those teeth."

In a distant corner of their site, François said proudly, "Here we cache the food." André saw they had ample provisions to make it to the spring. He unconsciously patted his stomach, remembering his hunger.

They showed their supply of high wines—less than Antoine had stocked.

"It's going down fast this year. Because of the XY post, we've used much more than usual," François said.

"Do you know about cutting down the high wines, and how much to offer?" André asked. "That would help me. Antoine did it at our post."

"Jean-Baptiste, he gave that task to me," Vincent said. "Me, I am good at it."

Next they walked around the palisade, checking the post wall. Several hundred feet away was the XY post—a long cabin and a small shed. A half-dozen small bark-covered tepees surrounded the other post.

"So close to our post?" André asked.

"That's where the chiefs wanted it," Vincent said apologetically. "So trading is easier for them."

André wanted to hear about "their" hunters.

"With Ducharme so close," Vincent answered, "we cannot call them 'ours' anymore. The Ojibwe, they trade here, and they trade there."

André was getting tired—his ribs ached from the effort and sapped his energy. He suggested they return.

Back inside, he studied the credit book Jean-Baptiste had left. Despite the indistinct handwriting, he made out familiar names, like Bobtail Bear, Runs When He Walks and many hunters he knew. He would have to get used to competition.

He pointed to unfamiliar names, starting with the largest remaining debts. "Who are these hunters? Tell me about them." As the three *engagés* told him what they knew, he continued down the list, making notes on the size of their families, their particular skills, how often they visited. He examined Jean-Baptiste's journal with noteworthy events. He matched the remaining trade goods on hand with an inventory list. Late in the day when he was finished, he closed the record books and turned to the men, who were hovering nervously.

"How long have you been at this post? And how long in the fur trade?" André asked. "Tell me about your families."

They answered perfunctorily.

No longer able to wait, Vincent asked anxiously, "Well, André, are we doing well?"

"Vincent. You are the most senior. What do you think?"

"If they bring us the furs they owe, we are fine. Because of that XY post, this year we have had to give more goods for the furs."

Vincent looked scornfully toward the rival post. "'Our' hunters, they visit both houses to get the best deal. We offered fancy chief coats to some. But Ducharme, the snake, gave more. And he offers high wine before the trade, after the trade, whenever they visit. They forget to hunt. Me, I think they owe him more and more."

"Maybe we steal the pelts?" Luc offered. "To get them first."

"*Non.*" André was firm. "We cannot carry over many debts this year. But we must get those pelts owed to us." He looked at each of them in turn. "Or the *bourgeois* could close this post!" It was how Antoine had suggested he approach their situation, if it was precarious.

Their jaws dropped.

"You heard the rumors at the *rendezvous* last summer?"

They nodded in shocked disbelief. After supper they were quiet, the three smoking, saying little.

"Would you like me to read from this book?" André said, to break the silence. "It is the adventures of Robinson Crusoe, a sailor who was stranded on an island."

"Not for us. Most nights we play cards, or maybe a game on the checkerboard."

André opened the book to read to himself, but after turning a few pages, he realized he didn't remember what he had read. Plus, the fun of reading it aloud, despite Mouse's interruptions, was gone.

The position will be much harder than I thought. Harder than Antoine realized. This is not the way I wanted to begin. But now we all know the worst that could happen, and together we can try to make the post successful.

CHAPTER 44

The next day, André paid a call on the XY post. With only two rooms—one for trading and one for sleeping—it was smaller than his post. He found Jean Ducharme and his *engagés* playing cards and smelling of liquor.

"Look who's here!" Ducharme said. "It's André Bon-à-rien. We thought you would visit us yesterday. That's when we were ready."

"Didier. My name is André Didier."

"André here paddled with Antoine Felix." Ducharme looked him up and down. "Like I did before I took this post."

Of course, they know this. Everyone here knows everyone else's business. They knew when Jean-Baptiste fell, when Chaboillez's messengers left, when Jean-Baptiste died. They probably added stones onto the burial mound. They expected me to arrive here days earlier. They knew everything—except the exact words Chaboillez wrote in his letter.

"We heard you died … er, thought you … got lost in the storm."

"I dug down for a few extra nights."

Ducharme introduced his men—Black Jacques, Petit Jacques, Etienne—who merely grunted and returned to their card game, smoking and whooping at their wins or losses.

Antoine would not condone playing cards or drinking alcohol in the daytime. Their behavior confounded André.

They ignored him, perhaps to show they felt he was too young to be an equal, so he scanned their trading counter to note what trade goods they had plenty of and what was missing. *Only a small pile of blankets, kettles and iron tools. No fancy things—he already gave many gifts to Bobtail Bear and his band. Wonder how much is in his fur storehouse? Antoine already has half his credits in.*

Finally, André was irritated. "Ducharme, come see me. I have much to do today."

The men cackled. "Do? Press pelts? Hunters won't start coming in for two, three more weeks."

On the walk back, he noted that Etienne had made the same comment Luc had. *They expected me to be dead.*

He flashed back where the tree had fallen on him. He stopped short. *The tree dropped at the same moment we came upon it. The dogs dashed after rabbits. Could someone have released rabbits right then? Had the tree been tampered with? Is this how Basile would try to get revenge?*

Then he stood up and straightened his shoulders. *I haven't worried about Basile since the tree fell. And I'm not going to let him bother me any more. We survived alone across the country. We got out from under that fallen spruce. Revenge and bitterness can eat him up. But not me.*

Yellow Eyes jumped at him, almost knocking him over and causing his tender ribs to smart again. André played and talked with her as she wagged her tail and licked his hands. He felt the pang of loss as looked toward the burial mound where he had placed Arrow and added stones for him.

At suppertime, Ducharme sauntered by.

"I came to see you. We are out of meat. You have some?" he asked casually. "Our hunters, they hardly ever bring in game. Nor rice."

André was not yet ready to be friendly. "Press them to hunt. Make it worth their while. They store enough food for their families, and they know how much food we need to survive."

"Little Mr. Know-it-All. Aren't you important?"

That stung, but Antoine had said it would be hard for older men to take direction from a newcomer, and a young one at that. He knew it was a bad start. It would be better to be civil, and take the high road, as Father Goiffon had always counseled. He took a deep breath.

"Why did you not trade for food?"

Ducharme shrugged. "We tried when we arrived but your post had taken most of their surplus. This winter there is little game. Everyone is hungry. The hunters, they barely feed their families. They took a moose some weeks ago, and shared the meat with us. But it is gone."

André took him outside, where he cut off a haunch of venison and added a bag of rice. Ducharme nodded gratefully.

"We could work together."

Ducharme shook his head. "*Non*, I am sorry. The XY Company, they do not allow. They wouldn't like me asking you for food, but I come as a friend."

André knew he was right. The North West Company did not encourage camaraderie either. They believed XY infringed on trading arrangements that "belonged" to them. The Ojibwe saw it differently.

"Is there enough business for both of us?"

Ducharme had started walking to his post, but he turned back. "*Oui*, of course there is. And plenty of pelts. But we give high wines so the hunters, they come to us first."

"That is costly. It destroys their incentive."

"André, this business is changing. High wines, it is what they want, so we give it."

He marked the loan in his book. *Food for a few days. But then what?*

From talk at the *rendezvous*, he knew the company's profits were unpredictable, that small posts—like Antoine's, like this one—might be closed if profits stayed down. He knew the prairie fires made it more difficult to trap beaver and other animals close by, so the Ojibwe had to travel farther. There were not as many prime beavers as in years gone by—only the Athabascans in the far north had bountiful game.

He could not force Ojibwe hunters to trade only at his post. At the *rendezvous*, some departments in Canada severely pressured their hunters to remain loyal. But the hunters needed to get the best deals for their efforts—hunting beaver took skill and persistence. The best furs were obtained during icy weather, and the process of preparing the pelts took time. Native hunters would divide their pelts between traders—it guaranteed a better price for them.

The XY men are not bad people, only friends trying to do their jobs. And the business of trading furs is changing—Ducharme is right about that.

The next day brought snow, up to their knees but, thankfully, no bitter wind.

But no pelts and no visitors either.

"They know the post's new clerk is here," André said. "Why hasn't anyone come to trade?"

François shrugged. "It's too hard to get here?"

André decided to send Vincent and François out to visit the tribes to get some of the pelts they were owed, as Antoine had sent him and Emile. It would be quiet at the post and he could recover his strength while getting to know Luc better.

But he was alone when an Ojibwe brought in a small bundle of furs.

His first solo trade. He recalled Antoine's advice.

"*Boozhoo*," he said with a smile. "Hello and welcome. I am André."

"What will you give me?" the Ojibwe man said abruptly, opening his bundle on the trading counter.

All the trappers who traded at Bear Tooth Rapids were new to André. "What is your name? Did you take debt this fall?"

"No debt. I come from Lake that Speaks."

Then his name, whatever it is, will not be in our credit book. "That's a long trek, maybe a week away. I traveled through your area some years ago," André said, trying to find friendly ground. "What brings you here?"

"Uncle north of here. I visit him."

"Wise to bring pelts to trade when making a long journey," he said to encourage him. He named a few Ojibwe elders who might be his uncle but the new trapper shook his head. He did not want to chat.

"What is your name, so I can write it in our book?"

"What do you give? Maybe better at other post." This hunter was planning to negotiate for the highest offer, which irked André, though he tried not to show it. But why not divulge his name, or his uncle's?

While André sorted the pelts, mentally grading them, the Ojibwe looked around. Wishing his Bear Tooth Rapids *engagés* were around this day to help with the trade, he named his offer.

"No rum? I go to other post," He stowed the pelts in his pack, retied it and left.

After the man left, André was troubled—by losing his first trade, but also something else. Something he couldn't identify.

CHAPTER 45

The next day, two Ojibwe arrived, weighed down with pelts. Luc identified them as Red Deer and Geese Flying High, well-known tribal leaders.

André's heart soared.

Then his heart tripped. Both wore silver medals suspended on colorful ribbons. Red Deer sported a shiny top hat to which he had added an edge of raccoon tail. Geese Flying High wore a white flannel shirt and an olive vest, fancy clothing like the *bourgeois* wore. They were "made chiefs," hunters of note. *Had Ducharme awarded them these symbols of importance? Would they expect special treatment?*

André said, "Greet them, Luc, while I check the credit book." He discovered their autumn debts had mostly been paid off. Both were accomplished hunters—and men of their word. *They have come to find out who I am—this is my first test. As the new head of this post, this must go very well.*

Remembering Antoine's words, he took a deep breath. Standing tall, he smiled and said, "*Boozhoo.* Hello. I welcome you. Thank you for coming to trade here. *Miigwetch.*" Then he introduced himself as the new chief trader, just come from the Moose Horn River, mentioning Antoine's name. That gave them time to size him up. He glanced at Luc, who complimented their hunting prowess.

In turn the Ojibwe spoke of the health of the tribe and how the weather had affected hunting for food and pelts. He listened to them carefully—and relaxed. *I like these men. This trade will go well for all of us.*

Red Deer hefted his bundle of furs, which included a huge black bear, onto the trading counter.

"Oho, what a bear," Luc said, rubbing his hand through the thick fur. "Me, I want to hear the story of how you got this bear."

Red Deer told of how the large beast got wind of the raccoon he was removing from his trap. He quickly threw the raccoon away from the bear to distract it. It gave him time to dash for his gun, leaning against a tree. He managed to kill the bear with a single shot. The Great Spirit had allowed him to harvest this bear to feed his family—and the raccoon, the tail of which was on his hat, along with several of the bear's claws.

Then Red Deer pointed to the extra trade goods he wanted— his furs were more than what he owed. André nodded, satisfied with the deal.

Among the pelts that Geese Flying High brought were four creamy soft deerskins and a thick moose hide.

"Your wife spent much time tanning these skins. The moose hide will make excellent moccasins." André looked at his own worn footwear, thinking it was time to have a pair made for himself. "Thank you for bringing them early."

After paying off his debts, Geese Flying High chose blankets and a pair of ax heads. André marked the completion of both trades in the log book and showed them how he had listed their credits. They signaled their acceptance.

André thanked them again for trading at the Bear Tooth Rapids post, and offered them gifts—a file, an ice chisel, beads and ribbons. They appraised the items and nodded to each other. He gave them a generous amount of tobacco—a spirit gift. Hoping instead to establish a different way to do business, he gestured to Luc at the soup pot and suggested a meal.

They declined. "We go back. Tell others you are good man. We will see you again. *Gigawabamin menawah.*"

"*Oui,* I will be glad to see you again," Andre echoed. "*Gigawabamin menawah.*"

After they had shut the door behind them, André smiled, relieved that this trade had been a success. He had enjoyed the ritual.

"Good trade, André. Now others will come." Luc clouted him on the back.

"Ouch." André hugged his ribs. "I am sore today. Healing is taking longer than I thought."

"Sorry. I forgot," Luc said. "But their sled, it had another bundle on it. Maybe they go to trade with Jean Ducharme."

"Which way do their tracks lead?" André asked. When they stepped out the door, Luc pointed out their arrival and leaving were different directions.

"Did they bring us as much as the other post?"

"More. They trade here long time. They want to meet you."

André thought for a while. "This year all our hunters took less debt than a year ago. Quite a few held over debt from the year before."

"And now it is divided between us and XY," Luc pointed out. "They owe both posts."

Something to ponder.

That night, he began to write down all the Ojibwe animals he remembered: *makwa* for "bear," *amhik* for "beaver," *nigig* for "otter," *wawashkeshshi* for "deer," *maengun* for "wolf." He struggled with "fox" and "moose" and would have to ask. Next trade he would use more of their language.

Vincent and François returned, pleased with the number of furs they had acquired. While the others organized the furs in the pelt shed, André sat with them, holding the account book, not strong enough to lift much.

Suddenly they heard a great pounding, crashing and yelling in the direction of the XY post. And then a gunshot—also from there. More shouting. Then quiet.

Everyone stopped their work and looked toward the XY post.

"A gunshot?" André was shocked. He gazed at his men with concern and curiosity.

Vincent shrugged. "This we have heard before."

"Oho, someone is mad," François said. "But who today?"

"Best to let them work it out," Vincent said. "If it is bad, if they need our help, they will come here." That matched another bit of Antoine's advice, not to interfere.

Later that evening, he mentioned the close-mouthed nephew visiting his uncle. "How often do new people, new hunters stop here to trade, or talk?"

"Now and then," Luc said. "We don't know all the hunters and trappers that come by."

"If a man is looking for someone, we do not ask too much," François said.

Which reminded him about tracking down his brother, Denis. Which brought Basile Roche to mind. It made him feel anxious, but he asked anyway, "Do you know Basile Roche?"

"But of course," said Luc. "A leech. Roche, he hooks onto someone, sucks them dry. He has tried to work on each of us. Twists himself onto us in some way." His face soured. "I have not seen him for some years. Which is good for me."

François said, "Basile, he knows everyone—traders and tribes. Not on a brigade for years, though. No one will have him."

"Me, I heard he had an accident. I thought he was dead," Vincent said. "Why do you ask—is he back in these parts?"

"No, and maybe he is dead." André shook his head. "He never visited Antoine's post, but the tribes there all knew of him. Roche was cruel to them."

"Not a good person to have around our posts. Not here, not next door," Vincent said.

Should I confide in them? Maybe together we can unravel the puzzle. But they were not friends, like Antoine, Mouse and Emile. He sighed.

In the very back of his mind, he reconsidered Basile Roche's threat. *I was afraid of him when I was in the woods, but it was trees and cold, not a person, that almost killed us. If I could face death in the woods, I will be able to face Roche. I can forget about him. Fear and worry will not help me.* And he put the problem aside.

CHAPTER 46

After a few weeks, André began to feel in charge of the post's financial situation. Despite Bousquet's inconsistent record keeping, smudged markings, unclear writing and tally marks that didn't add up, he understood the post's business and the pelt shed was beginning to fill up. He discovered he enjoyed the tasks of head clerk.

Until one cloudy day, when the door to the trading room flew open and three solemn Ojibwe men and one woman stormed in, wrapped in woolen *capotes*. One held a long flintlock gun, but they carried no furs—this must not be a trade.

The *engagés* froze.

"Hello and welcome to Bear Tooth Post," André said. "*Boozhoo*. I am André Didier."

Silently they examined him, communicating to each other with their dark eyes. Finally the oldest man broke the silence.

"You take place of Jean-Baptiste Bousquet?"

"*Oui,*" he nodded. "Yes. How can I help you?" He asked them to sit. They did not.

"I am Iron Shield." He pointed to the others. "My sons—Hides in Tall Grass and Elk Speaker—and my daughter Sky."

"Tea?" André motioned Luc to heat water in their teakettle.

"Jean-Baptiste marry with Sky in summer. This ties our band with you, the traders. She live with him in this post—until he died. Cared for him in his last days. We bury him." He jerked his head in the direction of the mound of stones.

André gulped, and glanced at his men who stood stiff and fearful. They had kept the marriage a secret from him.

"They," Iron Shield angrily gestured with his eyes at Vincent, Luc and François, "sent her back to our village. Did not provide for her. You must."

207

"What do you want of me?"

"You marry. Or we not honor debts."

Marriage? Out of the question! André felt like he had been whacked on the side of his head. He glanced at Sky, who kept her face hidden under the hood of a new *capote*, her shoulders slumped as if to make herself invisible. *How does she feel, once married to an important fur trader, but suddenly a young widow? And how old is she?*

"Is Sky ready to marry again? What does she want? It is barely a moon since ..." André heard her stifle a sob. Her brothers closed ranks in front of her and he could see only a wall of blanket-coats.

André remembered Antoine's advice, to take his time with difficult decisions. He took a deep breath. "I must think on this. We will talk of how to best honor the marriage."

They all stood in silence for long minutes.

"In one week we return." As a group, Iron Shield and his family turned and left. At the open door, André watched them move away. Surprisingly, Yellow Eyes frolicked near Sky's legs for a few seconds and she leaned over the dog and said something he could not hear.

The tea was finally hot but the guests were gone. André sat down, mug in hand. "Men, we need to talk."

Vincent said, "We didn't think she would come back. That's why we didn't tell you."

"But if you marry her, that takes care of it," Luc said with hopeful eyes.

He stared at Luc. "Be sensible. I'm too young to marry. You didn't want to, or you would have spoken about this earlier. What kind of person was she? Did you like her?"

"Sky, she was young, but she wanted to marry," François said. "She looked at our Jean-Baptiste with starry eyes. And he was so happy this year. This summer they marry, when we were gone. He did not go to the *rendezvous* this year—we took the pelts."

"Me, I didn't know her," Vincent said. "They spent many days at her village, not so much here. But she had a small lodge outside our post, for afternoon visitors. She liked that more than being inside the post. But we burned it after ..." He looked frantic at revealing yet another secret.

"So you sent her back and removed all traces of her at the post?"

Vincent, Luc and François would not meet his eyes.

"This marriage is like a treaty—it binds us to their band," André said. "We didn't break it, true. But it is broken, and now we are not trustworthy in their eyes."

"You asked them, is she ready to marry again," Vincent said. "That was a good question."

André took out the credit book to study Iron Shield's entries. Judging by the numbers of pelts they brought in, he and his sons were skilled hunters. But more entries near their names were changed, words crossed out or blurred by water droplets than any other names of hunters in the book.

"Some parts of this are very hard to read. Did Jean-Baptiste give her family special treatment—more goods from the post?"

"Maybe. We were not always in the trading room when Iron Shield came, but his sons, they often left with nets or twine, a length of cloth, a fire steel."

"Did you give her Jean-Baptiste's personal things?"

Vincent looked shocked. "No. Should we have? Me, I said they should go to Lachine. We don't know where his family is. Or who they are."

"Were any goods given to the family after his death?"

Vincent looked at François and Luc. All three shook their heads.

Maybe that could remedy the problem. But it wasn't a complete solution. André took a deep breath, inhaling the aroma of tea. *What would Antoine counsel? What would anyone—Joseph, Father Goiffon, Denis—suggest? What would Iron Shield's family value most?*

He fretted that he didn't have an answer. And only one week to come up with one.

CHAPTER 47

Some mornings later, two Ojibwe bringing furs mentioned a herd of elk they hoped were moving across several hunting areas. Five families planned to collaborate in a hunt.

After they had completed their transactions, Luc's eyes sparkled. "André, I have idea. Me, I am a great hunter."

Vincent agreed. "Luc, he hears, sees, smells game. He knows what the animals do."

"But of course," Luc said modestly. "I watch them many, many hours when I am a young boy."

"Will you shoot one of the elk? Could you be sure to get one?"

"André, it is their hunt," Luc began. "So *non*, I do not shoot. But Iron Shield and his sons will hunt. Maybe I go early, find a way to help them."

"And take a flintlock for Iron Shield's sons to use," François suggested.

If we could help Iron Shield succeed, maybe that would help us work together to solve the problem.

"Here is my plan: I stand without moving—like a tree," Luc continued. "When elk come, then I make big noise. The elk, they don't come by me, they go a different way, toward the others. So the others, they get the good shots." When Luc left that afternoon, he took two guns, shot and powder.

A few nights later, Luc returned, eager to tell the story. He had loaned the extra firearms to Iron Shield's sons. After scouting clearings, the hunters sighted the herd. Once the men had positioned themselves, Luc's noise-making forced the elk towards them. Each family took at least one animal, and they had celebrated with a feast to end the starving time.

When Iron Shield returned at the end of the week, only his youngest son stood with him.

"*Boozhoo*, I greet you," André said. "I heard you did well on the hunt."

"Seven elk in all—my sons shot two. Luc is good man."

"How is Sky?"

"You spoke true—she not ready to marry."

André's shoulders relaxed and he felt relieved. Then he said, "For Sky to remember Jean-Baptiste, we have gathered his things—his blankets, his shirts and a worked silver cross."

One at a time, Vincent laid the items on the trading counter.

"To honor the marriage, we also give her gifts—four lengths of wool and three of linen cloth, this paper of needles, colored beads and threads and ribbons." Luc and François placed these on top of the other items.

"To your family, we offer tobacco." André handed them a large twist of the post's best Brazilian tobacco. "A spirit gift."

He could see appreciation in Iron Shield's eyes.

André held out a tall black top hat, trimmed with a silk ribbon on its brim and around the crown. "And I present this hat to you." With ceremony, he placed the hat on Iron Shield's head.

Iron Shield looked pleased.

"We hope you continue to trade here, at our post," André said.

"At next moon we bring pelts."

"*Miigwetch*. I thank you," André said, bundling the mementos and gifts. "See you again. *Gigawabamin menawah*."

They left with dignity.

The *engagés* looked at André and smiled and he felt reassured.

Yellow Eyes barked outside. When André opened the door, he saw Iron Shield bending low, his face inches from the dog's head, ruffling her fur and speaking softly to her.

True to his word, Iron Shield returned within the month—wearing his new hat—to complete his credits.

Then he added, "The new dog, with the yellow eyes—she is good. I will trade for her when we bring more pelts for the guns." As Iron Shield left, Yellow Eyes wagged her tail and barked. André was jolted. *Now what should I do?*

He asked Yellow Eyes. She licked him and danced around. *Does that mean she approves?*

The XY men had heard him. "André, you talk to a dog? You are a "Crazy Dog Talker."

On the canoe voyage, others made fun of the questions I asked Gerard or when I "poled" rocks to learn how a setting pole felt. So I don't care if they don't like me talking to a dog—Yellow Eyes is a good friend.

Though spring was approaching, their pelt storehouse was not full enough to give him confidence. Once the tribes left to go to their maple sugar camps, would furs come in? Not long after that, André and his men would head to the *rendezvous* with the pelts—and Chaboillez and the other partners would decide about next year's posts. If this post didn't do well, it might be closed and that would reflect on him.

Ducharme might amble over to request meat or wild rice. Then he would disappear for days. Sometimes many hunters camped outside the XY post, while other times it was empty, not even smoke rising from their hearth. André did not know if either his post or the XY post was a rousing success or a huge failure.

He had mixed feelings. *I'm more comfortable as a trader than I thought I'd be. But if we failed here, I could go back to Antoine.* He didn't know what to say to Vincent, François or Luc.

Then he would pick up his book, trying to find answers in the story of Robinson Crusoe.

CHAPTER 48

Early one morning, Ducharme burst in to the Bear Tooth Rapids post. "Petit Jacques, he is sick. André, you went to school so you should know how to make him better. You must see him."

"Cure sick people?" André choked. *Medicine? I studied history, physics, geography, English, mathematics, Latin—but not medicine.* "My mother said trillium for pain, willow for a headache, dogwood for a fever. Will that help?"

"*Non.* Have you learned nothing useful?" Ducharme said disgustedly. "School—*pas!*"

"What is wrong with him?" André wondered if it had been too much high wine, but he kept silent.

"He has the bad humors."

Luc said, "My grandmother, she cured the bad humors. With a leech she bleed the sick person. Then she pull it off, spit on the cut and put the big leaf over it. But we have not right leaves until summer. Many times I see her. The sick person, they get better fast."

"My father, he had the bad humors too. I saw the leech they used—a big one, it was. Afterwards, my father felt good," Ducharme said. "*Oui,* bleed him, André. That's what Petit Jacques needs."

"But what is wrong with him?" André's mind scrambled for useful information. "Does he have a toothache? Is he coughing? In pain?"

"I do not know how to say it. Come see him. Then you will know."

"Does your post have a medicine box?"

Ducharme shrugged. "*Non.* We traded it. We do not read so why do we need a medicine box?"

"Does ours?" André asked.

"Someone dropped it on a portage," Vincent answered. "Most bottles, they broke. But I show you." He unearthed a wooden box with a dozen compartments, half of them filled with shards of brownish glass. Four small corked bottles remained, but chemicals or water had obliterated their handwritten labels. A diagram of its contents was attached to the lid, in faded unreadable handwriting.

André opened and sniffed each bottle, trying to identify its contents: tarry, bitter, sharp, sour. He couldn't take a chance. He unwrapped a small oiled cloth packet.

"Ouch!" he said, surprised. It contained three very sharp blades.

"Oho, lancets. Better than leeches," Luc said, pleased at this development.

Nothing else in the box seemed useful. With Ducharme tugging his arm, André and the Bear Tooth Rapids *engagés* hurried to the XY post.

Before they entered, Ducharme pulled off his neckerchief and wrapped it around his nose. "You have one too?" he asked. "You will need it—our place, it stinks!"

They followed his example and quickly discovered Ducharme had spoken truly.

Petit Jacques lay in his bunk in his nightshirt, unaware of the bad smell. His face was mottled and bloated and his eyes darted back and forth. He seemed ready to explode with anxiety.

"Does your head hurt? Is it your breathing?"

Petit Jacques shook his head vigorously. Then he placed his hands on his stomach.

"Your belly?"

Petit Jacques sighed and closed his eyes.

"Something you ate didn't set well with you? Or something you drank?"

Petit Jacques shrugged.

"What did he eat?" André asked.

Etienne counted off their meals on his fingers, "Venison, bear, bear, bear, fish, fish, venison."

A constant diet of meat would certainly affect his body.

Berthe usually placed her hand on a patient's forehead. André did the same—but it told him nothing. He picked up Petit Jacques's hand, again like Berthe, and placed his fingers along his patient's wrist. Its rapid beat surprised him.

"Ducharme, your wrist, please."

Ducharme was offended. "But I have not the bad humors. Why me?"

"Anyone, then."

"All right, me."

André placed two fingers on Ducharme's wrist, then lifted one. Aha! his heart pumped slower. He tested Petit Jacques's wrist again—racing. *Interesting. What should I do about it? If I don't help, they will think I'm not using my education. But they don't understand that medicine requires special skills. They think going to school gives me knowledge to handle every problem.*

"This not a good season to find the leeches," Luc said. "I run back for the lancets?"

"My father, he was bled into a cup," Ducharme added helpfully. "Here is my cup. I will get rags."

André too had seen a patient bled, but now he felt stymied and looked away. *What if I make it worse? This problem is impossible.* Then he remembered Joseph's words. *You can do nearly impossible things if you take enough time. So I should listen and think.*

While he waited for Luc to return, André pressed his patient for information.

"Petit Jacques, have you ever been bled before?"

He shook his head, his eyes large and sober.

"Do you want me to bleed you now?"

"*Oui,*" Petit Jacques answered quietly.

"Ducharme, wash the cup and keep it in hot water. Tell me when it is very hot." He tried to appear calm while he examined Petit Jacques, selecting a place to make a cut in his skin. *Where will I do the least damage?*

"Do you not think we should start on his arm?" Luc suggested.

"Behind his knee," was François' opinion.

Etienne was worried the treatment might not be effective. "Me, I remember they put a leech in the armpit of my uncle."

"Maybe. But I will begin on his back," André said. "Petit Jacques, please pull up your nightshirt and lean forward." With that, he slid the lancet's edge lightly on his patient's back. From a small incision, blood oozed, then welled out, dark and red. All their eyes were riveted on the blood.

"Ducharme, the cup." André placed it over the cut. "Now Petit Jacques, you can lean back to rest."

"Ooh, so hot!" squeaked the patient.

"Luc and François, turn the hourglass and sit with him for half an hour. Then come for me. I may need to make a second incision."

Vincent and André strode back to their post, glad to again breathe fresh cold air. André hid his anxiety, fearful that he might have failed. That half-hour was the longest he could remember.

When they returned to see the Petit Jacques, Vincent chattered the whole distance. They pulled out their neckerchiefs again to cover their noses. But they saw the door wide open—the room was being aired out.

Petit Jacques was smiling and lively, chatting with his mates. His face was pink.

"You are well?"

"Me, I have never been better."

"You amaze me, Petit Jacques. Stay leaning back, while I remove the cup." He slid it out, full of blood, and wiped up the drips with the rags.

"Ducharme, dump this out and get me a cup of clean snow." When he returned, André clapped it over the cut.

"Eee, it's cold!" Petit Jacques squealed.

After a few minutes, he directed Petit Jacques to sit. "May I test your wrist?"

His pulse had slowed. "You are cured. Eat lightly today and tomorrow. Easy on the high wines." When André was satisfied that the incision would close, he had Ducharme wrap a bandage over the cut.

"*Merci*, André," said Petit Jacques.

"You have done it. There is more to your school than I thought." Ducharme was amazed.

André smiled.

"But, I am sorry," Petit Jacques said sorrowfully, "I have not a *sou* to pay you—I lost all to Etienne in game of cards, *piquet*, it was, was it not Etienne?" He did not meet André's eyes.

"No matter," André said. "We help each other." On the way back, he marveled how it worked out. *When we return to Lachine, I should ask Father Goiffon for books on medicine. And also find out what Berthe knows.*

CHAPTER 49

During the midday of a spring snowstorm, the trading room door blew open. Wind and snowflakes drifted in as Makes Thunder, André's friend, stomped his feet. He carried the flintlock gun he had taken debt for at Antoine's post, along with a lumpy pack, which he dropped in the corner.

André was astonished—true, Bear Tooth Rapids was closer to Makes Thunder's new winter camp, but he believed that Makwa and Crow Man had saved all their trades for Antoine's post. *Was Makes Thunder transferring his allegiance from Antoine? Had he been a customer at Bear Tooth Rapids? No—his name was not in the credit book.*

"*Aaniin*, André. Hi. How are you? *Aniish na?*"

"*Aaniin*. I am happy to see you."

After Makes Thunder shed his snowy *capote*, they stood back and surveyed each other, looking for changes.

Makes Thunder was lean and straight. A speckled brown feather hung from his braided hair.

He has survived an ordeal and completed his vision quest. I wonder what the feather signifies. André knew he could not ask outright. Instead he said, "You are now a full member of your band."

"True. Now I am called Thunder," Makes Thunder answered. He paused, holding up his gun. "I hunt the new way. This makes it not so hard."

André held out his hand and they shook. "*Boozhoo*, Thunder. Hello."

Thunder studied his friend closely, now the post's chief clerk. "You too are now a man."

André nodded. Besides taking on the post's responsibilities, he had grown wiser on the trek to Bear Tooth Rapids. *That was my own ordeal and vision quest.*

"But I am still called André," he laughed. They talked of the difficulty of winter vision quests. Then he turned to business—the health of the tribe, the numbers and kinds of pelts being harvested. Finally, when nothing seemed to begin the trade, he asked, "You have made a long journey today?"

"Since daybreak we are on the trail."

"We? Makwa is coming? And Crow Man?"

"My sister. She is outside."

"Why? It is snowing. She should come in."

"You ask her. She not listen to me."

André opened the wooden door, but Little Berry was not there. He followed her moccasin prints around the corner of the building. She stood, snowflakes like white stars on her black hair, assessing their post as well as the raucous XY post. Yellow Eyes was licking her hand.

"Little Berry, come inside. Some tea to warm you?"

She met his eyes for a second, then looked at her feet.

He reddened, unsure of what to say as she stepped inside the door and handed him her *capote*, which smelled faintly of herbs. He placed it over the trading counter and stood for a moment, trying to clear his suddenly-jumbled thoughts.

Her dark hair was shiny, braided with leather strips and beads. He caught the faint herbal scent again. The deerskin tunic she wore was trimmed with beaded floral designs around its sleeves and yoke. The patterns were repeated in her knee-high leggings.

She too was taller—no longer the child André remembered. He was startled at her grown-up beauty.

"Please join us." André gestured at the stool near the fire and she sat, looking down.

He poured tea into china cups and handed one to her, one to Thunder. For an instant, their fingers touched, sending a rush through him. He dragged over a stool for himself. She said nothing.

Floundering, André resumed his conversation with Thunder, who told of how the band had struggled in their new winter site to trap enough fur-bearing animals. Without the meat they depended on, they had frequently been hungry. As the weather eased, they, and others, had traveled farther to find their quarry.

"This year we have little extra after we pay our debts. Next year is better, I think. Young beavers will be big enough to harvest."

André was impressed at their decision to trap only adult animals, though it limited them. Some bands took animals of any size—perhaps their need for goods was greater. "Have you seen Antoine yet?"

"Yes, friend. Last week, with my father. I brought him the rest of my pelts. Antoine says to you '*Boozhoo.*' Hopes you do well here."

He was pleased by Antoine's greeting, more than he could express. The tea cups now empty, André stood. "You have something in your pack to trade?"

"Not me. I carry for her."

She had said nothing, but André was sure she had followed every word.

"Little—Berry, you would like to trade?" *It does not feel right to call her "Little" any longer.*

She untied the heavy pack and pulled out furs—several martens, an almost-silver wolf, a black fox, a nearly-blond beaver. He handled them, assessing their worth.

They were of unusual quality. The dark brown marten pelts were silky and glossy, and the long hairs of the wolf pelt were paler gray than any he had seen. The fox pelt had the claws attached, though the bones had been cleverly removed. Of the beaver she had brought, André had never seen a pelt of that color. Each skin was soft, smooth, well-tanned. She had taken extra care to clean and brush them. They would fetch a nice price.

Berry watched while he wrote her name in the log book and listed her furs. She knew exactly what she wanted—fabric, a small copper kettle, a knife and two spoons, a scissors, needles and thread, thimble and beads. She spoke little in the exchange but her meaning was clear.

"I should have offered you a gift first." André held out tiny silver bells, ribbons and lace—what he thought Marie-Thérèse, the wife of his brother, Denis, would like. Then he added a package of vermilion pigment.

With a shy smile, Berry nodded—she was satisfied. She glanced at her brother. He stood and packed the trade goods and gifts into a bundle. They wrapped themselves in their woolen *capotes* and opened the door. The storm was over and the late afternoon sun painted rosy streaks in the nearly cloudless sky.

"Is it far to your lodge?"

Thunder nodded.

Outside, they bent to tie their snowshoes with long leather bands. Thunder hoisted the bundle onto his back. But Berry hesitated.

From her sleeve, she pulled out a small bag of deerskin, buttery soft and light. One side showed the outline of a canoe on a river, trees and leaves and a sun, embroidered with colored beads. On the other side, she had embroidered his name, "André," in black thread.

André was taken aback. *How did she know how to spell my name?*

She took out a piece of birch bark. On his previous trip, at a time when they were so much younger, they had played "talking leaves" in the village, and he had written his name and hers, along with other words. In a flash he remembered her small gifts to him—pretty rocks, a fuzzy tail from a red squirrel, maple sugar candy. *She used to be Thunder's little sister. But no more.*

Berry pulled out a long deerskin strip and, stepping close to André, tied the bag around his neck and tucked it inside his shirt. He smelled the herbs again. This time they made him a little dizzy.

Stunned, he reddened.

"*Mii ... Mii ... Miigwetch,*" he stuttered. His "thank you" seemed inadequate for the gift she had presented. "*Gigawabamin menawah.* See you again, I hope."

She nodded to her brother who set a quick pace towards home. She followed, striding gracefully.

André stood outside for some moments, unsettled. He fingered the decorated bag.

No sooner had he come inside and the door closed behind him than Vincent said with a huge grin, "Maybe next year she will marry. It should be you." His eyes danced.

"Unless you have the sweetheart back home," added Luc, his black eyes merry.

"Or you have one here, and one there?"

Oh! André sat down to their laughter, his face getting hot. Something he had not thought of. *But I'm too young. I'm fifteen.* Then he understood Jean-Baptiste's gifts to Sky and her family, gestures of affection and courting. Sky had been married to Jean-Baptiste to cement allegiances with the bands, but there was much more to the relationship. Now the possibility jolted him personally. For the next week they teased him about her.

CHAPTER 50

Slowly the cold released its hold on the land. Huge grayish chunks of ice tumbled in the current. Water from the melting ice overflowed the banks of lakes and rivers. Ponds swelled. Paths across woods and swamps became waterlogged. Mud sucked the moccasins off the unwary. Moving about was impractical.

Hunters, who in winter brought their pelts by dogsled, now sat idle in their camps, waiting to travel again on the water.

Both posts were busy now, preparing for the *rendezvous*. André and his crew used the time to work with the pelts. Those crawling with lice were beat thoroughly, piled with salt and beat again. The cleaned furs were folded, mounded and weighted down with stones for a week. The furs were organized by kind, size, quality and condition.

One evening a young Ojibwe boy arrived. André had not seen him before. Panting from having run, he glanced anxiously around.

"Ghost Crow and Crooked Horn? They not here?" he asked breathlessly.

"*Non.*" André shook his head. "Luc, go ask at the XY post." Minutes later, Ducharme, credit book in hand, and his men returned with Luc.

When the boy understood the answer was no, he sat, a great weight crushing him.

"What is amiss?" André asked.

"I am Split Rock," he said. His older brother Ghost Crow and their cousin Crooked Horn had been too impatient to wait another day to bring in their pelts. Though the morning was raw and windy, they had left camp, paddling the length of Buffalo Lake. The laden canoe carried much of their winter's work. After they had shoved off, the wind had increased, making big waves with white crests. They had not returned home.

"They are gone," he said brokenly. "The spirit of the lake took them."

It was silent for some time—the only sound was their breathing.

André's book showed Ghost Crow and Crooked Horn were competent hunters who planned to double their harvest of furs. With a wealth of trade goods, they would be known as men of substance.

"How many pelts did they have with them?" Ducharme asked.

The question seemed ruthless to André, but he also needed to know. Split Rock shrugged. "Many. Canoe was low in the water."

"What of their families?" André said. "Wives? Children? Parents?"

"My brother took care of his wife Blue Flower and three children and our mother." Split Rock bent his fingers to count the children—half-size. "Crooked Horn had a wife, her mother, two children."

Nine people would no longer have a hunter to provide for them.

They urged Split Rock to stay and eat, but he left immediately to tell his band the devastating news.

Their debts would be subtracted from the profits of the posts. That was business. But André was conflicted. *How should our post assist the families? It is wrong to leave them with nothing.*

The next day, Split Rock returned, clutching Crooked Horn's paddle, which made their deaths final. The tribe had already begun mourning.

André felt the loss in his gut—it reminded him of Gerard's death. And his own near-drowning.

Split Rock then showed them a scrap of bark, marked with animal shapes and straight lines. "We found this."

"*Miigwetch,* Split Rock. Thank you. This will help."

André consulted with Ducharme to determine how many pelts Crooked Horn and Ghost Crow had taken debt for and what they had brought for repayment a month earlier, when they came by dog sled.

Together they examined the tally marks on the scrap. To André, the animal with long teeth and a broad tail looked like a beaver—twelve marks. A paw with long claws was most likely a bear—one mark; an elk horn—one mark; a striped tail, perhaps a raccoon—fourteen marks; the tail of a fox—three marks. Finally smaller animals neither André nor Ducharme could decipher—twenty-nine in all.

"More furs than they owed," Ducharme said. "A lot of trade goods." He shrugged and left, his part finished. The loss would hit both posts hard.

"What goods did they want the most?" André asked.

Split Rock named blankets and iron tools among the items they had planned to take home.

André nodded. "We will bring gifts to the families tomorrow."

"Not yet," Split Horn said. "Their spirits are …"

"We can send tobacco now," Vincent started, "but André, the tribes, first they must escort their spirits on their way to the Great Spirit. We will not be welcome until they are finished."

"That is when we will visit," André said. "We will bring all the trade goods they had expected to provide for their families,"

After Split Horn had left, Vincent said, "That is kind, André. Most traders are not that way. Chaboillez not do this."

"I know. To him the post is business. But for me it is different. These men were … friends. The gifts will come out of my wages." He took out the credit book and entered his own name.

André set aside trade goods for the grieving families—a stack of blankets, two nesting kettles, a half-dozen awls, fishhooks, combs and a mirror, and gifts for them as well.

When they were sure the families would be ready, the Bear Tooth Rapids men delivered the goods. The young widows greeted them, accepting the gifts silently.

On the trip back to the post, they hiked past Buffalo Lake, which now was calm, clear blue and sun-lit. André's eyes misted. *Such a lovely spot for this tragedy. This visit is the hardest one I have ever made.*

He watched as a flock of large white birds that he hadn't seen before cruised over the lake and landed in a bay, scooping up fish with their bulging beaks.

André imagined the lake swallowing two strong men and their canoe full of furs. It brought to mind Gerard's drowning in the Ottawa River—and his own brush with death in Lachine. But today, like the day the brigade had left Lachine, the waters were sparkling and beautiful.

Ghost Crow and Crooked Horn did not escape the water's icy clutches. Nor did Gerard. But somehow I did.

Another thought burrowed in his brain. *And so did Basile.*

A few days later Iron Shield came in. "Your dog with the yellow eyes. Before you leave for *rendezvous*, I will trade for her."

André knew he could not take Yellow Eyes in the canoes, nor could he have her run alongside.

"Sky good with animals. She should have dog, and this one will have pups soon."

It was a shock to him—he had not noticed Yellow Eyes getting rounder in the belly.

"Maybe having the dog will help her," André conceded. "Yellow Eyes is a good dog." He was not yet ready to give her up. But it would have to happen.

Before Iron Shield left the post, André noticed how Yellow Eyes favored him—a special bond had already developed between them.

CHAPTER 51

"Time to think about which Ojibwe to honor as 'made chiefs,'" André said. He listed the most unusual items on their trading room shelves: "Three officers' uniforms, two red and one blue; one tall beaver hat; a variety of linen and calico and checkered shirts; silver and bronze medals on black ribbons; five brass snuffboxes ..."

"Last year we presented our best silver medals to Red Deer and Geese Flying High," Vincent answered. "Ducharme, he already gave them the fancy *bourgeois* clothes and the beaver hat. But for us they settled credits early. They helped with families of Ghost Crow and Crooked Horn after their canoe sank. How about we offer the red officers' coats?"

André marked it down in his book.

"Iron Shield got a beaver hat," Luc said. "He is good hunter. He brings in more pelts than he takes debt for. We could give him a snuffbox?"

André noted it in the credit book.

When François suggested giving shirts to Eagle Man and Treetop, André protested. "So far they only brought in half of their credits. I hope they had a successful winter."

"But they bring best beavers—clean, no lice," Luc argued. "And they live far away."

"True, they are due to come in soon," Vincent said. "Luc, he is right. They are good trappers. If they deliver more than they owe, maybe each a calico shirt."

"What about Has Horns? He paid off his debt and more—and so did his brother Elk Nation. Medals could go to them."

For several days they considered their trappers and the trade goods each man valued most. As the Ojibwe came in to settle their credits, André and the *engagés* added these special gifts. With profuse speeches, they thanked the hunters for their hard work and encouraged them to continue trading at the Bear Tooth Rapids post.

To their surprise, the shiny snuffboxes and the linen shirts were the most coveted.

After a week of warmer days, André and his men could not put off a cold, wet job that no one liked—pulling their canoes up from the water where they had been sunk to keep them from drying out over the winter.

All four of them waded in up to their knees, then hips, in the dark chilly river, not far from the jagged rocks called Bear Teeth.

As the water crept up his legs with each step, André felt anxious, his face tight with anxiety. Cold and fast, it reminded him of falling into the St. Lawrence, and of losing Gerard in the Ottawa. He had not been this deep in the water since ...

He took a deep breath. *My Ojibwe friends showed me not to be fearful in a river. They taught me to swim.* Then he remembered why he stopped playing in the water that afternoon at the New Fort— Basile had heaved large stones at him. *But I can do this.* Resolute, he carefully placed his feet though the water numbed his legs. *I hope my ribs are strong enough. They've been fine for a month.*

Suddenly, Luc slipped on a loose slippery rock and tumbled head-first into the rushing waters.

François' powerful arm reached down to grab Luc's shirt. "Help me, André." Together they hauled Luc back to the shore, pounding him on the back as he choked and spluttered. Luc slumped over trying to catch his breath.

"Falling usually happens to me," André said, embarrassed to admit his clumsiness.

After a few moments, Vincent asked Luc, "Can you help now? Because this job, it needs all of us."

They waded in again until they were nearly chest-deep, and leaned over the canoes to remove the heavy stones which weighted the canoes down. Carefully they lifted the canoes, tilting them gently to let the water pour out. Then they floated them to shore and turned them over to dry.

While outdoors, they peeled off their soggy leather pants and moccasins, and laid them over bushes to dry. Inside, they removed their shirts, and wrung them out. Over a rope strung across the room, they draped their sopping shirts, underwear and woolen socks, which might be dry by morning. But damp or not, they would have to be worn. Their threadbare wardrobes had no spares.

They felt chilled after their stint in the river, so François added more wood to the fire and they wrapped themselves in blankets. Darkness was coming on, so they were sure no hunters would come by. They looked forward to a quiet night.

After André wrote their accomplishments in the day book, he settled by the fire to finish the last pages of Robinson Crusoe while François and Luc played a game of fox and geese on the checkerboard.

"Halloo. Are you there?" Ducharme called.

Luc and François dived toward their bunks, scattering the game pieces. Closest to the trading counter, André scrambled to tie a *capote* around himself and dropped to the low stool, only his head visible. Vincent grabbed the blue British uniform coat not yet given to a "made chief," struggling to fasten its many brass buttons.

With barely a knock on the door, Ducharme walked in, white clay pipe in his mouth and a mug in his hand.

Vincent swore—he had buttoned the buttons out of order. Then he realized his bare legs showed beneath. He looked for a hiding place. None. He collapsed onto the floor, red-faced, alongside André.

Ducharme made himself at home, sitting on the three-legged stool near the fire. The wet shirts and socks dripped in a fast rhythm, some on him, which he didn't seem to notice. He gazed around at their trading counter.

"Watched you pull up your canoes today. Too early for us. Diving Loon and his sons, they will lift up ours next week. We're much closer to the rapids and the water is too cold." He paused for a long smoke. "Besides I'm getting old for that kind of work. Don't you think?"

No one spoke.

"It's a job I hate. I'm surprised you don't. But then, you are younger." Another pause, to drink from his mug.

"Didn't I see you swimming, Luc? You like the water?"

No answer.

Ducharme sipped from his mug, reveling in their discomfort.

"Isn't anyone here?" He made a snorting sound. "You're not talking."

André sighed. Ducharme was here to needle them. Could take a long time.

"You lifted your canoes so fast—we should make a deal. You could pull up our canoes instead of Diving Loon and his sons. We could ... we could ..." Ducharme did not finish the offer—he was laughing so hard he could not keep the jest going.

"Come out. Join me," he was finally able to snort out, between sputters of hilarity.

It was ridiculous, André realized, hiding their nakedness. "You win," he laughed, and laid the *capote* on the counter.

Luc and François unrolled themselves from beneath their blankets and sat down.

"Miserable buttons," Vincent sighed. "With so many buttons, how did the British win the war against the French?" He pulled off the coat, popping a button that he would have to sew on later.

They all laughed.

"I came over to get some meat for supper. Me, I thought you were asleep, warming up," Ducharme said. "But hiding?—so much better. Black Jacques and Etienne, they will laugh. The telling, it will not be nearly as funny. But I will do what I can to make a good story."

The Bear Tooth Rapids *engagés* laughed again. They would be the butt of that story at *rendezvous*. Didn't matter. Somehow the tension that had built up during the winter over the competition for furs and the high wines mattered less now. They were compatriots, doing the same hard work together, receiving the same minimal pay, living the same adventurous life.

After more banter, Ducharme left with a smile, preparing the tale to regale his men.

The next day, Vincent examined the canoes. He hesitated to interrupt André's work on the inventory. "The owl canoe, it is sound. A few leaks, but it will go to the New Fort and back. The other, our otter—it has split its sides in four, five places."

André remembered the feel of birch bark abraded by rough boulders. He thought of submerged rocks ready to splinter the canoes, of rushing waters pressing against the sides, of long portages where the canoe-carriers scraped against sharp tree limbs. He recalled many nights on the Ottawa and Mattawa rivers, sealing the seams of the Montreal canoes.

"Perhaps we should have a new one built. Who is good with canoes?"

"Kingbird," Vincent answered. "I will ask if he is around." He looked over at the temporary bark lodges near the XY post and ambled over to admire the canoes resting on shore and chat with the owners. Kingbird, he was told, was at his sugar camp.

"Pass a message that we could use his help," Vincent said to the Ojibwe hunters sitting there.

The following day Kingbird made a special visit to the Bear Tooth Rapids post. He studied the thickness of birch bark sheets that formed the shell of the canoes. He peered inside, lifting the cedar slats that protected their floors. He turned them over and rubbed his fingers across the stitching.

"Owl canoe is good," Kingbird said. "Otter canoe—too old. The two swallowed by Buffalo Lake in old canoe. You need new canoe."

Kingbird did not name the two hunters who had perished, but were in everyone's minds.

André glanced at the Bear Tooth Rapids *engagés* for their agreement. He nodded at Kingbird. "When can you start?"

A new canoe was a big expense for their post, but necessary to safely transport their cargo. André frowned to think of Chaboillez and the other partners reviewing his accounts.

CHAPTER 52

As the days lengthened and warmed, geese and ducks returned, flying high. Birds twittered in the trees, nesting nearby, slipping from branch to branch. Plants sprouted tiny green leaves, and shoots poked out of the earth.

One day while working outdoors, François shouted, "I see you. You cannot hide from me."

Curious, André hurried to see what he had found.

"It is the ferns. They are growing again." François proudly thrust a handful of coiled green stems at him.

André fingered one. *Like the curved top of a violin.* "A fern?" he said uncertainly. "We can eat this?"

François uncurled its delicate fringes. "*Oui.* Little, like this, it is tasty. Over there is another."

Those days crossing Superior without enough food, Toussaint and Pierre found greens like this. Others were so afraid of getting sick, they didn't want to take a chance.

"Show me more."

"Get a basket." They crawled through the brush and filled a *makuk*, a birch bark basket, with the small green fern tops. François was ecstatic.

André was pleased—their daily fare had become monotonous.

"My stew tonight, it would be better if I could find wild garlic," François said, looking at the ground. "Garlic is like a grass, but hollow."

When they did not find any, he said, "No, maybe it is too early. We go again, you will see."

From then on, François scoured the woods daily for edible plants, and taught André what to look for. On their hands and knees, they searched for mushrooms. "They grow by the dead trees." One day the two collected twenty odd-shaped brown mushrooms like the ones the cousins had found.

François dug roots. *Are they the same as the lumpy roots that Toussaint and Pierre dug? And how do you make them into something we can eat?*

"This shoot, it is milkweed. Bitter now, but if we boil it enough, it tastes like asparagus. Later, we can eat the flower bud and the pod. But only after boiling."

Hearing the foods mentioned made André hungry.

"Do you know this one? Feel the stem—like a square. It adds to your tea and makes happy the stomach. Smell."

André noticed a distinct aroma on a small jagged leaf—mint. He hoped he could find it again.

"You know the poison ivy?"

He was embarrassed to admit he did not.

"See that? It has three leaves on one stem. Don't walk there. You step in it one time—you will not forget. It burns and you want to scratch and scratch and scratch. For a long time. It gets all over your skin."

André's plant education continued. During the next weeks he learned which mushrooms would not make them sick (and two that would), how to find the root with arrow-shaped leaves that was like a potato and the wild garlic that had eluded them before. *Berthe will be pleased to see what I've learned when I go out in the woods with her.*

Though most Ojibwe had moved to their sugar camps, temporary lodges were pitched outside the XY post. Ruckuses continued. The Bear Tooth Rapids men could not ignore the noises, especially when they were outdoors. So they became accustomed to the sounds of fighting. They began to see new problems.

Hunters asked often for high wines. Easy enough to refuse—their stock was very low, and carefully rationed.

Children or their mothers wandered over for something to eat. Ducharme had little enough food for his men, none to spare, so people came to André—it became a daily occurrence.

"What can we do about this?" André asked his men.

François offered to boil bones to start a broth, adding to it each day—wild rice, a rabbit or owl, roots or greens. "If we have more mouths to feed, I add more dippers of water," he said.

André and François counted out what food supplies they would need for the remaining days before their journey to the *rendezvous*.

Of what was left, François said, "This much we can spare."

"I will mark the bags we need with vermilion pigment. And put them in the corner," André said. "The rest we can share?"

"Careful, André." Luc was cautious. "Always we run low in the spring. These are their woods. They are better hunters than we are. When we leave, that is the time to give any food we don't need."

"But they will not yet gather much food until summer," François argued. "We give this to them now. Good for next year's business."

It reminded André of the days on Lake Superior with nothing in their food bags. *We would have welcomed anything then. And so will these people. They shared what they had—and we will also.*

Animals also were hungry. Ojibwe hunters saw paw prints of bears out of hibernation, and claw marks on trees. After François discovered wolves pawing at the post's caches, André and his *engagés* decided to go in pairs to do chores away from the post. Nights, they took an ax or gun.

CHAPTER 53

Over the winter and spring, broken kegs and ruined birch bark containers collected around the posts. Antoine did not tolerate a mess at his post. "Refuse, it draws wild animals. Burn what you can not use," he had said. André and his men often built small fires to rid the post's yard of trash.

The XY men had no such standards. In addition to debris circling their site, they dumped food waste and animal bones in an open pit.

One spring night, three Ojibwe trappers were sleeping in a bark tepee outside the XY post. An empty cask of high wines had been tossed outside. Inside the door flap was their bag of dried meat.

While they snored, a starved he-bear sniffed the inviting scent of meat and followed his nose. The bear grunted and snuffled as he approached, but the sounds did not wake the sleeping men. He reared on his hind legs, his paws swatting at the bark slabs covering the tepee to get the prize he wanted. Growling, he ripped away the tepee's willow framework, and it began to topple over.

The bear's claws slashed the man nearest to the door flap. The bear was too close and the man could not move away. A second man was trapped by the tepee's falling framework, the third twisted in his blankets—none could swiftly reach their guns or knives.

A bone-dry sheet of birch bark from the tepee dropped onto the embers of their fire. Instantly, it blazed into fire.

Flames quickly spread and grew into a roaring fire. Stunned, the bear grabbed the bag of meat in his mouth and lumbered off.

By now the hunters had untangled themselves and yelled for help, running, beating at the tepee fire with their smoldering blankets.

Sparks floated upwards, igniting oak leaves hanging on the trees, and landed on the roof of the XY post. Its dry slabs of bark ignited immediately. In minutes the roof began burning.

The acrid smell of smoke woke the XY men. Bare-footed, Ducharme pushed through the door, his arms full of post records. His men staggered out wrapped in blankets, carrying trade goods, personal items—whatever was close at hand.

They dropped their loads near the river and raced back to carry water to toss on the burning building. But the small pots of water barely slowed the intense flames. Watching the Ojibwe hunters, they used their blankets to beat back the fire.

The yelling from the XY post did not wake André and the *engagés* who were accustomed to noise. Instead Black Jacques beating on their gate roused them to action. Seconds later, they smelled smoke and rushed outside, not sure what was burning. Seeing the blaze on the roof shocked them and they rushed over with pots and blankets.

But it was not enough. The stunned XY men slumped in exhaustion, no longer trying to put out the flames, but simply watched.

The Ojibwe hunters, injured by burns and bear claw slashes, disappeared into the forest. Their wounds would be tended elsewhere. Their tools were charred or bent but might be usable in another way. Many goods they had traded for, and tobacco and gifts, were lost—their winter's work gone.

Finally the fire slowed, having caved in a corner of the post roof. While a few flames still flickered, André tossed dirt and leaves in the air to make sure the wind was not blowing towards his post buildings. He needed to be careful.

François boiled black tea and brought a cup to each man. André noticed how the strong hands of his neighbors shook—their way of life was over. It was a silent group, stunned at their personal losses.

After the fire died, they made their way through the ashes and wreckage. Some of the trade goods had been damaged by ashes and falling embers. The separate XY pelt shed was intact, with most of the furs they'd been promised. Ducharme's fear—that the XY company would lose money on them and their contract would not be renewed—was real. They might also have difficulty getting to their *rendezvous*.

"Stay at our post," André offered. "We can double up on bunks."

"*Non.*" Ducharme shook his head, his pride wounded. "I need to see to my business."

"When you have made your plan, tell us how we can help you."

After breakfast, Ducharme sent Black Jacques and Petit Jacques to visit hunters in their camps—news of the fire would pass quickly. With fewer trade goods, it might be harder to collect their debts.

Ducharme and Etienne sat with the Bear Tooth Rapids men to consider possibilities.

A new roof on the post? Ducharme's heart was not in it.

They decided the XY men would sleep and live in the pelt shed though it had no fireplace.

"What are we—that we can't stand cold?" Etienne muttered. "We cook outside. *Nous sommes voyageurs.* We are voyageurs—we care little for comfort. Besides, it is spring."

André and Luc piled the XY furs along the most protected corner of the burned post. Vincent added bunks to the now-empty pelt shed while François cut a window and tacked oiled paper over it for light.

Ducharme and Etienne sifted through the smoky ash-covered heaps to locate the rest of their personal items and trade goods which they moved to their new quarters.

Alone, André considered the fire. The bear had caused it— Vincent and François had followed the huge paw prints. But something sinister stuck in his brain. The posts had been rivals, and only recently friends. Then this new tragedy hit. *Why? Was something else behind it?*

In the busyness of running the post the last few months, André had rarely thought about Basile and his threats. He wondered briefly at Basile's whereabouts, with the threat open. *Or maybe Roche is dead. I don't care any more.*

A week after Yellow Eyes had her litter, Iron Shield and Sky arrived, with two pairs of beautifully beaded moccasins for André. Iron Shield and André watched as Sky murmured to Yellow Eyes and handled the puppies. André was sad and delighted at the same time.

"*Miigwetch*, Sky. Thank you," he said, his voice thick.

She glanced up at him, and smiled.

"I didn't think I could say goodbye to Yellow Eyes. But you will give them all a good home."

He reached over to pet Yellow Eyes one last time and handed Sky his fur-lined mitten which had his scent. Perhaps Yellow Eyes would remember him, though now the dog was more attentive to her puppies.

Now I need something to remember them—a yellow rock for Yellow Eyes, an arrowhead for Arrow.

CHAPTER 54

For the next weeks, the men worked long hours to get ready for the *rendezvous*.

Vincent knew instinctively how many pelts made a ninety-pound bale, though André had to count—forty large beavers, or eight to ten bears, or only two buffalo robes. Luc and François compressed the bundles and wrapped them with canvas covers. Luc sewed the corners of the cloth tight while François tied the bales with moose hide ropes.

"Three years ago—or was it four?—we ran out of the canvas," François said proudly. "What a year! So many furs. On the last bales, we had to put one beaver pelt on top and one more on bottom. And paint the numbers on the pelts. Not very pretty, though."

If we run out again, we will exceed their expectation. Then the bourgeois won't close this post.

For each finished bale, André carefully listed its contents in his inventory. Then he painted a corresponding identification number on the bale, and marked "BTR" for Bear Tooth Rapids and "NWC" for North West Company so they would not get mixed up with another post's bales at portages, or at the *rendezvous*.

André was relieved his men were more proficient at the art of making bales than he was. Antoine had growled at Emile and Pretty Mouse and him for their sloppy attempts.

"When it looks like that, your bale, it will fall apart on the portage," Antoine had predicted. "We pick it up, drop it, toss it, sit on it—a thousand times. It breaks open and the other brigades, they laugh. Antoine's bales—they must be tight." So their poor ones had been redone to his high standard.

In closing the Bear Tooth Rapids post for the summer, André fretted over each detail, whether important or trivial—it was hard for him to separate the two.

They were bringing fewer prime beavers, more fishers and martens and other small animals. The pile of bales was smaller than he had hoped. Their canvas wraps were not as squared as Antoine's, and the moose hide strips that tied the bales were looser.

As André thought about trade goods the post would need for the next season, he realized that the Ojibwe did not accumulate extra pots or guns, and only replaced broken things—a worn blanket or a pot with a hole from overheating it in a fire. They seemed to own enough tools like guns, knives, fish hooks and chisels. Fabrics and tobacco—and high wines—were the only goods they consumed.

Their post had barely enough liquor. So next year, they would probably carry more. *High wines created problems for the XY post. Drinking is getting worse. What could I do differently?* The heavy responsibility made him sad, and confused.

Ducharme and his men closed their post one cloudy morning. Not expecting to return, they were stiff-faced and silent while loading their canoes and preparing to leave. After helping them, the Bear Tooth Rapids voyageurs stood idly. It was hard to say goodbye, so different from the excitement of leaving Lachine or the *rendezvous*.

André ached at their unhappy farewell. Suddenly, he grabbed a spare paddle, and shot a spray of water at them as they shoved off. They laughed in surprise—it broke their anxious mood.

"We look for you next year," Luc called. "Somewhere."

"Somewhere. *Nous sommes voyageurs*," they yelled back. "We are voyageurs."

"And friends," André shouted.

"*Au revoir*, friends. Until we meet again. *Au revoir*, Crazy Dog Talker."

The XY men had chosen a route André was not familiar with. That opened the question of what rivers were the best to travel.

"What other ways can we get our furs to the New Fort?" André asked.

"Depends," Vincent said. "Which do you like better, portages or rapids?"

"Which way did you go last time?"

"We took the route Jean-Baptiste told us to paddle, but the rivers were shallow and we made many *décharges*," François said. "The otter canoe did not like it. Me, I would not go that way again."

He explained the other choices: One route was downstream but had long portages and *décharges*. The other way started against the current and was longer. Though it had the most demanding carries, it had the fewest and they were short ones. André and his men discussed each choice.

"We are voyageurs—we paddle. I hate to portage, if I don't have to," Luc said.

We are voyageurs—*nous sommes voyageurs*. That decided it. They would start their travel upstream, like the XY men.

They next discussed provisions for the journey. Because of sharing food supplies with the Ojibwe families and the XY men, their surplus was small. They would need to trade for fish along the way to supplement their meals of wild rice and game but, if they stopped before dark, François and André might forage for wild greens or roots.

"Kingbird will bring the new owl canoe tomorrow," André said a few days later. "We can leave for the New Fort soon. Here is what I know we have to do. What have I forgotten?"

André named the last tasks he was responsible for in order to close the post: Test the canoes, cache or give away anything they did not want to bring with them, pack the trade goods, load the furs, tally the account book and write the final entries in the post journal. Some tasks were his alone while others he could supervise.

"A short list," Luc grinned. "Me, I say we go tomorrow."

"*Non, non*," François answered. "Tomorrow two Ojibwe women come to work in our garden. They will tend the turnips and carrots until we come back. The day after?"

As André gathered his personal items, he wrapped the book of Robinson Crusoe in its oiled cloth cover before tucking it into his pack. *What an amazing kindness, to have shared this book with me. I wish these men had been interested in hearing the story.*

When he picked up the pulley, he recalled his trek from Antoine's post. The near-disaster had taught him to rely on himself.

As he tucked the bag embroidered by Berry into his shirt, he discovered a small group of red beads securely attached. *It's a berry, for Berry!* He had hoped to see her again, but Thunder and Berry had not stopped before moving to their summer campsite. *Maybe I will look for something at New Fort for her.* The plan made him smile.

CHAPTER 55

Finally they set out on the new route. They traveled against the current, paddling swiftly. With vigor, they sang the song for returning home—"*C'est l'Aviron Qui Nous Mène,*" "It is the Paddle That Moves Us On." Singing brought them joy. Once more they were voyageurs, pleased to be bringing pelts to the *rendezvous.*

They waved at Ojibwe fishing, watched otters play and slide on the banks of the river, navigated over beaver dams and steered around boulders.

This country is beautiful now. André noticed with pleasure the sounds of the forest, the insects, frogs and birds, and the greening of the trees, with occasional fragrant flowering trees or deep moist earthy scents filling his nose. *Next time I want to stay all year and see each season. This is where I belong—not France.*

"I'm glad you gave Kingbird our last silver medal for this canoe," Vincent said while they paddled. "This one, it rides smooth and true."

On a pipe break, they talked of the events of the year—the fire at the XY post, the fights and ruckus, the drowning of the hunters Ghost Crow and Crooked Horn.

"Their deaths hit you hard, André," Luc said.

Now that they were away from the post, André told them about the fears that plagued him. "I nearly drowned in the St. Lawrence—and most of that winter I couldn't look at the river. I was scared to go on the brigade. At every *décharge,* my fear came back. Then, my friend Gerard LeMoine drowned in the Ottawa. I wanted to save him, but couldn't. It was his place as *gouvernail* that I had to take."

"*Oui,* we heard about that at last summer's *rendezvous,*" François said, crossing himself. "I was a *milieu* in his canoe one year. Gerard, he was a good man. It is hard to lose him."

"But we did not know—until now—you were friends with him," added Vincent.

"When those young men disappeared into Buffalo Lake," André said, "I relived those lonely days without Gerard. Nobody talked about him, and that made it hard for me."

"Is that why your face, it was so white when we took up the canoe from the river?" Luc asked. "I fell, but for you maybe it was worse. You were remembering."

"Me, I hate the *décharges*," said François. "I slip every time, but perhaps you do not see that."

André had been so intent on his own problems he not seen others' mishaps. He relaxed. Talking to them was easy.

Each pipe break, each conversation opened him up more.

When the topic turned to Jean-Baptiste Bousquet, André confessed his misgivings in taking over. "I thought I'd only be here a month until he regained his health and then I could go back to Antoine's post. Becoming your head clerk shook me—I wasn't ready. I didn't know how do it."

"*Oui*, we know. You talked to Yellow Eyes about it often," Luc laughed.

"A dog as a friend—that is new to me," said Vincent. "Hard to let her go to Sky."

"Such a year," Luc said. "Other winters, it was quiet and lonely."

"Me, I like the quiet," François said.

"I didn't have much time to feel lonely here," André said. Then he added gratefully, "You made me welcome. *Merci*. You have made me rich in friends, and in life."

Late that afternoon, they paddled past the lush spring growth—and then trees broken and pointing all directions, some on top of others and thick roots exposed. The devastation from last year's storms shocked them—they had not seen it before.

"This whole forest, here it is down," Vincent said in awe, "but over there, nothing was touched. Like our checkerboard. I did not know last year's storms hit this area."

"On my way to Bear Tooth Rapids, some forests were like this," André said soberly. Fingering the yellow pebble and arrowhead in the bag around his neck, he told them about the tree that crushed Arrow and finding a way to lift it with his pulley. As he spoke, he felt the awfulness of that journey lift from his shoulders.

"We knew the trip from Antoine's post was hard," François said. "We wondered what happened. You arrived all scraped, your *capote* torn and your ribs wrapped with rope. We waited—but you didn't say a word about it."

This is what Joseph—and Antoine—meant when they said to trust your fellow voyageurs.

～•～

Not long after, they paddled around a rocky bend in the river. Vincent pointed to a narrow cleft in the woods. "Our portage, it is there. I see it."

When they pulled the canoes ashore, the men looked at each other and sighed—the path was full of dead branches and debris from last year's storm. Crossing this portage would take much longer.

"They said it was a short portage but steep and rocky. This will make it worse."

"But why didn't someone tell us the trail was covered with fallen trees?" Luc said. "Ducharme, didn't he and his men go this way?"

"*Oui*, but they turned off at Wolf Creek to get pelts. That's where they'd portage," François said. He had twisted his knee while loading and it hurt him to walk on uneven ground. "If it is all this bad, maybe we go back to the post? My knee will be better in a day or two."

"Wait here, François." Vincent looked dubious. "Me, I will look. Then we decide." He reached for two bales, about to start the portage.

"I'll go with you. Leave the bales, but take an ax," André said. "I'll get another one. Two can clear the trail faster. Luc, can you unload for François?"

Vincent grabbed the tools and they began.

The trail was rocky and steep, with roots snaking across. Rain had made the few level places slippery. Tree limbs and loose rocks were strewn across the path. Vincent and André began to cut away limbs that would cause them problems. On a few places they could follow the path, but others required much clipping of branches. And then they found trees blocking the entire way.

"The way this tree fell we have to go a long way around. We have to make a new trail here," Vincent said.

"It's the only path we can take," André said. "We can't crawl over tree trunks while carrying two bales on our backs and our hands full of paddles and supplies." *But it makes me uneasy.*

"If this clearing takes too much time, we will have to camp at the start," Vincent answered, "or the far end."

André didn't respond.

The forest is silent. Birds aren't chirping. André glanced around. No birdsong, no insect noise, no movement. He peered ahead to see what made the birds fearful. *Probably a predator—a bear or wolf. Maybe a moose. We should be careful.* It made him edgy.

Another large dead tree angled precariously across the portage trail. Other trees had fallen close by—there was no way on the narrow trail to go around.

"We can go under that one," Vincent suggested. "The trunk, it is high overhead."

"Wait!" André looked sharply at the tree base. Squared splinters—made by an ax?

"*Non*, Vincent. Stop!"

Too late.

CRAAACK!! The huge tree crashed down toward them.

Vincent leapt left and André right. But not far enough. A heavy branch hammered André to the stony ground, knocking the air out of him. His heart thudded.

"Vincent … where … are … you?" he gasped, his breath ragged.

No answer.

CHAPTER 56

André waited for his brain to clear, and thought about where it hurt most. Rough bark had scraped skin off his arms and hands—they stung. His knee had hit something and throbbed. His ribs ached—but not so much as before. *Maybe only bruised.*

Leaves surrounded his head, like being in a small green house. Beneath him, fist-sized rocks on the outcrop pressed into his back and side. He tried to brush the biggest ones away, but they were solidly embedded. His ax? Not reachable. André peered through the closest branches to look for Vincent, but could not see him. He called again.

Silence.

Rest a moment. Then find what is trapping you. His eyes followed the trunk. Worst and most dangerous, the main tree had fallen a foot above him. He held his breath, waiting for it to fall. It remained hung up in the air. *It's held up by a limb or two, like an arm against the ground. I'll have to be careful, but I think I can get out before it gives way.*

It quivered. Had it already done in Vincent? He glanced again at the teetering trunk. Carefully he pushed aside branches and rocks. *A few more and I can almost sit. Then escape.* He opened his mouth to yell to Luc.

No need. He saw movement out of the corner of his eye. *Luc! He already caught up to us! Probably helping Vincent first.* André blew out what little air he had. "Luc! Here I am!"

Then he realized this man was thicker, darker. Not Luc. Instead, beside the base of the tree stood the familiar figure of—Basile Roche.

"Not Luc," a gravelly voice rasped. Roche laughed but started coughing.

André's heart sank as he peered through the branches. Close up, the man didn't look much like the powerful Roche of old. His body was broken, misshapen. His left leg was bent at an odd angle and his left arm dangled uselessly.

Alive. Roche is not dead.

Basile saw him staring. With the handle of his ax he touched his bad leg and then his bad arm. "Don't pity this body. I have you in my trap, like a mouse," he taunted. "You will not escape. I only needed to fell a few trees on this portage to catch you."

A trap? Had Roche tampered with the tree? Of course—the ax shavings. Letting nature take the blame instead of confronting me directly.

André exhaled. *Now what do I do? Take enough time. Keep him talking so I can think. The branches will hide me.*

"But this body, it is your fault. And for it you will die, slowly. I will watch and laugh as the breath is squeezed out of you. My nephew will arrange some accident to end Denis' life and get the land in France. It will be my land. My estate. All mine."

André shuddered. "You made the tree smash down on my way to Bear Tooth Rapids."

"*Non,*" Basile scoffed. "It was not me. It was your fears that made you think such a thing. But it gave me this idea."

"It didn't kill me," André said quietly. *Keep him talking.*

Basile jeered. "I wanted you to hurt, to worry, to suffer because you have made me suffer. All I had to do was plant seeds of doubt. Your fear would do the rest." He made his voice high and sneering. "'Where is Basile now? Is he watching me?' From the shadows, I spied on movements, your post. The Indians, they told my men. They did not realize they were doing so."

So I was being watched. Roche planned this for a long time. But I will not cower. André shifted his legs, his shoulders. *Keep him talking. How can I stop him? Where is my ax?*

"You can't get out," Roche snarled. "I have you exactly where I want."

While Roche gloated over his success, André's hand felt for a loose rock. But all were deeply buried—he couldn't gouge out any. He stretched his arm wider, continuing to search by feel—and then one moved. Only an inch, but he probed and dug until he could tighten his fist around it. He slid his free arm slowly, quietly. *One rock, one chance. Has to be enough. The angle is awkward so I will aim for the biggest place, his chest.*

"It was easy, like a cat playing with a mouse," Basile sneered as he fingered the sharp edge of his own ax. "I used your fearfulness against you. You are trapped, worthless mouse. But today I end this game. *Adieu*, André Bon-à-rien. It is your day to die."

André watched and waited. *Be ready.*

Finally, Roche braced his legs. He lifted the ax with his good arm. Swung it backwards, high over his head.

Now. André flung the rock as hard as he could. Into Roche's belly.

He heard the CRACK of Roche's ax hitting the branch.

The tree dropped several inches closer to him. He tried to move. Couldn't—the branches held him down even more.

Roche's bad leg buckled. He tumbled toward the quivering tree trunk. Screaming in frustration, he let go of the ax and grabbed at the trunk with his good arm. Missed it.

His knee gave out. He struck the trunk.

The trunk smashed down. Twisting Roche underneath. Crushing him.

The trunk struck André's shoulder and knocked him flat.

GYAAAHHH! The most unearthly scream. It stopped.

The forest was utterly silent.

André was stunned. He gazed up at the teetering tree, suspended a half-inch above his nose. His heart raced. Sweat trickled across his cheeks and down his neck. *When will it drop the rest of the way? I must get out.*

What holds it up?

"André, was that you?" Vincent yelled. "Did you scream?"

"Vincent! You are alive!" André said, relief flooding his voice. "I thought you were dead."

"Alive, *oui*. Not dead. For that I thank this rock—it holds the top of the tree over me. Oho, my head, it hurts. But now I have my breath back I will be fine. My back, it is on the ground. I see nothing but branches."

André took a deep breath. If he pushed away branches surrounding himself, could he scramble out? Or would the tree fall down completely? He couldn't wait—he anxiously moved one branch, and another, and another, until he had a clear space. He crawled out. *Why didn't the tree drop all the way down on me?*

"Vincent, where are you?"

"Over here." He followed Vincent's voice, and started to free him. "Are you hurt?"

"*Non*, not so much, but I am bloodied. Who screamed?"

"Basile Roche. He was waiting for me."

"Roche? He is here? Why?"

"The tree that fell on us, he chopped it—to trap me, and kill me. I tried to stop him—I threw a rock. But I think he stumbled or the tree fell on him. I don't know for sure."

"Then he is dead?" Vincent said. "I hope so."

André felt the same way. He wanted to walk away, paddle away, continue on to the *rendezvous. Roche is dead, and never again will I worry about him coming after me. This chapter will be closed, forever.*

But he remembered suffering under the tree in the winter forest. Even if Roche was his sworn enemy, he was a person in trouble. André didn't want to, but helping a fellow voyageur—and a relative—was the right thing to do. He sighed.

"Vincent, we must help him."

"We? Then first you get these branches off me. If you pull that one toward you, then I can get out. Yes, like so. Now give me a hand."

Together they found Roche, sprawled at the base of the tree covered by branches. Deliberately they cut away small branches until they could see his head and shoulders. A widening pool of blood soaked the earth under his shoulder—sliced by his own ax. A branch, thick as a man's arm, was thrust into his chest.

"Can we get him out?"

"I don't think so, André. He is alive, but not for long."

"Please help me. I must do something."

Vincent looked at the tree. "Too much tree. But we try."

"My pulley could help lift the tree off. Go back and get it, and ropes. Tell Luc to hurry and François, if he can."

"But pulling the branch out of his chest—that will be a big problem. How do we stop the bleeding?" Vincent started back, calling to Luc.

"Help is coming, Basile," André said, leaning over him.

Basile grunted and opened his eyes. His face was ashen, his lips blue.

"You ... destroyed ... all my ..." His voice was barely a whisper.

"What?" André bent closer to hear.

Roche's arm whipped out. He slashed a knife at André's face.

André jumped back, a streak of red growing across his cheek. He kicked the knife away from Roche's hand and wiped the blood off with his shirt sleeve. "Basile, we can help you." *Vengeful to the end. Do I want to save a man who hates me so much?*

"You ... will die ..." Roche choked as blood filled his chest.

André shook his head. "Neither of us needs to die." He cut away more branches and chose trees where he could set up the pulley.

Vincent returned with Luc and François, and the pulley and ropes.

252

"My nephew … he knows. … will stop you," Roche gurgled. "Will come after you. You … will not know … when …"

They wrapped the ropes around the tree and tied the pulley in place. When they were ready to grab the rope and heave, they looked at Roche.

Basile tried to raise his fist, but instead coughed and spewed a stream of blood. One halfhearted breath and then he lived no more.

"It is too late, André," Luc said.

They stood, looking at the branch piercing Roche's broken body. *That's why the tree didn't crush me—Basile's body held it up. His death allowed me to live.*

"A bad man," Vincent said. "It is over for him."

"Basile, he was the one who haunted you?" Luc asked.

André nodded, and turned away. "Can we bury him?"

"You want to bury him after he threatens his nephew to come after you?" François asked.

"He was related to me. A distant cousin."

Vincent gazed at him and then Roche. "*Non*, André, we cannot. The tree, the digging—the work will take us more than a day. We must go to the *rendezvous*."

"But we could pile stones over him," François said, "like we did for Jean-Baptiste."

As they dragged rocks to cover Roche's body, they talked.

"Basile lay in wait for me at the *rendezvous* at the New Fort," André said. "He threatened me when my friends were not around. His words wormed their way into my brain—my fear of him ate at me. Coming to Bear Tooth Rapids alone, I was afraid, worried he would set a trap along the way. But after the tree fell on me and the dogs, I found my own way to survive, and I couldn't waste my energy on fear. At Bear Tooth Rapids, I didn't have time to worry. So I decided his words were idle threats—until today."

"He shadowed you," Vincent said. "Waited to kill you."

"When Roche's name was mentioned at the post, you became tense. I see why," said François.

"Me, I wish you had told us. Maybe we could have helped," Luc said.

"*Merci*. I thought I had to get over the fears by myself, and learn how to take care of problems. Even though before I left, my foster father told me to trust my friends—and so did Antoine."

As they completed the burial mound and stood around it in silence for a few moments, André knew it was only right to speak words about Basile's life. He recalled the Bible verses he had spoken over Gerard's cross of canoe paddles. His mouth wouldn't say the same words with Roche in mind. Roche didn't deserve them.

Instead the words "smite the enemy" and "vanquish the foe" came to him. *That's how Basile saw me, and I was afraid of him. I fanned my fear into a fire and upset myself. But I never wanted to smite or vanquish him. Now I have to release Basile, forgive him. Unless I do that, he will be a stone forever on my heart, like the stones that we placed over him.*

Finally an image came into André's mind. He said, "Here lies Basile Roche, a lost sheep. Ste. Anne, keep him under your wing, like you have us."

The feelings of forgiveness would take longer, but words were a beginning. *Joseph said I would have to force myself to do hard things. This will be one of them.*

"He was a voyageur," said François. "Like we are."

"No more *rendezvous* for him," Luc said. "His last portage."

"Basile Roche was kin," André said. "I worked so hard to find my brother, but Basile was here all the time. As strange as it is, with him wanting to hurt me, I wish him peace." They recited a prayer and began to leave.

André looked at the tree-strewn trail they had tried to clear.

This carry was supposed to be short and rough—and it was. After today, no path will be as hard as this portage. Each thing that happened helped me somehow—falling into the St. Lawrence, steering the canoe through a tornado, getting Arrow and the sled freed, being the head clerk. Fearing Basile.

I weathered those problems. Each time I found a way through. I'm no longer the frightened youth who left Lachine—I can face whatever challenges come next.

He glanced past the pile of stones over Basile—just ahead was the end of the portage and the stream where they would load up and start paddling again. That path was clear of trees.

Basil's last portage, but our first. His end, our beginning.

Then he put his foot out, to return for their fur bales and canoe. Miles away at the end of this and other portage trails, and after much paddling, they would reach the *rendezvous*.

For us, the cycle of the voyageur continues.

FRENCH GLOSSARY

Visit *www.nikkirajala.com/resources* to hear how the French words are pronounced.

Adieu	Farewell. (when people will not meet again, as at death)
Allez	Go!
Allons	Let's go! (person giving command is leading)
Au revoir	Goodbye (literally "Until I see you again.")
Avant	Primary steersman in the bow of the canoe
Beaucoup	Very much, as in "Thank you very much."
Bon-à-rien	Good for nothing
Bourgeois	Owner of the fur trade company, a high-ranking company officer or gentleman trader from the upper class, the boss
Capote	Woolen coat, made from a heavy blanket
Crèche	Cradle or stable scene of Jesus, Mary and Joseph
Décharge	Process of guiding a canoe over a rapids too dangerous for a loaded canoe (which may be fully or partially loaded or unloaded, due to danger or water depth)
Engagé	Voyageur, person engaged to paddle and portage in the fur trade
Gouvernail	Steersman, second in command a canoe, steers from the stern or back
Je suis voyageur.	I am a voyageur. (spoken with great pride)
L'Enfant Jesu	The infant Jesus
Livre	Money used in the fur trade. Voyageur contracts listed wages in *livres*, but men might be paid in Spanish pieces of eight or English shillings and pennies. After the French Revolution, the money system

changed quickly and it is difficult to determine the value of a *livre*. At that time French Canada used barter culture more than money.

M' aidez!	Help me!
Marchons!	Let's go! March! (implies hard work or struggle)
Merci	Thank you.
Merci beaucoup	Thank you very much.
Mon dieu!	My God!
Milieu, milieux	Middleman, middlemen; paddlers in the middle of the canoe
Non	No
Nous sommes voyageurs.	We are voyageurs (spoken with great pride).
Oui	Yes
Pas!	Not! (very dismissive)
Rendezvous	Annual meeting of *bourgeois* of the fur trade, including voyageurs from Montreal and winterers from inland fur posts
Rubbaboo	Stew made from dried corn and pemmican, a staple in voyageurs' diets
Sault	Rapids, cascade
Sou, sous	Money, a very small coin, a penny
Tourtière	Spiced pork meat pie eaten in French Canada
Tuque	Tight-fitting knitted cap worn by voyageurs
Un, deux, trois	One, two three
la Vielle	The old woman, a poetic description of the changeable Lake Superior
Voila!	Aha! Oh look!
Voyageur	Canoeman transporting trade goods along fur trade routes, an *engagé*

OJIBWE GLOSSARY

Visit *www.nativetech.org/shinob/ojibwelanguage.html* for more words. Spellings vary in many of these words.

Aaniin	Hi
Amhik	Beaver
Aniish na?	How are you?
Boozhoo	Hello
Deedeens	Blue jay (also *deen de se*)
Maengun	Wolf
Makuk	Birch bark basket
Makwa	Bear
Miigwetch	Thank you.
Nigig	Otter
Geezheebasun	Tornado
Gigawabamin menawah	See you again.
Misakakojiish	Badger
Pemmican	Dried bison, pulverized and mixed with fat and dried berries. A staple food of the voyageurs who lived in the interior. The first high-energy food
Wattap	Spruce root, used to repair the canoe lacings
Wabizhashi	Marten
Wawashkeshshi	Deer
Windigo	Evil spirit, a cannibal or ogre. (Spellings vary.)

ACKNOWLEDGMENTS

Thanks so much to many people:

My voyageur ancestors—what a hard life, but lived with vigor!

My mother, Agnes Peloquin Rajala, who introduced many of the characters in Book 1. She signed me up for my first Girl Scout canoe trip into the Quetico. Her collection of books on the fur trade has provided me with amazing research.

Those who answered my questions on aspects of the fur trade:

Patrick Schifferdecker, site director at North West Company Fur Post in Pine City, Minnesota;

Jeremy Ward, curator at the Canadian Canoe Museum in Peterborough, Canada;

Joe Winterburn, tinsmith and researcher at Fort William Historical Park in Thunder Bay, Ontario;

Dave Kless, re-enactor;

And guides at Mille Lacs Indian Museum and Trading Post in Onamia, Minnesota.

Also:

The helpful staff at Professional Office Services, Inc.

Supportive family and friends who realized Basile Roche was still alive and frequently asked about the progress of the next book.

My advance readers—Jean Leiran, Mary and Dan Rethmeier, Kathy Knudson-Mestnik, Bruce Regan, Lowell Olson, Charlotte Stephens—whose insightful remarks improved every page.

John and Linda Peck and Steve and Wendy Gessell, who shared their expertise about edible wild foods.

Lowell Olson, who described the physics of paddling and how the pulley should work.

Ken and Sylvia Raschke, who showed me stones which inspired the pulley.

Dan Rethmeier, who improved my French.

Joseph Young, for title wizardry.

Carol Jessen-Klixbull, for the best professional copy editing.

My brother Brian and sisters Kitty, Kris and Mary, whose contributions are too numerous to list.

And Bill Vossler, my most exacting reader and best friend.

For more information,
visit *www.nikkirajala.com*